BUR

D1765348

DA

3

Linington, Elizabeth　　298427

Crime on their hands

BURLINGAME PUBLIC LIBRARY

Burlingame, California
344-1164

1. **UNLESS OTHERWISE DESIGNATED, books** may be kept for two weeks and may be renewed once for the same length of time.
2. **Overdue fees will be levied on all magazines, books, and phonograph record albums according** to the schedule posted at the main desk.
3. **DAMAGES AND LOSSES** of Library-owned property will be paid for by the borrower.
4. **RESPONSIBILITY** for all books taken on his card rests with the borrower as well as for all fees accruing to his card. Notification of loss of card does not free the borrower of his responsibility.

PRINTED IN U.S.A.

CRIME ON THEIR HANDS

DELL SHANNON

Elizabeth Linington

CRIME
ON THEIR
HANDS

William Morrow & Company, Inc.   NEW YORK

BURLINGAME
PUBLIC
LIBRARY

Copyright © 1969 by William Morrow and Company, Inc.

All rights reserved. No part of this book may be reproduced or utilized in any form or by any means, electronic or mechanical, including photocopying, recording or by any information storage and retrieval system, without permission in writing from the Publisher. Inquiries should be addressed to William Morrow and Company, Inc., 105 Madison Ave., New York, N.Y. 10016.

Printed in the United States of America

298427

In tragic life, God wot,
No villain need be! Passions spin the plot:
We are betrayed by what is false within.
———George Meredith

Gift 5.95 Feb '75

ONE

Mendoza finished his coffee and looked around cautiously for any livestock before shoving his chair back. "Everybody's in the back yard," Alison told him. "And you're going to be late."

"I know, I know." He took up his hat and made for the back door. On the top step of the porch, he surveyed their yard full of assorted pets. Clapping on his hat, he said, "And for the love of heaven, if you go anywhere, remember to lock the car."

"Well, really, Luis," said Alison. "It's not a thing that's likely to happen to anybody twice, the stray dog stowing away in their car."

"I'll take no bets on you," said Mendoza gloomily. Cedric, the large shaggy English sheep dog who had stowed away in Alison's car, was galumphing happily about the yard after the twins. El Señor, their alcoholic cat, had a wider streak of caution than his mother and sisters and was still keeping a wary eye on Cedric. The other three were ignoring Cedric at the moment, Bast busy washing, Nefertite stalking a butterfly and Sheba asleep in the African daisies; later, if they didn't fancy their own lunch, they would scrounge Cedric's under his benevolent eye and let him wash them afterward instead of attending to the job personally. "Livestock!" said

Mendoza. "What next? A stray hamster—a lost parakeet. ¡Vaya! And you the soft-hearted sucker—"

"I'm only going up to the market," said Alison. "I'll lock the car."

"See you do." He kissed her hastily, took out his keys and made for the garage. Mrs. MacTaggart, sitting on the bench under the tall alder tree, knitting, rose to corral the twins; Alison watched the animals as Mendoza backed out the long black Ferrari. He waved to her, the twins waved to him, and Cedric barked.

"Livestock," said Mendoza to himself. His own fault, saddling himself with a redheaded wife. And he was going to be late at the office; it was a quarter past eight.

He switched his mind from Alison and thought about the case-load they were working. An average-to-middling case-load for Central Homicide, L.A.P.D. *Dios me libre*, the rape-murders cleared up: that Rooney, off the Ten Most Wanted list, had come apart and confessed to those. The Garcia thing was thrown in Pending, not a smell of a lead. They now had another liquor store holdup shooting, and not much on that. They had a two-year-old boy beaten to death, brought to the general hospital by the mother, who said her husband had done it. But when they'd had a look at the home address —an old apartment over on Boyd—they'd found a five-year-old girl tied to a bed and also bearing marks of beating, and by the few incoherencies they'd heard from her, Mama hadn't been backward at mistreating her offspring either. There was now a warrant for homicide on Mama, to be served today; they were still looking for Papa, one Giovanni Echevarrio. They also had, since late yesterday afternoon, a sixteen-year-old girl dead of another botched abortion. At least that was what it looked like; the autopsy report wasn't in yet. There was the usual unidentified corpse, and the latest suicide. While doubtless something new would show up before long, it was an average work load right now. And at least it was nice weather—as usual in late March, mild and sunny.

He walked into the office at ten to nine, just as Hackett's tall bulk preceded him. "Better late than never," said Hackett.

"Pot calling the kettle—you're just coming in too."

"I," said Hackett, "have already been out. The first body of the day. Just more paper work, a guy walked in front of a car over on Temple. Drunk, maybe. Tom and Matt are out spreading the word we want that Echevarrio."

Lieutenant Carey was lounging beside Sergeant Lake's desk, idly chatting. "What do you want?" asked Mendoza. Carey belonged down in Missing Persons. "Don't tell me you've got a new body for me too?"

Carey grinned. "About six weeks old, but relax, it's not yours." He followed Mendoza into his office and Hackett drifted after them, disinclined to start typing up the report on the traffic victim. "It's a funny little thing—I don't suppose it'll make much work for you, I'm just passing it on as per request. About a month ago—oh, thanks," he accepted a cigarette and bent to Mendoza's lighter "—we had a request in from Dubuque, Iowa. Chief of police there. Seems this young fellow left town, driving, heading for L.A. to visit an aunt and uncle here. One Howard Hollister, twenty-four —young man of importance, no drifter, inherited a sizable amount of money from the parents. Part owner of some manufacturing company there. He was driving a bright red Maserati Vignale 3500 convertible, 1963 model. He—"

"¿Cómo?" said Mendoza. "Sufficiently noticeable."

"Yeah. Well, he never got here, and his sister finally put in a missing report. Nobody'd seen or heard from him since the day he left town, February first. He was coming down through New Mexico and Arizona, so all the states along the way were asked to look for him. Right off, a pretty firm identification of the car showed up. One of the border examiners at Needles. He noticed the car, naturally, and he also noticed part of the plate number—the last three figures of it, 777. But if that was Hollister's car, and Hollister's plate number is IS-5777, there's something a little funny, because the border guard says that was ten days ago it passed over into California. Hollister left Dubuque on February first, was reported missing the tenth. And now they've found his corpse over in Arizona, and the autopsy says he's been dead at least five weeks, probably nearer six."

"Where'd they find him? And why not sooner?" asked Hackett.

"Oh, sergeant—Arizona?" said Carey. "All those wide open spaces—prospector stumbled across him, about forty yards off the highway. He'd been shot. No ballistics report yet. But if he was shot by a hitchhiker, about five miles from the California border—which is where he was found—six weeks ago, why didn't the Maserati come into California until ten days ago? Was whoever shot Hollister still driving it? Not that that's your headache—the sheriff of Mohave County's responsible for finding out. But he's asking the usual cooperation from all metropolitan forces—will we please put out a bulletin on the Maserati."

"Yes," said Mendoza. "All right, we'll put out a call for it and see what turns up. That is a little funny—of course whoever killed him may have sold the car—"

"Not our job," said Hackett through a yawn as Carey ambled out. "Thank God. Enough on hand as it is. God, that Echevarrio—and I know, I know, we've seen it before, but I never get used to it. It is simply beyond my imagination how anyone could—"

"Conforme," said Mendoza absently. "He'll turn up somewhere. A bum. On the welfare. According to his wife he wouldn't have had more than ten bucks on him. The autopsy report on that Delaney girl ought to be in. Maybe Percy Andrews can give us this-and-that on—"

"Abortion ring? He'll only tell us," said Hackett cynically, "you want the lock-picker, you can always find one."

"Where's George?"

"No idea—he was here when I went out on the traffic call."

So, something else new in. Mendoza yawned too and lit a new cigarette. Palliser and Grace were off on Tuesdays. He got up to ask Lake to call the morgue and jigger up Bainbridge on that autopsy, and Matt Piggott and Tom Landers came in.

"So you finally got here," said Landers.

"Any luck on Echevarrio?"

"Oh, we haven't been on that. We were starting out on him when a new call came in, so we took that. It—"

"What's it look like?"

"Well, depending on what the lab might turn up, maybe a mystery," said Landers. "Though if it was the simple break-in after loot, more often than not they're not very smart, and the lab may pick up some prints. And on the other hand, there wouldn't have been much loot there, which anybody should have known, so—"

"Run-down old place over on Magnolia just off Washington," said Piggott. "Poor old Negro woman, about eighty. Looked as if she was beaten and strangled. Her grandson found her about eight o'clock. Doesn't live with her, just came by. But there were some mighty funny things about that place, you ask me." His long dark face wore a thoughtful expression. "I didn't like that sheep's heart."

"Sheep's heart?" said Hackett.

"That's what the internes said it was. Sheep, goat, something like that. Raw. With a piece of black velvet ribbon tied around it," said Piggott. "In the bedroom. On a chair. Just sitting there."

"A raw sheep's heart?" Mendoza was fascinated.

"Well, by the looks she was living pretty close to the bone," said Landers, "and you know some of them like the outlandish meals—"

"But a black velvet ribbon," said Mendoza; and Sergeant Lake looked in.

"New call—squad car. Cortez Street. Woman strangled."

"*¡Por Dios!*" said Mendoza. "Was I thinking, an average load? Come on, Art." Hackett got up.

Cortez Street was just this side of the Hollywood freeway, in a huddle of little streets some fifteen blocks from the Civic Center. Not the very oldest part of L.A., it was still old and shabby and run-down; the blacktop of the streets was cracked and potholed in places, and the single houses and four-family apartment buildings were aged and mostly unpainted. The one they wanted was probably the oldest house in that street, and the only two-story single house on the block: best General Grant style, a big old house once important, and once, probably, surrounded by its own lawns and garden, before the city grew up to it. It was a frame house with a porch across the front and down one side, and in the bay window facing on the front porch was a hand-lettered sign reading "Room For Rent." There was an ambulance in front of it and a little farther along a black-and-white squad car. One of the uniformed men out of the squad car was standing on the sidewalk awaiting the men from Homicide, and beside him was a dispirited-looking thin man about forty. Along the block, a few curious knots of neighbors had collected to stare at the ambulance.

"Lieutenant, sir," said the uniformed man formally as they came up. "I'm Robinson, sir. My partner's inside. This is Mr. Heffner."

"How do," said the thin man unhappily. He needed a shave, his eyes were bloodshot, and he had a cut over one eye that had bled and formed a dark red scab. He had on an

ancient, ragged pair of tan chino pants and a white shirt
without a tie, and his prominent Adam's apple bobbed as
he nodded at them. "You deteckatives? I never met any before." He felt the cut with an obviously shaking hand. "Honest to God. Mis' Milliken. Honest to God, take your life in
your hands these days, live inna big town. All the punks—the
hoods. The robbers. Don't care *what* they do. Honest respectable widow-woman like Mis' Milliken. Honest to God."

"We'll want to talk to you," said Mendoza. "If you'll stick
around, Mr. Heffner?"

"Sure, sure. Anything you want to know," said Heffner
mournfully. "If I just hadn't tied one on last night—fool thing
to do, but how'd I know this was gonna happen? Honest to
God, when I saw her— These hoods. Comin' right inna person's *house*. I think I'll go back to Marysville."

There was a square entry hall, with a thin flowered rug,
a plain table by the door with a mirror over it. Stairs straight
ahead; a door opening on either side of the hall, and a long
straight hall going back beyond the stairs, probably to the
kitchen premises. The right-hand door was open, and voices
sounded from that room; Mendoza and Hackett looked in.
The two internes were lounging at the foot of the bed, the
uniformed man just inside the door. "So what can you tell
us?" asked Mendoza, his eyes on the body on the bed.

"Looks as if she was strangled," said one interne. "Maybe
last night."

The woman on the bed was elderly, a woman at least in
her sixties, possibly older. She had struggled against attack:
the chenille bedspread was pulled half off the bed, and a
cheap china vase, a couple of paperback books, a pair of
glasses, and an alarm clock had been knocked off the bedside
table. The bed had been made up and she had been dressed:
she was wearing a faded pink cotton housedress, thick
gray cotton stockings, and one felt houseslipper. The other

13

one was on the floor. The room—probably originally the parlor of the old house—was large, perhaps eighteen by twenty, and besides the old high-backed bed held a large old-fashioned bureau, a low chest, and an old marble-topped commode. All the drawers had been pulled out and dumped, and the contents strewed over the floor—clothes mostly.

"There's another one upstairs," said the other interne. "Nobody told us about that. Hadn't found it till after they called in, I suppose."

Mendoza raised his brows and started out to look. "Room to your right at the head of the stairs," said the interne.

Upstairs, a thin strip of cheap carpet down the hall: three doors to left, three to right, and a single door across the end of the hall. Once this had been the home of a propertied family, when the city was young, before these streets down here had become the nearest to a slum L.A. possessed. But everything in the house looked clean, the furniture dusted, the old pine floors polished. He looked in the open door of the first right-hand room. Hackett came up behind him.

The ordinary furnished room: old threadbare rug, painted bedstead, painted chest, an old sagging upholstered chair, a small bedside table. And a dead man. He had been in bed, the bedspread folded back, and he was wearing blue pajamas. He lay sprawled half off the bed, legs trailing to the floor. He was not a young man; gray hair, and a china dish on the bedside table held a pair of false teeth in water. Beside the bed was a pair of shoes, one with a tall built-up sole, a surgical shoe.

"Knocked around some and strangled, for a bet," said Hackett. "Break-in for the loot." Drawers were pulled out here too.

"No bets," said Mendoza. "Let's find out who they were." There was a lab team on the way; the internes could take the corpses. Nothing looking very abstruse or mysterious here; the all-too-common break-in, if it didn't really often end with homicide. They went downstairs and told the internes to take the bodies. Out on the porch, the melancholy Heffner was sitting in an ancient rusty glider round from the front door. The uniformed men had already gone, back on tour.

"You found them, Mr. Heffner?" Mendoza offered him a cigarette.

"So why else do I call cops? No, thanks, I don't smoke. Any sense, I wouldn't drink," said Heffner. "Nor I don't, usual—who's got the money? Oh, a beer or two in summer —you know. But yesterday—well, everything at once, know what I mean, first I get fired off my job and it wasn't no fault o' mine neither, I was workin' at the S. P. an' they're layin' off accounta railroads ain't doin' so good, I seen that for myself inna newspaper. So all right, I can prob'ly find another job O.K., I ain't particular what I do so long as it's honest work, only I kinda got thinkin' about goin' back to Marysville, that's my home town, see. I don't know. Big town, kinda a rat race like they say. Anyways, then I have the accident. Never had an accident in my life, drivin' twenny-five years. I'm careful, never had a *traffic* ticket, honest to God. Goin' down Temple about twenny miles an hour, careful, an' this fool kid in a VW runs into me—an' now I ain't sayin' as my old Ford was tip-top A-number-one shape, but honest to God that about finished her. An' the fool kid's a Mex and he ain't got insurance. I get into an argument with him, an' this cop puts the arm on both of us. Disturbin' the peace. I like to disturb that kid's peace all right. An' then the mechanic says maybe two hundred an' fifty bucks, fix up the Ford. Well, it was—you can see." He felt the cut over his eye. "So I go an' tie one on. Not that it *takes* much, me not bein' a drinkin' man. I had maybe five, six whiskies, in at this bar up on Glendale Avenue. I got home O.K.—sorta instinck, I guess, acourse I lived here nearly three years—don't remember comin' home, but I must've—an' then this morning—"

"You rented a room here? From—"

"Mis' Milliken. Sure. Mis' Gertrude Milliken. Nice respectable widow-woman," said Heffner. "It's a nice place. She kept everything nice an' clean, homey, you know. But these days, my God, these hoods, break in, take all you got. Kill you. I think I *will* go back to Marysville. Kind of peaceful, small town like that."

"How did you find Mrs. Milliken and when?"

"Oh, well, when I got up about six I had kind of a headache—not bein' used to drinkin' like I say—an' took some aspirin an' went back to bed. I got up for good about, maybe eight thirty, an' she was awful good-natured, you know, nice jolly woman, times when I'd been outta work before or not feelin' so good she'd invite me to breakfast, make things for me special—not that she did board, but she was nice, a good woman. And all alone in the world, never had any kids and her husband dead. So I come downstairs, and well, there her door was open an' I saw her. Poor soul. These hoods. So naturally I call for cops. An' while I'm waitin' for 'em, I think about Nordhammer."

"Nordhammer?" said Hackett.

"Sure, sure. The right front room upstairs. I got—had—the middle room on the right. Nordhammer on one side, Forstein on the other. Nordhammer—I don't know his other name—he'd been here a long time too. Very nice guy, he seemed like. I don't see much of the others, just sleepin' here like, mostly. Nordhammer, he kinda worked for you guys. He—"

"For us?" said Hackett.

"Well, kinda. He hadda job, one o' the guys like janitors, up at that place in Elysian Park where the young cops get trained. I heard. Learn how to be good cops. He helped clean the rooms an' wash windows an' like that, see. He had to wear this special shoe, he's got one leg shorter than the other, but it didn't seem to hamper him none, spry as all get-out he was. But he's had the flu, last couple o' days. Off work. Mis' Milliken was talkin' about it just the other day—Sunday. An' she was an awful kindhearted lady, she felt sorry, him sick and nobody to look out for him—she'd been takin' him soup an' like that. Anyways, I know he was home yesterday, still sick, so I thought maybe he'd heard somethin'—the hoods —an' anyways he ought to hear about poor Mis' Milliken, so I went up an' knocked on his door an' when he didn't answer I—"

"You opened the door. So we'd better have your prints to compare with any we pick up," said Hackett. "You weren't here most of yesterday?"

Heffner shook his head. "Left usual time for work, seven A.M. I got fired about four o'clock—me an' some other guys —an' I started home an' then the fool Mex kid run into me, an' what with the cop an' all, an' then gettin' the Ford towed in an' the mechanic sayin'—I ended up in that bar along about eight, I guess, an' I never got home till maybe ten."

"All right," said Mendoza. "Do you know the other roomers here? If there are any?"

"Oh, sure. She had six rooms to rent. Middle one on the other side's been empty about a month, since old Chester went to live with his married daughter. He was gettin' too old to take care o' himself, alone. He sold papers on a corner uptown. Who else? Well, old Forstein's got a pawnshop up on Temple. He's a nice old guy, kinda serious, awful religious —Jewish, you know. And across the hall there's two young guys, brothers, share the front room—Fairbrother the name is—they both work at the S. P. too, but they're regular Brotherhood men, you know, not just like carwashers, I think one's a fireman an' the other's an engineer, I don't know them too good. An' inna back room there's Mr. Jarvis. He's retired on the pension."

"Any idea where he spends his time? He's not here now?"

"He'll likely be up in Echo Park. Goes there every day to watch the boats and swans," said Heffner. "Terrible shock it'll be to everybody. Mis' Milliken. As nice a lady—but these hoods, they don't *care* what they do, honest to God. Break an' steal, kill people—"

"Would Mrs. Milliken have had much of value in her room, would you know?" asked Hackett. "Did she keep cash at home? Jewelry?"

Heffner shook his head, feeling the cut over his eye. "Damn fool," he said, "me. Tying one on. I musta fallen down against somethin', cut my head. No, acourse not. She wouldn't *have* much—poor respectable lady, gettin' along best she could. She owned the house—I know that—she an' her husband bought it. He was a railroad man. We all pay the same, ten bucks a week. If you wanted she'd do your laundry for an extra dollar. She did mine. But outside that . . . Jewelry? Well, she had a wedding ring. Naturally. All I ever saw."

"Well, thanks very much," said Hackett. He and Mendoza exchanged a glance. The crude break-in, after any loot immediately available: probably at an hour (early evening?) when only the landlady and the flu-stricken Nordhammer were at home. And the abrupt shutting-up of any outcry. Possibly, with two corpses, two or more looters. And probably the homicide not intended. See what the lab came up with.

They left Heffner still sitting on the old glider looking mournful and feeling his cut and went back to headquarters. But Hackett did not at once start to type up the report on the two new corpses. They found George Higgins waiting to tell Mendoza about another one.

It looked, in fact, as if Central Homicide's average caseload was rapidly getting escalated.

Higgins had come to work that Tuesday morning feeling more than at peace with the world. Mary had scolded him for extravagance over Laura's birthday present, but she hadn't really meant it; and it was just as much fun as he'd always thought it would be, having a wife and family (Bert Dwyer's good kids) to look after. The birthday party had been bedlam, Mary said, but everybody'd had a fine time, and Laura, now officially ten, had nearly strangled Higgins in gratitude for the wristwatch. And the doctors were now saying Stevie's brace could come off next month, and with exercise and therapy he'd be as good as new.

Higgins started typing up the report on yesterday's suicide (and how anybody could get to the point of that was beyond him, but people did come all sorts) and had just signed it and sorted out the triplicate copies for their different destinations when Sergeant Lake hailed him. Landers and Piggott had gone out on something, and Hackett on something else, the boss wasn't in yet, and Henry Glasser was typing a report across the communal sergeants' room.

"Something new?" said Higgins.

"Something new," said Lake. "Crandall Street, just down from Beverly. Squad car just called in."

Higgins went down to the lot for his car and drove up to Crandall Street. There was a squad car; there was a much annoyed and voluble citizen by the name of Fisher. A bookkeeper at the Broadway department store. "It is a *continual* nuisance, these *irresponsible* and *thoughtless* people, forever parking right *across my driveway*—I am expected to be at my desk by *nine sharp*, and when I find my driveway *completely* blocked—I have complained to the police before, but the nuisance has continued and really this is the *last straw!* I did enquire of the nearest neighbors, it has most often been that Gibbs boy, that disreputable old Ford of his—but when I finally *looked* at the car— And what Mr. Lowther will say, I'm half an hour late now but *not* my fault and of course one must cooperate with the police—"

19

The ambulance, summoned by the squad car men, came up as Higgins examined the car.

The car, parked carelessly nosed in to the curb, its rear end half across the driveway of the old but respectable four-family apartment building, was a 1963 Chrysler 300, blue, looking fairly clean, with California plates. There was a man slumped over in front; he had been sitting behind the wheel and had fallen sideways half into the passenger's seat. From what Higgins could see, his clothes were conventional: gray suit, white shirt, tie. His face was hidden. By all appearances he had been shot, and at close quarters: there was a powder-blackened bullet hole just above the right ear.

"We haven't touched him," said one of the uniformed men, "but you can see, sir, there—"

Higgins saw. The right front door of the car was open. Had been left open, the squad car men confirmed. Higgins inserted his head and shoulders and looked.

The Chrysler had bucket seats in front, and what was called a console between—an armrest, also a lockable compartment, flat between the seats. And the obvious bullet hole in the head of a dead man—but Higgins knew that head injuries, even from bullets, were tricky; sometimes, with the fatal wound, people lived for days.

The dead man had, apparently, not been killed outright, even with the bullet in the head. Had, apparently, made some effort to—what? Some effort toward something, anyway.

There was, on the console of the car between the bucket seats, half under the man's left hand, a synthetic-leather pocket memo-pad. It was held open by the dead hand. It was stained with blood, dried blood. There was a ballpoint pen, evidently fallen from the man's right hand, rolled down into the passenger's seat. Gingerly Higgins reached in and edged the memo-pad from under the hand, across the seat. Handling it carefully by the edges, he got it out and looked at it.

Across the little blank page was scrawled, painfully, one word,
with a dark stain of blood just below it. One word, in over-
large letters:

Jewels

Higgins thought that Mendoza was going to be interested
in this one. The slightly offbeat one.

TWO

"Jewels?" said Mendoza. "Jewels?" He smoothed his moustache absently.

"You can see for yourself," said Higgins. He and Hackett were sitting on either side of Mendoza's desk; he reached into his breast pocket and brought out a plastic bag of the type used by the lab. "I went right to the morgue with the body —the lab's towed the car in by now—and got everything on him, got Scarne to dust it right there. Nil. Nothing much that'd take prints. But offbeat you can say, all right. Wait till you see."

Hackett craned over Mendoza's shoulder as the contents of the bag came out on the desk blotter. The memo-pad— Mendoza picked it up. The first page bore the ordinary notation in a neat hand, *Rose 9 P.M. home.* It was the second page that held the bloodstains and the single mysterious scrawled word.

"He went to a little effort to get that down," said Higgins. "He must have known he was dying—at least badly hurt. And he uses all the strength he's got left to work that pad out of his pocket and write that down. Why the hell? What did he mean?"

"I'll be damned," said Hackett. "That is a funny one. Jewels."

22

"The rest is maybe funnier," said Higgins, lighting a cigarette. Mendoza laid the memo-pad down and considered the other items on the blotter. Two billfolds, neither new nor old: a ring of keys. A folded clean handkerchief. Three address books, one blue, one red, one black, that one looking well worn. A dollar thirty-seven in change, including a Canadian nickel. "That was from his pockets," said Higgins. "He was wearing the rest. Nothing much to be got from his clothes —ordinary. Local and national labels."

Mendoza turned the jewelry over with one forefinger. One fourteen-karat gold tietack set with a black star sapphire. One gold-plated wristwatch, fancy rectangular shape with a wide gold mesh band, a Longines. One fourteen-karat ring, set with a large square onyx stone with a diamond chip in the middle. One pinkie ring, fourteen-karat, set with what looked like a diamond but was more likely a zircon. "*¡Así!*" said Mendoza. "Quite the natty gent. A bit too natty. Was he a pickpocket?" He picked up one of the billfolds.

There was a wad of bills in it: forty-seven dollars, mostly in ones. There were cards in the plastic slots, starting out with a Social Security card. No photographs. Except, you could say, one: the one on the driver's license. For some time now, California drivers' licenses had been embellished with a photograph of the driver, a photograph snapped without warning, usually as the unsuspecting, innocent applicant was cleaning fingerprint ink off his thumb. Mendoza vividly remembered his own late experience: the photograph, duly appearing on his new license, made him look like a particularly sinister gangster. This license he was looking at had been issued to one Rex Richard Carson, in 1967. It was a four-year license, and that said his driving record was good. And whoever and whatever Mr. Carson had been, Mendoza felt some respect for him, for even under such adverse conditions he had been photogenic. Rex Carson, who had been thirty-five in 1967, was described as six feet, 170 pounds, hair black, eyes blue, complexion medium, and by the photograph he was a good looker. The black hair was slightly wavy, he wore a slight smile on his wide mobile mouth; the features were regular, a square chin with a cleft in it, and a high forehead. "This is him?" asked Mendoza, and Higgins nodded.

"Glamour boy."

Past the license was a card that bore the legend in elegant script, *Forrester's School of Dance for Children, Miss Shirley Forrester, Owner and Supervisor*, with an address on Hyperion Avenue in Hollywood. On the left-hand bottom corner it added, *Mr. Rex Carson, Representative and Talent Scout.* Mendoza raised his eyebrows at it and flipped over the plastic slot. Another printed business card. *Patti's Model Agency, Training and Placing*, an address on Vermont. Lower right-hand corner, *Mr. Rex Carson, Representative.* "Such a busy boy," said Mendoza. The next slot held the card of some outfit called *Match-Mates, Inc.*, address on Hollywood Boulevard. *Mr. Rex Carson, Agent.* "Well, well," said Mendoza, and picked up the other billfold. The first was tan leather; this was dark brown alligator.

The first plastic slot held another driving license. No picture on this one; it was an Oregon license. But the description on it, of one Mr. Robert C. Conway, was remarkably like the description of Rex Carson, and they were the same age. "Now just fancy that," said Mendoza. No money in this one; only a collection of snapshots in the bill compartment. They were all candid snapshots of Rex Carson—if that was his name—mostly with other people: mostly with women, only two showing him with two different couples. Some two dozen snapshots.

"The address books are interesting," said Higgins. Mendoza looked at them. The first one had the initials R. R. C. inside the front cover; the second the initials R. C. C. in the same place, and the third the initials W.W.

"*Maravilloso*," said Mendoza mildly. The address books had

a miscellany of names and addresses noted in them. The first one listed addresses all around the L.A. area, the other two had listed a dozen or so Oregon addresses. Most of the names were female.

"Jewels," said Hackett. "What the hell—a con man? There's an address for him here—" he stabbed a blunt forefinger at the California driving license. "Alexandria Street in Hollywood. At least a place to start—"

"I've been there," said Higgins. "The manageress of the place wasn't there, I couldn't raise anybody. I put a seal on the door and told the lab—they may have got up there by now. It's an old apartment, just a place to sleep, about seventy per I'd guess."

"Yes, and somebody listed in here," Mendoza nodded at the address books, "should be able to tell us this and that about him. He may have a record—we can ask. It certainly looks—and if he was a con, either amateur or pro, quite a few people might have had some reason to want to take him off. But . . ." he picked up the memo-pad again, shook his head at it. "*Extraño*. Jewels. Jewels? It might not have one damned thing to do with his getting shot, George."

"When he made such a try at getting it down when he was dying? Those bloodstains—"

"We don't know that. Maybe he was just sitting there in the car with X, talking—talking business, and he was just jotting down a note for himself when X shot him. And he fell and bled onto the memo."

"It's not a bit like the writing on the first page, the one about meeting Rose at 9 P.M. When he wrote down that *Jewels*, he was—"

"Drunk," said Mendoza irritably. "We don't *know*, damn it. Yet. See what the autopsy says. You said the car was carelessly parked—he could have been tight. Wait for it."

"You think it's funny too," said Higgins. "He could have been, but I don't somehow think he was."

"Jewels," said Hackett. "Even if he was, it's a kind of unlikely word to put down on a memo-pad, Luis. This *Rose 9 P.M.* is the sort of thing you write on a—"

"Both of you good detectives," said Mendoza sardonically, "are arguing ahead of your data. Wait for the autopsy. Wait to see what shows in his apartment. Wait to hear what all the people in the address books can tell us about him. ¿Cómo? It's just another one to work—and a couple of others have priority." He got up and opened the office door. "Jimmy! That Echevarrio warrant come through yet?"

"Just now. And the Delaney autopsy."

"*Bueno.* Who else is here? Henry—" Glasser was just emerging from the sergeants' office. "You can go make the collar on Mrs. Echevarrio."

"Anything to oblige," said Glasser amiably.

"That thing," said Higgins with a grimace.

"And we ought to get a formal statement from Heffner on the rooming house thing. You might go fetch him, Art. There's not much more we can do on that except get hold of the other roomers, who probably can't give us any help—see what the lab turns up. Where's Matt and Tom, Jimmy?"

"Couldn't say. On that new one, or hunting Echevarrio."

"Well." Mendoza took the autopsy report and stared at it unseeingly, smoothing his moustache. "Go see if Heffner's still there, Art. At that, we might as well get on this Carson— I'll take those cards, George, and you can start out with the Carson address book. The R. R. C. one. I do wonder what the W. W. stood for. Woodrow Wilson. Walter Wood. Oh, Jimmy. Call Records and ask if we've got him listed. Under Carson or Conway." Lake glanced at the license and took down the description in rapid shorthand.

"Jewels," said Hackett thoughtfully. "I have the feeling this is going to be one of those wild ones."

"I'm the only one allowed hunches around here, Arturo," said Mendoza. He went back to his desk and looked over the autopsy report, which was expectable. The botched abortion. He was irritated. Hackett all too right, in the big city anybody in the market for an abortion could get one. It was in the cards they'd never find the abortionist who'd done the crude job on sixteen-year-old Jean Delaney. Higgins had seen the mother yesterday, said she seemed to be a respectable woman. Bewildered and shocked. Well, sixteen-year-olds these days, no matter what kind of a home . . .

The respectable widow Gertrude Milliken. And the flu-ridden Nordhammer. Was the house door locked during the day? The front door hadn't been forced. It could be that she didn't bother to lock up unless she was going out, to market or somewhere. And at night. See the other roomers; had they all been at home last night? See what the autopsy said about time of death. But provisionally, Mendoza was thinking that that X (or possibly a couple of X's) had made his attack at a time when Mrs. Milliken and Nordhammer were alone in the house. The woman at least had probably made a little noise.

There was also, he remembered suddenly, the raw sheep's heart with the black velvet ribbon around it. Piggott's poor old Negro woman beaten and strangled. Oh, yes? He hadn't heard anything about that yet.

Well, it was early in all these cases to do any serious thinking. Wait for more facts to drift in. If they did. Meanwhile, the only ones that offered any immediate profitable action were, of course, Delaney and the new offbeat one: Carson-Conway-Blank. There was this and that to be done on Milliken; but admit it, that looked like the ordinary crude burglary for small loot, down there, ending in unintended homicide.

It was eleven fifteen. Mendoza gazed down absently at the bloodstained memo-pad. *Jewels*. The billfolds. The little heap of slightly too gaudy jewelry. The autopsy report—terse description of a sixteen-year-old's unpleasant snuffing out. *Dios*, he was going sentimental: in all probability a cheap little tramp. But, sixteen: sixteen, whatever its moral state, was really too inexperienced and immature to judge—people or anything else—and it didn't seem fair. Nothing said life had to be fair. Some people thought Something was managing things, so that in the end everything turned out fair. Mairí MacTaggart trotting off to Mass. . . . And just maybe, he thought, Something was. In the very long run. *The sins ye do by two and two—*

He hoped Alison had remembered to lock the car. Unlikely be damned, he thought, any lost-stolen-or-strayed animal making a beeline for the one soft-hearted sucker . . . That Cedric. He grinned at the autopsy report, got up and reached for his hat.

In the anteroom, Lake, with a martyred expression, was smoking a cigarette. He was still doggedly trying his experiment: never a smoker, he had read somewhere that smokers who quit usually gained weight, and he was trying it in reverse instead of counting calories. Even cops, thought Mendoza, came all sorts. He said, "I'll be down in Vice awhile, Jimmy, and then out. Until after lunch anyway. When Henry gets back, chase him over to that Milliken house, see if any of the other roomers have showed. If not, he might check the S. P. for those Fairbrothers, and look up Forstein at his pawnshop. Probably a waste of time, but we have to do the routine." Turning to the door, he met Piggott just coming in. Piggott had a man with him, a sullen unshaven dark man in shabby clothes.

"Sit down," said Piggott. "We'll get to you in a minute. . . . There he was big as life at the apartment. I ran into Henry going to collect the Missus, and went along, and there he was."

"Echevarrio," said Mendoza, pleased. "So, start in on him. I'll see you later."

"But I wanted to tell you about that other thing—see what you think," said Piggott plaintively. "Something mighty queer there, and—" Glasser came in with a sullen dark woman in flashy clothes and too much makeup.

Mendoza hesitated, thinking of the sheep's heart. "Time later, Matt. Get busy on Mama and Papa. Tell them all about their rights and ask them if they want lawyers, and—"

"And wipe their noses and hold their hands," said Piggott. Mendoza laughed and went out.

"Now what the hell do you expect from me?" asked Lieutenant Andrews down in Vice. "You're old enough to know better, Luis."

"I didn't really expect much, Percy. But any smell—"

Andrews shut his eyes and leaned back in his desk chair. "Once in awhile we do get the organized ring. More often it's one like that old doctor we picked up last month—you were in on that. But any time, in the big town, a girl wants it, she can find it. Asking around. What you say, and by this—" he looked at the autopsy report "—this was probably an amateur job. But you can't even be sure about that—could have been the drunk ex-doctor or some bungling practical nurse." He shrugged. "Anyway, I can't give you any leads. Sorry."

"Just looking," said Mendoza. "Little shortcut if you could."

"Sorry," repeated Andrews. "If anything turns up along that line I'll let you know, but—"

It was an old block of business, on Vermont Avenue down from Santa Monica Boulevard, a shabby tired-looking block where the lackadaisical wind rustled old newspapers and all the flotsam and jetsam of refuse along the gutters, and the green and yellow monsters of city buses sighed out their diesel fumes to the old-fashioned clang of the automatic traffic signals. The building fronts hadn't been painted for a long time; they were a uniform drab dark brown brick. Mendoza had parked at a public lot down the next block; he came past a dirty-looking chain drugstore on the corner, where the bench on the sidewalk under a bus stop sign was occupied by a very fat Negro woman, a longhaired unwashed beatnik male-question-mark, and a neatly dressed young blond girl chewing gum, past a photography shop, a dry cleaners, and a women's hat shop, to a narrow door with a transient-looking cardboard sign, *Patti's Model Agency, upstairs, walk in please.* He walked in. The stairs were uncarpeted and steep. Up one flight, he came to a landing and another door. *Patti's Model Agency. Come in.*

Mendoza went in.

Pretty obviously this had been an apartment living room at one time. A modern desk square in the middle of the room and a cheap modern low couch and two matching chairs tried to make it look like an office: there were reproduction Picasso prints on two walls. Mendoza wrinkled his lip at them. A bell had rung discreetly as he opened the door; after a moment the door beside the couch opened and a woman came in.

He sized her up rapidly, cynically; and with his experience —prior to the time he had saddled himself with a redheaded wife—that, Mendoza was good at. She was pushing forty, probably, and doing a good job at looking less. Her figure very good under a plain black dress high-necked and tight-skirted. Good legs, in dark nylons, and medium-heeled black patent pumps. She was dark, probably with the help of a good tint, and she had fine fair skin just beginning to show dryness around the eyes, at the jawline. Her blue eyes looked tired, but the automatic pleasant smile she flashed showed good teeth.

"And what may I do for you, sir?" Her voice was thin and high. Just a trifle surprised at Luis Mendoza, his elegant tailoring and suave manner, here. He brought out the badge, introduced himself.

The blue eyes rounded; she was genuinely astonished.

"What on earth do the *police* want of *me*? I don't—"

"I'm sorry, I don't know your name, Miss—"

"Page. I'm Patti Page. But I don't—"

"Miss Page. Do you know a Rex Carson?"

"*Rex?*" she said. "Mixed up with *police?* What's he done? I was afraid he might get in trouble, he just doesn't— Yes, I know him. But he wouldn't do anything really—"

"I'm sorry to have to tell you, Miss Page, that Mr. Carson is dead. He was found shot this morning." Mendoza watched her.

She didn't go into hysterics. She stared at him and said dazedly, "Rex? Sh-shot? Where?"

"In his car, downtown."

"Oh." She sat down suddenly on the couch and began to cry gently. She sniffed into a handkerchief fished out from her brassiere and said, "*Shot.* But who'd want to shoot Rex? Why, he was in here just yesterday—he said—he said—" She cried for a little while, and sat up and blew her nose, and looked at Mendoza dully. "Well, I guess I could imagine some reason. For somebody. My God. My God." She looked vaguely around the room, the brave cheap little room pretending to be a smart office, a business. What clients would she get? The high school kids, stenographers in small offices, dreaming of the glamorous career. And Patti, probably, doing the same twenty years back. Heading for Hollywood with high hopes? And Carson drumming up new clients for her? She was staring at him. She said, "Rex *dead.*" She wet her lips. "We were going to Vegas this weekend. He said, a little windfall, let's blow it, honey. I hadn't seen him for a couple of months—he came and went, you never know when— My God. . . . It's like—I don't know—like something laughing at you. Life. What you want, and what you get. Rex—what'd you say your name was?"

Mendoza repeated it. "If you'd answer some questions, Miss Page. How long had you known Mr. Carson?"

"About—four years. About that. . . . He didn't *mean* anything," she said in a low voice. "Anything—wrong. He just—I knew that—he just—liked to be comfortable. A very sweet guy. He wanted everybody to be happy. He just—well, some people can't stand routine. You know. But—but he liked things easy and nice. Oh, I didn't kid myself about him, Mr. Mendoza—honestly I didn't. I knew he was lazy, and he—he didn't think about money just exactly the way most people— He never paid back that hundred I lent him, the time his sister died back East and he had to pay for the funeral—but I've been down on luck too, we've got to help each other. It was just how he was. Always thinking up schemes to— I knew that. But he was—fun to be with. A sweet guy. Only he—slid out from under." She raised her eyes to Mendoza's, to see if he understood that. "Some people are like that, they can't help it. And I guess—" that was very low "—some other people made to—just make excuses and—and not care. I knew him, but—"

"Had you lived with him, Miss Page?" asked Mendoza conversationally.

"It wasn't anything permanent," she said flatly. "He was such a nice guy, Rex—you couldn't *count* on him, but once you knew that, what'd it matter? You take people the way they are. I know I was a fool, so maybe I was a little better than all the others he'd sweet-talked—not that I know who any of them were, but there's bound to have been others. You get tired. You get so tired. This piddling little—well, I try to give the girls some value for the money, teach them how to walk and talk and wear clothes—turned a couple of old storerooms behind this into a makeshift gym. But it's not exactly like John Powers." She fumbled at the cigarette box on the coffee table; Mendoza leaned forward and snapped his lighter. "Thanks. I know I was a fool," she said bitterly. "But you take what you can get. I knew how he was. He never meant anything serious—about me. Just, if he couldn't get anybody else, or maybe thought I'd be good for a twenty-buck loan— Oh, he *liked* me—he liked everybody, you've got to understand that. He wanted everybody to like *him*. It was a kind of need he had. But it was—out of sight out of mind. I hadn't laid eyes on him since January, when he got a couple of new girls to sign up for the course. He said he'd been out of state, but I don't know if he had. He showed up yesterday, took me out to lunch, and said let's go to Vegas for the weekend, he'd had this little windfall. He—kind of woke you up, you felt on top of the world when you were with him— I always fell for it."

"A little windfall," said Mendoza gently. "Did he say from where?"

She shook her head. "I'm not a fool. I knew him—in my head. Probably he'd borrowed the money, or got it by some little finagle. I don't know. But—you take what you can get out of life. And he was such fun to be with." She started to cry again.

"Well, there you are," said Higgins. "The jewels. And what does it say?"

"God knows," said Hackett.

Among the various things on hand, Carson-Conway had struck them both as the possibly offbeat, interesting one. Anything a little different was a relief, in the welter of day-to-day routine. Whatever Mendoza might say about that scrawl on the memo-pad, pending the autopsy report (he *could* have been drunk), that was offbeat.

Hackett had duly fetched Heffner in and got the formal statement, while Higgins typed up the preliminary report on Rex Carson-Robert Conway. They had then had a quick lunch and checked back with Scarne at the lab. A lab team had been through the Milliken house, and a report would be sent up. Checking in at the office, they heard that Glasser had delivered the Echevarrios to the facility on Alameda and gone over to the Milliken house looking for stray roomers. No word from him so far. They ran into Piggott at the office, and heard a few tidbits about the other new case and some peculiar things that had showed at that place. And then, no new calls being in, they had gone up to Alexandria Avenue in Hollywood to the shabby old apartment where Rex Carson had most recently lived.

The manageress's bell went unanswered. There were a couple of lab men, Duke and Willis, poking around. Carson's keys had been sent down to the lab. They had dusted the place, for what it was worth—a waste of time in a way, Carson having been shot in his car, but you never knew what evidence would prove useful. It was an anonymous sort of place, small living room, bedroom, bath, kitchenette. The closet held a wardrobe of natty gents' clothes, four suits, sports clothes, five pairs of shoes; the drawers of the rickety old bureau the expectable underwear, handkerchieves, socks. There was a sketchy stock of food on the kitchen shelves, in the old refrigerator; he hadn't done much cooking at home. Liquor on one shelf, all opened bottles: bourbon, gin, vodka. There was a little desk in the living room but it was absolutely empty; evidently he never used that at all. No checkbooks or credit cards anywhere. The strictly cash-and-carry operator unusual these days; but if Carson had been at least a borderline pro con-man . . .

"So, the jewels," said Higgins.

"What the hell could it say, George?"

"You tell me."

The jewels—if such they were—had been in a locked metal box on the shelf of the bedroom closet. Duke said there were some good latents on it; he had lifted them. The jewels—if such they were—were now spread out on the diminutive kitchen table in the little kitchenette. The only other item in the box had been a scrap of paper, the roughly torn-off half of a used envelope, bearing the brief notation *Harry OS-94563.*

Looking most important of the lot, there was a ring, either white gold or platinum, set with what looked like a good-sized diamond solitaire.

Next, there was an old-fashioned-looking gold ring set with an amethyst. A cameo brooch, also old. A garnet brooch. A garnet ring—several small stones. A small opal ring. A thin gold bracelet. A brooch set with three small opals and three diamond chips. A topaz ring. A turquoise ring. An old pendant watch, not running. A pair of single pearl earrings for pierced ears. And, in a new-looking white velvet box labeled inside *Keller's Jewelers,* a very new-looking gold ring set with a pale blue stone.

"What makes sense?" asked Higgins. "I don't care what Luis says, that *Jewels* means something. Drunk, my eye. He made the hell of an effort to get that down. It meant something to *him.* What?"

"What indeed?" said Hackett. He picked up the topaz ring and stared at it. "What could it have meant? And where did all this come from?"

THREE

Mendoza got back to the office to find that Glasser had just brought in one Ronald Fairbrother; as they started to talk to him Lake looked in and said a Willard Jarvis had just come in, on the Milliken thing. Another of the roomers. They talked to them together, and a little emerged, possibly of significance.

Fairbrother, a nondescript balding man in the forties, explained that he and his brother Earl didn't *live* in California; they lived in Chicago. But they were both S. P. engineers, and on their regular runs they landed here for layovers of various lengths nearly every week. It was convenient to have the clean quiet room to go to instead of the more expensive hotel. Paid them to keep it on. He'd just landed here today from San Francisco and would take a freight out on Thursday for Chicago. Earl hadn't been here since Sunday, when he took a freight out east. So, count out Fairbrother, much shocked at the murder of such a nice woman as Mrs. Milliken.

Jarvis, a stout, hale old man with a halo of white curls, was shocked too; when he'd got home from the park Heffner had told him about it, and he had seen the mess in both rooms. Knowing the police would want to talk to him, he'd come right down. He knew where to come, he said, because he read all the true-detective magazines and a lot of detective novels and knew all about the precincts. And he gave them a little.

Mrs. Milliken, he said, always kept her doors locked. A lot of honest people around there but other kinds too, and she'd been careful. He had been a little surprised that she wasn't up when he left this morning—around eight thirty—she usually was. But the back door was still bolted; as usual he'd left by the back stairs and back door, more convenient to his room. It had crossed his mind to wonder whether maybe she'd caught Mr. Nordhammer's flu. A terrible thing—such a nice woman. And all alone in the world—she hadn't any relatives at all, he remembered her saying. "What will happen to the house?" he asked anxiously. "I've been settled down there—it's quiet and comfortable—and only the pension—"

Mendoza said he didn't know. "What about Monday, Mr. Jarvis? What time did you come home?"

Jarvis thought. About five thirty, he thought. He spent most of his days up in the park in nice weather. Reading or just sitting. When he came in yesterday, he said, Mrs. Milliken's bedroom door had been closed. He hadn't seen her at all after he'd seen her yesterday morning. He'd had an early dinner at a cafeteria uptown before coming home, and went up to his room and read, and went to bed about ten.

Mendoza exchanged a glance with Glasser. Her door had been open this morning, reason Heffner had seen her and called in. Had the killer still been in the house when Jarvis came home yesterday? Both Milliken and Nordhammer already dead?

No, Jarvis hadn't heard anything unusual after coming in yesterday. Mr. Forstein had come in about nine thirty, later than usual; he heard his door open and close; and Mr. Heffner came in—making quite a lot of noise—about ten. That was all. And he could not get over it, a terrible thing, two innocent honest citizens right in their own home—

"Yes, sir," said Glasser. "I guess that's all we want to ask you right now. We'll have a squad car take you back—" he began shepherding them out.

See what the autopsy reports said about time of death; but Mendoza was thinking now that it had probably been yesterday afternoon. Milliken and Nordhammer alone in the house. How had X got in, with doors locked? Some pretense— And there was the fact, of course, that none of the other roomers' rooms had been ransacked. Had X—or a couple of X's—panicked, having inadvertently committed homicide, and hearing Jarvis come home, got out as quickly as possible? That could be. And the anonymous thing; unless he—or they—had left any prints around, the permanently anonymous thing, for there didn't seem any way to pin down what loot had been taken.

He got up and went into the sergeants' office. Piggott was hunched over his typewriter. "What'd you get out of Mama and Papa?" asked Mendoza abruptly.

"Nothing," said Piggott, looking up from the report. "They both did some fancy swearing at me, was all. I did, naturally, have to tell 'em they didn't have to talk. These rules and regulations." Piggott was a pillar of a fundamentalist church and not a swearing man, but his expression swore for him. "I gave up finally and booked 'em in. But I don't think the fast-talking lawyer can get around the evidence."

"Let's hope not," said Mendoza.

"That other thing was what I wanted to talk to you about. The old Negro woman—Sadie Snyder. One way, just another break-in and the lout using a little too much violence. But she was on the pension, didn't have anything much. I know that says nothing. But the looks of that place—something queer," said Piggott seriously. "Mighty queer. But she seems to've been an ordinary honest old lady. No record. The grandson's got a regular job at a Sears warehouse. No record. His parents—old lady's son and his wife—have a little grocery store on Sixtieth. No record. Ordinary honest people. But that apartment looked funny. The things—"

"Lieutenant," said Sergeant Lake. "Art. Your outside phone."

"O.K.—later, Matt." Mendoza went back to his office and picked up the phone. "Where've you been?"

"On the legwork," said Hackett. "I'm out in Reseda now. Thought I'd better call in. I probably won't be back before I knock off."

"What are you doing out there?"

"On Carson. George and I divided up some of the names from that address book. Saw four or five people together, and then— Well, a little something emerged. I've got two or three more to look for before I call it a day. O.K.?"

"And what has emerged?"

"Too long a story to tell you now, on a pay phone," said Hackett hastily. "In the morning. Just reporting in what I'm on. I'll see you." He was gone before Mendoza could get in another word.

"¡Condenación!" said Mendoza mildly. And it was too early, but he called the lab to ask if they had anything for him on any of the recent cases. They hadn't.

"On that Milliken thing," said Duke, "we'll have to check out all the roomers' prints against what we picked up. And you don't know then it wasn't one of them did it." Mendoza said he didn't think it likely, though anything was possible. "Or, any strange prints, just because they were there it doesn't say they belong to a killer. I think we're just going through the motions. But I did notice one thing. Nothing very abstruse."

"What?"

"Well, there was a sign in the window saying *Room for Rent*, but all the beds were made up—all the rooms looked, you know, occupied. Which I suppose you noticed too, and—"

"Oh, really?" said Mendoza. "As a matter of fact I didn't." He thought a moment and added, "I may be calling you back."

He got his hat and went out again, sought the Ferrari in the lot downstairs and drove up to Cortez Street, to the Milliken house. He found Heffner, Jarvis and Fairbrother there, still talking about the nine days' wonder of murder crossing their peaceful orbits, and asked questions. They all trooped upstairs to look at the middle bedroom on the left, the one unoccupied for the past month, as all the roomers could testify. Mendoza stopped them on the threshold.

The room looked occupied, all right. The bed was made up with what looked like clean sheets. Nothing in the drawers of the painted bureau, but there were a couple of used towels on the floor, and some clothes—an ancient pair of gray slacks, a ragged white shirt, and an old pair of navy blue sneakers.

The roomers all told him they each had their own towel rack in the single bathroom at the end of the hall and never kept towels in their bedrooms. And the only reason that Mrs. Milliken would have made up the bed in here would be that she had rented the room. And it must have been just yesterday, because none of them had seen her last night, to hear about it.

"Mmh—yes," said Mendoza. A vague picture formed in his mind: the only snag was, of course, that Mrs. Milliken had evidently been careful about whom she rented her nice clean rooms to; she wouldn't have taken in the first ragged stranger who offered her two weeks' rent in advance. However—

He came out and looked up and down the street. Nearly dark, people just coming home from work, and housewives busy over dinner. Catch them tomorrow. He found a pay phone at the corner, called the office and told Lake to leave a note for the night men: somebody should see old Mr. Forstein—though it was unlikely he had anything useful for them. And then he went home himself.

As the Ferrari's lights turned up the drive, they caught Alison out in front, unprecedentedly cutting roses from the bush against the house. She waved at him as he slowed in surprise. "Oh, darling, would you mind coming in the front? Mairí's got a cake in the oven."

When he came in the front door and looked for her, she was putting the last touches to a bowl of roses on the dining room table. "A cake?" said Mendoza. "Since when do I annoy Mairí coming in the back door?"

"Hmm?" said Alison vaguely. "Oh, she just said— I'll get you a drink, *amante*. You sit down and relax—you look tired. Go on, sit down, I'll—"

Mendoza put away his hat and sat down in the living room, and she brought him a full shot-glass of rye. "Anything new?" she asked brightly.

"Not much," said Mendoza, yawning. "Couple of new ones, yes—one rather funny little thing, but I don't suppose it will be once it gets unraveled. Where are the offspring, *cara?*"

"Having their supper. Dinner in ten minutes, and then they'll be having their baths while we eat in peace. Thank heaven for Mairí," said Alison.

"Well, it occurs to me I don't see much of them," said Mendoza. "No father figure around. They do say—"

"Darling, they're only two and a half. When they're not going to bed so early—"

"There now, my lambs," said Mrs. MacTaggart from the door, "say goodnight to your father like good lambies and then off to our baths."

"Well, *señor y señorita, buenas tardes*," said Mendoza. "What have you been up to today, *niña*—?" as Terry ran to him.

"Terry," said Alison. Terry giggled and retreated from his hug, her dark eyes bright with mischief.

Johnny giggled and clapped a hand to his mouth, squealing. "We were good!" he said emphatically. "*¡Muy bueno!*"

"Well, that's a change for the better," said Mendoza.

"An'—an—Bast were *colérico*, Daddy—*muy colérico—*"

"Now, now," said Mrs. MacTaggart briskly, "your father's wanting his dinner, come along. It's all on the table, *achara*, but for the salad, so you'd best be getting to it—and these two a bit overexcited, come along, my lambies—"

"What upset Bast?" asked Mendoza as the twins were shepherded out. He finished his drink.

"What? Oh, the Robertsons' peke," said Alison. "She spat at him like anything. I'll get the salad."

As usual, it was a satisfactory dinner. Center cut pork chops broiled slowly, Mairí's own special creamed potatoes, the fat green Italian beans he liked, Alison's special rolls, the salad, and lemon tarts with whipped cream for dessert.

"What happened to the cake?" asked Mendoza.

"What cake? Oh, that cake," said Alison. "Why, it's for Janet—Mairí's sister. Tomorrow's her birthday. More coffee?"

There was a certain amount of subdued noise from the rear of the house, and then quiet as, presumably, the twins settled down. Mendoza glanced up from his coffee to remark that he didn't know Mairí could whistle, something new in lullabies, and Alison said she hadn't been noticing. As Mendoza came back to the living room while she cleared the table, Cedric the shaggy dog marched in with an air of something-accomplished-something-done, at this end of a busy day a dog was entitled to relax, and flopped down in the middle of the room. His blue-gray top needed a good brushing, but his white chest, paws and tail tip were immaculate. "Well, *bufón*," said Mendoza, "I take it you've supervised the bath and bed routine as usual." He wandered down the hall to say a proper goodnight to the twins, and was forestalled by Mairí at the door.

"They're settled down and near asleep now, for once, you'll not be disturbing them," she told him in dulcet tones. "You go relax yourself, I'll be fetching you another dram maybe?"

"No, thanks, Mairí." When Alison appeared in the living room fifteen minutes later he surveyed her suspiciously. "I've got the oddest feeling that something's going on around here."

"What? Don't be silly," said Alison. "What would be going on? Tell me about the funny new one," and she sat down to listen expectantly. Cedric yawned widely, his forehead mop falling back to show his one wild walleye, and the cats came stalking in, tails high. Bast made for Cedric and began to chew his right ear meditatively; Sheba and Nefertite got to Alison's lap simultaneously, and El Señor leaped onto Mendoza's knees and began telling him a long story in excited Siamese—El Señor had inherited his father's voice.

"I just have a feeling—" said Mendoza. But it wasn't until he was getting undressed, later on, that there was anything overtly suspicious to remark on. Alison was serenely massaging cream into her forehead at the dressing table, and Mendoza was just buttoning his pajamas when, quite distinctly and somewhere quite near, somebody whistled the first four bars of "Yankee Doodle." "What's that?" Mendoza shot open the window on the side yard.

"What?" asked Alison. "I didn't hear anything."

He looked at her disbelievingly. "I—there it is again." Just the first four bars, repeated four times. A prowler wouldn't—

"You're imagining things," said Alison. "If there was anything there, Cedric would have barked." Which was, of course, quite true. In the six weeks since they'd acquired Cedric—all through Alison's soft-hearted sentimentality—he had proved to be an assiduous watchdog. Doubtfully, Mendoza shut the window halfway; the nights were still cold.

As he was drifting muzzily into sleep, he thought he heard an owl somewhere nearby. Quite impossible, of course. Owls of any variety were practically unknown in urban Southern California.

When he got to the office on Wednesday morning, there was a report on his desk from Nick Galeano. Old Mr. Forstein had been interviewed; he was not helpful. On Monday night he had stayed late at his pawnshop working on his books, and when he came home the front hall had been dark; he knew the place and had not bothered to switch on a light, so couldn't say whether Mrs. Milliken's bedroom door had been open or not. And yesterday morning he had left the house early, six thirty, it was still not quite light and he had not glanced in that direction as he came down to the front door. *Old boy very shocked*, Galeano had added, *this is probably gospel.*

And now Hackett was retailing what he and Higgins had turned up yesterday afternoon on Carson. It was Higgins's day off—what else he'd turned up after they split the list would come in tomorrow.

"This Bill Collard," said Hackett, "at a men's store on Western. He says, Is that jerk still around, when I mentioned Carson. Carson owed him twenty bucks from a couple of years back, he said. Seems Carson worked at the same store awhile, six months or so that long ago. Collard called him a lazy bum, further said he—Collard—had always figured it was Carson who got Marjorie in trouble. Marjorie the former cashier at the café next door—nice girl, Collard said, but that Carson, the females just couldn't resist him. You gather Collard didn't think much of him. Said he wasn't surprised somebody shot him. And then we went to this dancing school for children. As per the business card. Miss Shirley

Forrester. I shouldn't think it likely," said Hackett dryly, "there was any romance there. She's about sixty-five trying hard to look forty, ex-chorus-girl type, hard as nails but the sweet front. The dear kiddies. That's the same old racket, if I read it right—minus the doubletalk, get your kiddy in the movies and retire for life. She talked about discovering talent in our budding youth and all, but that's it. And dear Mr. Carson such a live wire at finding talented pupils for her. Read, gullible parents."

"Mmh," said Mendoza. "I thought that game was dead long ago."

"So we're both surprised. Con games never die," said Hackett, "they just stay that way. She said she hadn't seen Carson for about two weeks. Then George and I split up, seeing there are a couple of hundred names in that damned address book, and the next one I talked to was a Mrs. Marion Childs. She's a divorcée, works at a dress shop in Hollywood, and has a ten-year-old daughter named Jeaneanne Marie. She thought Mr. Carson was a lovely young man, so intelligent and discerning, he said right away when he'd listened to Jeaneanne Marie sing and dance that she had exceptional talent and it'd be a terrible shame if she couldn't have proper training, and he got her in the course at special rates as a favor, only ten dollars a lesson once a week, it did seem expensive but you do have to pay for the best—"

"¡Caray!" said Mendoza. "What people fall for. But no animosity against Carson there."

"Anything but. Then I found Mrs. Eugene Campbell. I'd guess, substantial money—nothing spectacular but more than comfortable. About fifty-five, a widow. Smart dresser. Lives alone in an apartment-hotel in Hollywood. No children. Quite a nice woman, Luis," said Hackett thoughtfully. "But—lonely. A little bit foolish. She met him about a year ago when he rang her doorbell by—um—mistake. Wrong address. And they got talking. Can we guess he cased her a little? We can say for sure he was the charmer—insinuated himself easy. And there's no sex there—not likely—but I read between the lines. A woman alone, places she hesitates to go —no fun dining out alone, going places. Like that. I'd have a shrewd guess she picked up the tab, just to have the escort. Charming young man to amuse her, talk to her, flatter her. Maybe she gave him a present now and then. Worth a little of Carson's time, the good restaurants, the drinks."

"Y-e-s," said Mendoza. "But—"

"All grist that comes to his mill. That kind. Then I ran into something funny. Out in Reseda. There was this name, J. L. Lamson, and the Reseda address. It turned out to be a small-parts manufacturing company. Aircraft parts, I think. I had a time getting in—the badge finally did it. And Lamson turned out to be the owner of the company."

"And what did he have to do with Carson?"

"Nothing—he says. He says he doesn't know any Carson, never did know him, and when I ask what his name's doing in Carson's address book he says he hasn't any idea, but a lot of salesmen and so on do call on him soliciting business, people he doesn't know, and beyond that he really couldn't say and if I'll excuse him he has an appointment. The funny thing," said Hackett, "is that he was scared."

"*¿Por qué?*" Mendoza cocked a brow at him.

"Don't ask me, how would I know? But when I mentioned Carson's name—he was still looking at my badge to be sure I was bona fide—he started to sweat. He was all formal and polite on the surface, but he didn't like me at all, and he was very positive that he didn't know anything about Carson. In a hurry to be rid of me."

"You don't tell me. Why? Small-parts for aircraft. . . . A pattern, in a way," said Mendoza. "We'll see what George came up with. But it does just occur to me, Art— Carson living by his wits, sure, and he really doesn't look like the pro con-man, just the drifter, the lazy charmer who'd rather make it easy by the gimmicks than work the eight-hour day. All right. Just what's showed so far—Patti Page, these other women—the dancing school racket— What's that Match-Mates, Incorporated?"

"Couldn't say, George was going to cover that."

"Oh. Well, just by what we've turned up so far, he wasn't taking in even a living wage with the occasional sponging off his girl friends, the little commissions on the talented kids, the would-be models. He must have had some longer irons in the fire. I've got queries out to Oregon, but—"

"Well, we've got a lot more local names to look at," said Hackett.

"Nobody you've talked to so far admits to seeing him recently?" Hackett shook his head. "He was paying seventy-five for the apartment on Alexandria. Nick got hold of the manageress there last night. He'd lived there a couple of years, been away sometimes. Nobody there knew him—a place to sleep. At times," said Mendoza cynically. "And what with inflation—he must have had some better, surer game than all that. That paid better. The girl friends and so on were insurance, to fall back on."

"There was that phone number," said Hackett suddenly. "In with the jewels—I told you about that? Well, I meant to. The jewels. Funny little collection of stuff. I sent it down to the lab, see what it's worth. They've got experts on everything down there. But this little scrap of paper—Harry, and a phone number on it. I meant to have Jimmy ask the phone company to check it out."

"We had better do that indeed," Mendoza started to say, and Jason Grace thrust his head in the door.

"Conference," he said, smiling. "Just thought I'd ask all polite if I can put in my oar on that thing Matt's muttering about. Mrs. Sadie Snyder."

"If you have any ideas," said Mendoza, "by all means. It sounded—what I've heard about it—strictly routine. For the lab."

Grace put his head on one side, his brown face crinkling, his moustache neat as Mendoza's. "Well, sometimes, Lootenant suh, us cullud folk know a litty-bit about our own that a white man mightn't. If you get me."

Mendoza grinned. "The results are all that interest me, Jase. You've got an idea, go work on it." Grace half-saluted and vanished. "It just occurs to me, Art, instead of going through this address book at random—" he was glancing over the one marked R. R. C. idly, the one with the local addresses, leafing over pages "—we might check over the names first. There's something just on the edge of my mind—small aircraft parts—*Por Dios*, I can't—"

"Morning," said Landers from the door. "We've got a new body. In an alley over on Fourth. John went out on it." Palliser back today too. "There's a teletype in from the Oregon D.M.V." That query had been sent out yesterday. "They've got a license on file for a Robert Conway, that's all. No traffic citations on him."

"Helpful," said Mendoza. "How're you feeling, Tom?" Landers had got shot up last month; this was only his third day back on the job. Landers, feeling his shoulder absently, said he was O.K. "Damn it," said Mendoza, "do we ask every police force in Oregon if they've got a record on him?"

"Why?" asked Hackett. "He didn't show in ours, as either Carson or Conway. I don't think he was a pro, Luis. On the way, maybe. Maybe in time he'd have pulled something a little rawer. Maybe he had, and hadn't been caught up to yet. And I go along, he must have had some surer source of income than the piddling rackets, the women. The occasional things. But—"

"*De veras*," said Mendoza. Carson's prints had been sent to the FBI; time would tell on that. The quickest way to find out. But— He said suddenly, "*¡Demonios!* Didn't I just say—"

"What?"

Mendoza got up. "These addresses." He had been leafing over pages carefully. "You can get on with your list, I'll check this. Just for fun. Carson was found in his car over on Crandall Street. Probably shot right there—he'd been driving. And here's a Mrs. Rose Lamont, address on Mountain View. Which is about three blocks away from Crandall. I think I'll go see what she looks like."

As he passed Sergeant Lake's desk, Lake was just putting down the phone, saying, "New call—maybe another suicide, out on Wilshire."

"O.K., O.K.," said Landers. "I'll take it."

The four-family apartment on Mountain View had begun life as a large single house and later been cut up into apartments. Mendoza found Lamont listed, by the mailboxes, as occupying Apartment Three upstairs. He found the door open, climbed stairs past the former entrance hall of the house, and faced a door with a tarnished brass "3" on it. He knocked.

After a long moment the door opened to him. "Mrs. Lamont?" said Mendoza, and realized his mistake at once. The girl who had opened the door couldn't be more than thirteen or fourteen. She was thin and awkward, at the gawky stage: dark straight hair in a neat Dutch bob, and a pale clear complexion. She had on blue pajamas and a too-short pink chenille bathrobe, and there was an open book in her hand. Automatically his eyes deciphered the title: *Algebra for Beginners*.

"Oh, you mean my mother," she said in a thin reedy voice. "She's at the café. You could find her there. I'm only home because I've got a cold. It's just two blocks up on Beverly—

Rose's Eatery. She owns it. But if it's about insurance or anything like that she wouldn't be interested."

"It's not insurance," said Mendoza. "Thanks very much."

"She doesn't buy anything at the door," said the girl doubtfully. "It's more expensive."

"I'm not selling anything. I just want to talk to her."

"Oh, well, then," she said. "She's at the café."

He found Rose's Eatery up on Beverly and produced his badge. "Why, yes, I'm Rose Lamont—*police?* What on earth do you want with me?" It was a hole-in-the-corner place, short-order lunches and breakfasts, a counter and four booths, but it looked clean and quiet. She was a small woman, dark and rather harried-looking. About thirty-five, not bad-looking at all, her hair a little untidy, discreet makeup. She had big dark eyes. At this hour, there wasn't a customer in the place. Mendoza asked her if she knew a Rex Carson.

"Why, yes—why are the *police* asking—"

He told her that Carson was dead. "I'm sorry to have to bother you, Mrs. Lamont, but if you could tell me—"

"*Dead?*" she said blankly. "Rex *dead?*" The dark eyes filled with tears. "Oh, my dear Lord—oh, my God. They must have *got him* after all. He said it was awfully dangerous. They got him after all. The Russians. The Communists. He *said*—Oh, my dear Lord. Rex. We were—kind of engaged." She began to sob.

"Communists?" said Mendoza, taken aback.

"Oh, oh, oh!" she sobbed. "My Rex! Didn't you know he was a CIA agent? And he—"

FOUR

"Oh, you didn't know," she said, staring at his expression. "Oh, my, oh, dear, you'd better tell the government right away, they'll want to know, won't they? How—how did he get killed?"

"He was shot. Mrs.—"

"Oh, poor Rex. Oh, my poor dear—he always said it might happen, he warned me. But it just doesn't seem right, all he had to put up with and nothing going right for him—such a wonderful man, and so patriotic and all, the sacrifices he made for his country—" She blew her nose. "And I guess, somehow, I never did quite believe it'd work out for *us*. But it's a shock, coming so sudden—"

"Yes, I'm sorry," said Mendoza mechanically. "Mrs. Lamont, I'd like to ask you a few questions if you don't mind."

"Yes, sir. I'd like to help however I can, of course. Are you from the FBI? But if you didn't know he was—"

"Lieutenant Mendoza, L.A.P.D. I'd just like to hear how long you'd known Mr. Carson, and how you met, and—"

"Well, I don't know why you'd be interested in that, but if it'd help find whoever killed poor Rex—" She blew her nose again and lifted the flap beside the cash register and came out to his side of the counter. "I guess it's just as well there aren't any customers in, what they'd think—but it's a

BURLINGAME
PUBLIC
LIBRARY

shock. We always said it might happen. He had to go on these dangerous jobs, you know, for the government, he never knew when—sometimes he even went behind the Iron Curtain—and there was always the risk he'd be followed back here. And he said if he ever *was*, and killed—like that—why, the government'd just have to say they didn't know anything about it. On account of him being an agent. It'd be no good my asking about him. Oh, dear, I do think it's terrible, the things that go on these days! But I guess we better not have anybody coming in to interrupt—" Sniffing and dreary-eyed, she turned the *Open* sign on the door to read *Closed* and locked the door. She looked around helplessly. "Would you mind sitting in a booth, sir? Maybe you'd like a cup of coffee. I guess I'll have one."

Seated in the booth, the hot coffee in the usual thick mugs between them, he asked, "How long had you known Carson, Mrs. Lamont? Excuse me, are you a widow?"

She nodded mournfully. "Yes, sir. Since my daughter Mary was five—she's fourteen now. My husband was killed in an accident. I've had a lot of bad luck in my life, but some good too, I've got to remember. It's funny, even from the first I had the feeling Rex and I were going to have bad luck. It was sort of too good to be true—for me, anyway. I guess you've got to be thankful for what you get in life. And I have been truly thankful to Mrs. Eaton, she was a good woman, and we'd got on just fine together—I came to work here in 1959, nearly ten years back, she was getting on and couldn't take all the standing anymore, so she hired me and we took to each other right away though she was so much older. She took an interest in Mary too, never having had any children of her own, but I never in the world expected she'd leave all she had to me—that was four years ago when she died—the café, and her house, and nearly five thousand dollars in the bank. It's the apartment house where I live now, there's three other apartments that rent for eighty apiece. It was just wonderful of her, I couldn't get over it. But to get back to Rex, I didn't mean to—"

"Mrs. Lamont, did Carson have an appointment with you on Monday night?"

She nodded vigorously. "Said he'd be by about nine. He'd dropped in here that morning—he'd just got back from another of those jobs for the government—I hadn't seen him for nearly a month. I was so glad to see him, you can't think, and he said he'd come by that night. When he didn't, I was worried, but I thought maybe he'd had a sudden call—a man like him, in special government work, it's not like an eight-to-five job. But he never called or anything. And to think— oh, poor Rex! And only thirty-seven, it doesn't seem fair. All he sacrificed. My daughter Mary'll be all cut up too, she liked Rex—we were going to be married, you know—"

"Had any date been set, Mrs. Lamont?"

"Oh, well, no, he couldn't while he was on that sort of job, not fair to me or Mary. Not until he could be settled down, you know, and the government wasn't sending him on all those dangerous missions. He—"

"When did you meet him? Where?"

She sipped her coffee, refusing the offered cigarette. "I never got in the habit. You smoke, I don't mind, sir. Why, he came in here a few times, last year it was—last February, more than a year now. We got to talking a bit, he was such a friendly sort, sort of put you at your ease like, and we—well, liked each other right off. I told him how I came to own this place, and how kind Mrs. Eaton was and about my daughter Mary and all—poor Rex, always wanted a family he had, and his ex-wife didn't want any, couldn't be bothered—when I think of the trouble that woman made him, I could just wring her neck! It was just disgraceful, and him so long-suffering about it. But that was later. You understand, I didn't like to—to put myself forward or seem to—to be chasing after him, but he seemed so lonely and I finally did ask

53

him to dinner and, well, that was how it started. Of course it wasn't till later that he confided in me what his real job was. When we sort of got engaged. I mean, up to then he couldn't, naturally—confidential secret work for our government. Sometimes I'd wondered about it, I wouldn't see him for weeks and then he'd turn up. But *then*, he told me—in strict confidence, you understand—and I was so proud of him! He was a wonderful man, Rex was, so patriotic and of course he must have been awfully brilliant or the government wouldn't have given him all those dangerous important secret jobs to do. He was so anxious to have it all over with so he could settle down—he and my daughter Mary got on just fine, did I tell you? Of course Mary's bright too—she takes after her dad that way—always got her nose in a book, she wants to be a teacher of some kind, she gets all A's and I've been saving for her college a long time. But when I think how—"

"Mrs. Lamont, when you saw him on Monday—" But the tide swept over Mendoza.

"—that woman acted, it's just hard to believe. His ex-wife. He was such an honest man, poor Rex, and he had this alimony to pay—I never hold with it when a woman's young and hasn't any children—and it was awkward, with him being sent off on those terrible missions and the government having some rule about not paying till the fiscal month or something—I never understood that, but who can understand the way the government does things—"

"Mrs. Lamont. Did you ever lend him any money?"

"Well, that's just what I'm telling you. And for all I care, you can tell the FBI just what I think about it. I mean the CIA—terrible! Send a fine patriotic man like Rex over to those awful places to mix with Communists, just serving his country as best he could, and then— Why, the first time he had to go away after we knew each other, when he got back he was all behind on his alimony to that woman and she was making all sorts of nasty threats, he said. He was worried, and his government pay wasn't due for another two months. I lent him seven hundred dollars then to keep her quiet. And later on, the same thing happened again—"

"Had he paid any of it back, Mrs. Lamont?"

"What? Well, he would have as soon as ever he could," she said earnestly. "Like I told him, in a way it was *our* money— we were going to get married. As soon as the government stopped sending him on these missions. That time, the next time he went off, he had to bribe a man to help him get out of Russia safe, and then the first thing we knew his ex-wife— her name was Maureen—was cutting up about the back alimony again, five hundred it amounted to then— That woman! I said to Rex, where's her *patriotism?* And then another time—"

Mendoza finished his coffee, regarding her with some fascination. "Mrs. Lamont," he said rather loudly. "When was the last time you'd seen Carson before Monday?"

"Oh, a good month. He thought he might have to go away again then. I don't know whether he had, but I expect so, not coming by in so long. He just looked in a minute on Monday morning, and said he was coming to see me that night. And when he didn't come and didn't come, I was worried—but he'd've called if he could, I know. And besides, all this time, I've been telling myself—my great-great-great-grandfather fought in the Revolutionary War, Mr. Mendoza —we've *all* got to maybe make sacrifices for our country, and I hope I've always been a good patriotic woman—Rex and I did want to be settled down and married—my poor dear Rex—but after all the country comes first, and—"

"Did you try to get in touch with him on Monday night?"

"Oh, no. I couldn't. I never knew where to reach him, he was always moving around. The kind of work he was on— secret, you know. It was just as he could get away he'd come to see me. No, I just—waited. And he never came." Tears filled her eyes again.

"You were alone? At home? With your daughter?"

"Oh, Mary'd gone to see her friend Susan. I just waited— And he might have been lying dead all the while! Some terrible spy *murdering* him—" She began to cry again.

Mendoza extricated himself with smooth thanks, managing to avoid any commitments to get in immediate touch with J. Edgar Hoover and the White House. He started back to the Ferrari marveling at the female sex. And what a line to feed her—*¡por Dios!*—the funny thing being that, as was so depressingly the case with so many marks (of both sexes) taken by the cons, she was apparently sensible enough at running her little business, collecting rent from her tenants. And in a modest way—by pro con standards—she had been a good mark. The little café was in a business neighborhood; she'd get a good brisk lunch trade. Over on Mountain View, a modest street, taxes not yet astronomical. She had had the twelve hundred bucks to hand over. Out of her savings for Mary's college?

The female of the species—Kipling had not been infallible. What it always came back to, of course, was human nature. And sometimes—quite often—that old devil sex.

But unless Rose Lamont was a consummate actress, she hadn't had anything to do with taking off Carson. Carson-Conway-Blank. But he had, couldn't it be deduced, been on his way to see her when he was taken off. The body found only three blocks away. Oh, yes? What had he been up to in Oregon? When? And while twelve hundred bucks was a very decent take from one mark—still, over a year's time? Of course, put it all together—all his piddling little gimmicks— it added up. And considering what had shown, it was not surprising that somebody had finally got mad enough to use a gun on Carson. And it might have been almost anybody: one of the women he'd victimized, waking up at last, or learning that she wasn't his one and only romance: an annoyed boy friend of one of them. Any of the marks. And some men's names in the address books too: what had been his pitch—or pitches—with them?

Well, see what Hackett turned up today. . . . When he got back to the office Palliser was there typing a report. "Anything much?" asked Mendoza.

Palliser looked up. "Paperwork. Corpse over on the Row —looked like a natural death. *Vino* or a coronary. Or both. And wouldn't you know, Roberta's found a house she likes. At forty thousand."

"Inflation," said Mendoza. "Civil servants considered good mortgage risks."

"And who is kidding who? Any private insurance company," said Palliser, "doing the realistic thinking, would have doubled our premiums by now."

Mendoza laughed, went on into his office and looked at the little pile of papers on his desk. On top was something new: the autopsy reports on Milliken and Nordhammer. He glanced over them rapidly. Cause of death: Nordhammer, massive contusions to head, Milliken, strangulation; she'd been beaten too. Estimated time of death on both, between 1 and 5 P.M. Monday. So. Belatedly Mendoza recalled what Heffner had said, picked up the phone and asked Lake to get him Captain Welsh at the Academy. . . . "Mendoza, Homicide. I understand one of your maintenance men up there is one John Nordhammer, Captain? You know anything about him?"

"Old Nordie? Sure," said Welsh, sounding surprised. "He's an institution here—more of the boss-man on the job now. Been here for twenty years. You have to hand it to him, he's got a short leg, a lot of men just wouldn't try. But he's a good worker. What's Homicide's interest in Nordie?"

Mendoza told him, and Welsh was shocked. There hadn't been much in the papers: a paragraph on page three. Which in itself, reflected Mendoza, was silent commentary on this year of our Lord. The violence, thievery, assault on the person so all too common that, committed on the average unimportant citizen, it was no longer front-page news.

And, the promised lab report on the Milliken house not yet having arrived, he then settled down at last to read Piggott's extensive report on Mrs. Sadie Snyder. The poor old Negro woman, living on the pension, beaten and presumably robbed by the lout breaking in for whatever loot he could pick up—much the same as on Milliken and Nordhammer, only . . . As he read, his eyebrows climbed higher and he brushed his moustache the wrong way repeatedly and smoothed it back with irritated vigor. And he had casually said to Jase, so far as he'd heard it sounded like the routine thing? What the hell was this?

". . . Photographs made of entire scene will show nails in position, crosses of salt on floor as described, etc. . . ." ran Piggott's careful typing. "The body was in the kitchen, prone on floor. Approximately 600 old nails, all same size and thickness, were placed in a circle around the body. Nails placed in the form of a cross were . . ."

"You can see it in that photograph," said Landers from the back seat, pointing over Grace's shoulder. "The nails on all the thresholds, put in the form of a cross. And—"

"Show him the one of the sheep's heart." Piggott was driving. "That was what got me, Jase."

"And here," said Landers as he reached over Grace's shoulder to shuffle the eight-by-ten photographs Grace was studying. "Craziest setup I ever saw. Salt from the old lady's own kitchen, it looked like—spilled on the floor there, making more crosses, and in a circle all round the body, outside the ring of nails. And in all the other rooms—living room, bedroom, bathroom. And the garlic—talk about crazy—I didn't know what it was until I smelled it—scattered on top of the body, and then that sheep's heart—all bloody and raw— here's the picture."

"Um-hum," said Grace. "When you mentioned a little about it, I sort of had an inkling." He looked at the sharp glossy photograph, a good closeup. The ugly lump of raw red meat was placed in the center of the uncushioned seat of an old straight chair: a strictly utilitarian chair, once painted white and needing another paint job. There was a neat circle of black velvet ribbon tied around the heart, and on the chair seat around it was a precise circle of old rusty nails, each touching the next. "Unbroken circle," said Grace. "Yes. I think so. These Snyders, Matt. Willy, the grandson who found her. Educated?"

"I'd say so. Willy, anyway. I just saw his parents a few minutes—but they seemed like pretty average people. No pedigrees, not on welfare."

Grace laughed. "I don't think that aspect figures in."

"Well, I'd just like you to take a look—any ideas you may get— The Lieutenant's been busy, he'd maybe have a hunch. The lab didn't come up with a thing. No liftable prints, and there's no telling what was taken—the Snyders couldn't say." Piggott made a left turn and slid the car into the curb.

"I think I'd rather have a look at Willy," said Grace, still studying the photographs.

"Your fairy godmother just granted your wish," said Piggott. He slid out from behind the wheel and crossed the narrow sidewalk to the front walk of the little old white frame house. "Well, Mr. Snyder. I think I told you we'd put a seal on the door of your grandmother's place."

"You told me," said Willy Snyder. He looked nervously at them, blinked at Grace, well tailored and broad-shouldered between the slighter Piggott and the lank lean Landers with his boyish face. Willy was a medium-brown young man, reasonably neat in clean work clothes, with the straight Semitic features of North Africa: not a bad-looking young man.

"Well, as long as we're here, let's go in," said Grace softly, smiling. "My name's Grace, and this is Detective Landers, Willy. Where, Matt? I thought you said an apartment."

"Round back." Piggott got out a key. Around the side of the old frame house on this narrow street, down a cement walk, it appeared that part of the rear of the house had been made into a little apartment with its own front door. It sat close to the ground; a single springing rose bush was in bloom beside the tiny porch. Piggott broke the seal and unlocked the door, and Grace prodded Willy in ahead of him.

"I don't mean to put you gentlemen out any," said Willy. "I just thought—my daddy said—if the police was finished here, we could maybe fetch away Grandma's things. The rent's up the first." He looked at Grace from under downswept eyelids.

Grace was looking around interestedly. After the photographs had been taken, the body had been removed and the lab had taken over—there was still evidence of fingerprint powder here and there, but otherwise not much had been moved. The lab had probably taken a few of the nails for analysis, or had they? Why? The nails on the front threshold had been scattered, and on the threshold into the bedroom, but they were still there.

"Ah-hah," he said. He walked over to the fake mantelpiece above a little gas heater and picked up the photograph frame. A cheap dime-store leatherette frame: an enlarged snapshot of Willy and an older couple, probably the parents, a nice-looking couple serious-faced and obviously dressed up. "Turned to the wall. Like that when you first noticed?"

"Yes, that's right," said Piggott.

"And—" Grace strolled across and looked in the bedroom door "—that mirror in there turned to the wall too?"

"Yes, why?"

"Why indeed," said Grace. "It's a shame about your grandma, Willy. She was a nice honest old lady, just getting along on the pension, and the robber broke in and killed her, hah?"

"Yes, sir. That's right. It was awful. She wouldn't've had much for anybody to steal."

"Did he steal much?"

"What?"

"Did he get much from your grandma?"

"I don't know," said Willy. "I don't know how much money she'd have had. Not much." He looked covertly at Grace, and away.

"By any chance, did she have a favorite secret hidey-hole here to stash away her money? A lot of old ladies do." Willy muttered an unwilling Yes. "You know where it was?" Another mutter. "Well, let's just see if the robber found it, shall we? You go look."

"Well—all right," said Willy. Slowly he moved into the bedroom, approached the bed. It was an old-fashioned brass bedstead. Slowly he reached to the knob on the left rear post and unscrewed it. "Anything, Willy?" asked Grace.

"Glory be, they didn't find it," said Willy. He didn't sound very jubilant. He brought out a little wad of bills from the hollow post, and at Grace's gesture counted it. "Eleven bucks," he said. "I guess, what she had left of the pension."

"Yes," said Grace. "Funny he didn't find it. A lot of people know about those hollow posts. . . . Nice old lady, was she?"

"Yes, sir, she *was*," said Willy defiantly. He looked Grace in the eye. "She—she was a God-fearing woman, and she—never meant no harm to anybody. She didn't have much schooling but she knew the Bible, and—and almost first thing I do recall is Grandma teachin' me about the Commandments."

"Is that so?" said Grace. "She had a reputation for being a good one, did she? A white wi—"

Willy shied back two steps. "For bein' a good woman,

yes, sir. That's what I said. And—and she brung up all her children to be good Christian folk too, sir, my daddy and seven more. She brung 'em up to see that it don't matter what color, it's what's in your heart that matters and—good's good and bad's bad, you can't get away from it."

"And that's right, Willy," said Grace gently, "but that isn't all. There's good and bad that's just human, and maybe as old as people. You wearing something round your neck under your shirt?"

"No!" said Willy, backing away. "I—I go to the Baptist Church. I been baptized all regular."

Grace laughed softly. Piggott and Landers were staring, but Willy wasn't noticing them. His eyes were fixed on Grace, wide and fearful. "You got no *call,*" he said desperately.

"You know who it might have been?" asked Grace. "If you do, you'd really better tell us, Willy. Because it was the bad thing—the evil thing—to kill the old lady."

"You tell me *that?* I don't know anything about it." Willy licked his lips. "It was the robber. You got me all confused. I didn't say anything about—"

"That's right. You can take the eleven bucks to your daddy," said Grace casually. "And clear out the apartment any time."

Willy turned and ran. Grace got out a cigarette and lit it. "And what was all that about?" asked Landers interestedly.

"Human nature," said Grace, drawing strongly on the cigarette. "You ever catch yourself tossing salt over your left shoulder when you spill some? Say God bless you when somebody sneezes? All part and parcel of the same thing, so don't turn up your noses at those African witch doctors. I kind of thought when you mentioned the nails—" He reached out one well-shod foot and moved the two dozen scattered nails on the threshold of the bedroom. "Witches and warlocks, they don't like iron. Foils all their powers. Nor they can't abide salt. And witchcraft, you know, is basically the old religion—pre-Christian, and mostly anti-Christian, though not always, funnily enough. So by the logical conclusion, witches don't like crosses either. And anybody knows it's only common sense to turn a photograph to the wall, so it can't see you if you're up to something you'd just as soon not have known—"

"What the hell?" said Landers blankly.

"Same like with mirrors. But by what Willy said," said Grace, "I was off the beam a little. I thought she was—had the reputation of being—a real old-fashioned witch. Black magic. Evidently not. There are the other kind too. The good witches. White ones. But she certainly had the reputation of having the Power. And even white witches, so they do say, can cause a lot of discomfort in a good cause."

"Oh, now, really," said Landers.

"By that sheep's heart," said Grace seriously, "that could have been what she was up to. I've done some reading on the subject, you know." As well as a number of other subjects: Grace was the compulsive reader.

"What's the sheep's heart got to do with it?"

Grace emitted a long stream of smoke. "One of the common substitutes for the little wax doll. All sorts of variations. . . . People." He laughed. "The Snyders nice ordinary honest citizens, yes. Good Baptists. And Grandma a good Christian woman—as she might quite well have been, too. But having the Power. The reputation. By osmosis, a lot of people knowing that." He looked around the room, with its shabby furniture: a room obviously clean and neat, if poor and shoddy, before violence struck. "And after all, that is a thing pretty deep and old in human nature—and not just African human nature, either. Fellow I went to the Academy with, Joe Caravallo, college man too and a dropout from the Church, believed in the Evil Eye. Somebody, boys, thought Grandma had woven a spell against him, and he took what steps he could to circumvent it. After killing Grandma, he protected himself as best he could from her—um—avenging spirit. Surrounded the corpse with iron, left garlic on it— another potent talisman against witches, and who's to say no? He made the salt crosses, the iron crosses—and he'd have been very careful not to take anything of Grandma's."

"My Lord," said Piggott. "My good Lord."

"And," said Grace, "people are funny, aren't they? The Snyders all know that. That landlady in the front house— you'll have talked to her, and I'd guess she said she didn't know a thing, didn't hear a thing. Yes. Willy must have known when he found her, and saw all the signs. Probably panicked and called for cops before he had a second thought, or he'd have destroyed all the signs first. Good religious people, but—on the one hand, enough so to be a little ashamed of Grandma having the reputation—and on the other, deep down still kind of believing she really *was*, and ashamed of that. So, saying nothing. Making like the Tar Baby. Human nature, as I say."

"For God's sake," said Landers. "That's a funny one. Yes, I see it. But—"

"Satan still going up and down," said Piggott.

Grace put out his cigarette in a Woolworth vase of dead roses. "Not always Satan, Matt," he said seriously. "There's a Power on the other side too. Depends how it's used—and what for."

"I will be damned," said Mendoza interestedly. "You think that's what was behind it. *Es posible, de veras.* These things don't spontaneously vanish when people acquire electricity and indoor plumbing. To the end of her days, and her trotting off to Mass every Sunday, my grandmother carried a charm against the Evil Eye. I'd just been reading Matt's report. The offbeat one all right. That sheep's heart—"

"I seem to recall," said Grace, "there was a thing recently in England—reported in *Fate* magazine—sheep's hearts used in witchcraft rituals. These things crop up." He looked amused. "But young Willy not quite so much a true believer that he's wearing the *ju-ju*—concocted talisman of bones and herbs and so on—round his neck. Or was he? But I would take a bet. But as to giving us any idea who—"

"The lab report adds up to nothing," said Landers. They were sitting round Mendoza's desk; Grace lit a new cigarette and thoughtfully examined one of the rusty nails he'd brought away as a curio.

"That's the snag," he said. "It's very possible some of her neighbors know something. I can go round asking. If they'd part at all," he grinned, "it wouldn't be to any of you. If any race has any inborn traits except human nature, I guess you could say us cullud folk tend to be secretive."

"You'd better go and ask," said Mendoza, and the inside phone shrilled. He picked it up. "Yes, Jimmy?"

"That Fairbrother," said Lake. "He just called in. He says he's found some of his clothes are missing. Hadn't checked before. He says the others have looked too, and—"

FIVE

Grace said absently he was going back to that neighborhood to poke around on his own. Mendoza told Piggott and Landers he'd meet them in half an hour for lunch at Federico's, and feeling rather irritated started for the Milliken house. On the way he reflected that they weren't doing a damned thing about that Delaney girl, the abortion. He ought to see the mother; the girl might have said something, come out with some little thing that could be a lead. George had said, the mother rather stupid if respectable. There was also that liquor store shooting; they had a provisional Identikit sketch from the one witness; he wasn't pinning much faith to it but they had to go through the motions. The hunt through Records for a lead on that had halted temporarily when these latest cases erupted, but they couldn't just drop it, after all.

At the Milliken house, Heffner and Fairbrother were awaiting him on the front porch, wearing identical aggrieved expressions. "Look," said Mendoza, "you were all asked to check over your belongings for anything missing, when the lab men—"

"Well, we never thought you meant *clothes*," said Heffner. "None of us ever left any loose money here, at least I never did, and they said like jewelry and valuables. Not like *clothes*.

But when Mr. Fairbrother here found his good suit was gone, I—"

"Well, what seems to be gone?"

"My good suit," said Fairbrother, annoyed. "Second to newest, anyway. I keep a few things here, dress decent on my layovers. And a new white shirt and a couple pairs of socks. It was the socks I missed first, I knew I had a couple clean pairs left—"

"Yeah, and they took my *only* good suit," said Heffner. "And my new shoes."

Mendoza got vague descriptions of the clothes, and reflected, heading for Federico's, that that said a little.

Both men's suitcases intact; nothing like that gone, unless one had been taken from Mrs. Milliken's room. A suitcase in good condition in Nordhammer's closet. And Jarvis hadn't lost any clothes. So. Fairbrother and Heffner being much of a size, did that say that X took clothes that fit him? And already had a suitcase? *es posible.* The picture built up a little sharper. And damn it, he'd meant to ask around the neighborhood today; if she had rented her empty room to a stranger, forgetting afterward to take down the sign, there might be some noticing neighbor who'd seen him arrive.

He had a quick lunch with Piggott and Landers, and went back to the office, having steered them back onto the liquor store shooting. See if anything new was in, he thought, and then go see Mrs. Delaney and some of Mrs. Milliken's neighbors.

Something new was in: a teletype from the FBI in answer to the query on Carson's prints. Mendoza sat down to read it. In one way it was surprising, in another not. The FBI knew Carson solely from his army record. There was no criminal pedigree on him anywhere in this country, but a certain amount of other data. He'd been born in Newark, New Jersey, in 1930, attending public schools there and graduating from Newark High School in 1948. He'd been inducted into the army the same year. Evidently he had managed to suppress his maverick instincts in service, at least there weren't any black marks against him serious enough to get into his record. He had been given an honorable discharge in 1951. That was the last the FBI knew of him. While he was in the army he had listed his next of kin as Mrs. Erma Carson of an address in Newark; he had been unmarried up to leaving the service.

"Well," said Mendoza. He told Lake to teletype a query to the force in Newark, ask them to contact any possible family. Eighteen years back—but some people stayed put, of course.

"Art gave me that phone number this morning," said Lake, lighting a cigarette distastefully. "I asked the phone company to check it out, and they're usually cooperative. I think they use computers, otherwise it'd take them days, a place like this. Of course, it may not be a local—"

"What ph—oh, that," said Mendoza. In with the jewels. Carson. That was a funny little thing.

He went back to his office for his hat, and when he came out again the door was just closing after a uniformed man. Lake said, "Lab report. On the Milliken thing."

"Damnation," said Mendoza, but of course as the lieutenant he was the one who was supposed to keep all the threads separated and observe progress on the various cases being worked, so he went back to his desk to read the report. He skimmed rapidly through the descriptions of where and how prints had been lifted, analysis of material from under Gertrude Milliken's fingernails (supplied by surgeon), and the rest of the technicalities, to the last paragraph, which rose off the page at him and called forth an expletive.

"¡Porvida! With the phone to hand—Jimmy!"

"Three distinct latent prints," ended the report, "from the post of bed in bedroom, right front second floor—" Nordhammer's room "—check out as identified prints William

68

Ernest Schuyler, our records. Photostat record appended. You will note—" Mendoza noted arches, loops, whorls, tents. For the courtroom.

"What's up?"

"Who's here?"

"John. Still doing a report on the corpse on the Row."

Mendoza charged out to the sergeants' office. "And the lab is often very helpful, as it has been this time, but I suppose they had this a couple of hours ago at least—oh, well, they're busy. We know the X on Milliken, John. Anyway one X. Suppose you go try to find him. Here's his pedigree."

"Right," said Palliser. He looked it over. "Quite a pedigree." It was. Schuyler was now twenty-six, and he'd first been picked up by the L.A.P.D. at the age of thirteen. The juveniles got the little slaps on the wrist until they turned into legal adults. Petty theft, said the record, petty theft, burglary, attempted burglary, attempted robbery, mugging, assault; and the first adult charge, seven years back, was robbery from the person with violence. He'd got two years. He was out on that six months when he was dropped on for burglary and assault; he served a year of a one-to-three for that, and then in 1965 he'd been charged with burglary. He'd evidently got a tough judge that time, and a three-to-ten. He had served three years and was now out on parole, since five months ago.

"Rehabilitation they talk about," said Palliser, looking tired. "I don't see anything about his working with a partner at any time. Could be he's the only one we want for Milliken."

"It could be. Anyway, it's all very suggestive. Schuyler could have got religion and reformed, and just been looking for a nice cheap quiet room where he could stay while he went to business college. But that is very much the kind of caper he's pulled before, and his prints place him in the house. Probably recently, because Mrs. Milliken seems to have been a good housekeeper. Suppose you go see his P.A. officer and try to pick him up."

"Will do," said Palliser. "But what idiots they are. What stupid oafs. You'd think anybody would have better sense, for God's sake. With this record, leaving his prints—and only five months out—"

"*De veras*. You would think. The only reason we catch as many as we do, John," said Mendoza.

"I guess. It makes you wonder." Palliser shook his head, tucked the photostated record sheet into his breast pocket and started out. Mendoza went back to his office again for his hat, and when he came out Lake was just putting down the phone.

"Computers, like I said. They'd never have found it in this time otherwise. That phone number. OS-94563. It belongs to the Kit-Kat Bar and Grille. Brooklyn Avenue, Boyle Heights."

"Oh," said Mendoza. Just very slightly funny. He thought about it. Carson-Conway-Blank, not exactly the pro con-man, was on the surface respectable middle-class white collar. Well, come to think, probably so were some people in Boyle Heights. It was just that any cop, when he thought of Boyle Heights, thought of bar brawls, muggings, juvenile gangs and break-ins. He thought about that: where Hackett had come across the phone number. Harry, and just the number. It was about a hundred to one—or a thousand—that it had anything at all to do with Carson's murder; Harry might be a bookmaker, anything; but it had to be followed up, of course.

As he started back to his office, Duke came in. "Here's your pretties back," he said. He followed Mendoza into the office and dumped a plastic bag on the desk blotter. The jewels. Mendoza hadn't seen them before. The jewels—a grandiose word for it—found in Carson's apartment.

"So what about them?" he asked.

"What can I tell you?" Duke shrugged. "What do you want to know about them?"

"Are they hot?"

"Definitely no. I got a description typed up and took it up to Goldberg. He took one look and sneezed and said, quit wasting his time on garnets and pearls, a fence'd offer about sixty bucks."

"Oh." Mendoza looked at the little heap of jewelry. Garnets all right, the topaz ring, the opal ring. Small stones. Chip diamonds—he picked up the one large ring, a man's gold ring set with one large stone. "This a diamond? It looks as if it is. Quite a rock, if so."

"I don't know, could be a zircon, I suppose. Kind of thing the pro gamblers like to flash. Here's Willis's evaluation, anyway."

Mendoza picked up the one boxed piece. "This looks new."

Duke peered. "Yeah. There's a jeweler's name on the box —someplace to ask anyway."

"Well, thanks very much. Haven't you got a phone in working order down there?"

"What?"

"You got a make on those prints from the Milliken house, so you let me wait for the written report."

"Didn't Scarne call? He was supposed to, I guess he got sidetracked."

"Better late than never," said Mendoza philosophically. He looked at the odds and ends of semiprecious stones, the inexpensive jewelry—jewels, *vaya*, he thought—and put them back in the bag, with the lab's evaluation. Carson. And Harry. Well, anything that might give them a lead had to be looked at. He sat down at his desk, lit a deliberate cigarette, picked up the phone and asked Lake to ring that number. The Kit-Kat Bar and Grille on Brooklyn Avenue.

The phone buzzed in his ear seven times before it was picked up at the other end. "Kit-Kat Bar," said a rough voice.

Mendoza hadn't a clue as to what this was all about, or who Harry was. He was playing it by ear. He said, "I'd like to talk to Harry."

"Oh," said the voice. A man's voice, deep, sounding uneducated. "Uh. Harry ain't here right now. Uh—how'd you know call this number for him?"

Mendoza didn't hesitate. The voice wary—taking precautions? Why? Something funny about Harry. He said hurriedly, sounding annoyed, "What the hell's it matter, mister? I *got* it, don't I? So where *do* I find him?"

"Uh—" said the other man. "Well, you wanna make a deal some kind?" The voice had dropped as if its owner was nearly whispering into the phone.

"Why the hell else am I callin' him?" barked Mendoza. And what the hell this was—Carson, and Brooklyn Avenue, and the wary Harry?

"Oh. Well, all right, keep your shirt on. I—uh—I can have him here in—uh—half an hour. O.K.? You come to the bar, ask for Mike."

"O.K.," said Mendoza, and put the phone down. Fun and games, he thought. What *was* this? Undercover work, and all the cards wild. And Harry—whoever he might be—and Mike, at a bar in Boyle Heights, were a far cry from the kiddies' dancing school racket, Patti Page, and the incredibly credulous Rose Lamont. He said to himself, "A *su tiempo maduran las uvas*," and thoughtfully opened the top drawer. He stripped off his jacket, buckled on the seldom-used shoulder holster, loaded the Police Positive .38 and dropped a handful of shells into his pocket, holstered the gun and replaced his jacket. After all, one never did know—and he now had some hostages to fortune. At least three of them. Counting the livestock, eight.

"Schuyler," said Mr. Richard Nash. "That one. Don't tell me. Don't tell me." He took off his glasses and pinched the bridge of his nose. "So let's hear the worst. What's he been up to now?"

"Murder," said Palliser.

"Good God," said Nash. "Well, I suppose it was only a question of time. So we try him for it and he gets life and in seven years he's eligible for P.A., and for my sins I get him on my list."

"Let's hope not," said Palliser. He thought about the forty-thousand-dollar house Roberta had gone into raptures over. In for a penny in for a pound, he thought. A thirty-year loan—what was it but rent? And they had to live somewhere, and he was due for a raise in six months. Enjoy yourself while you could. And if they started a family, they'd want a house of some kind. A family—and then worry about them turning out delinquents.

"I'd take no bets," said Nash.

"Well, you've got an address for him?"

"I have. Theoretically it is a fine idea," said Nash, going over to the file case in the corner of his office. "The parolees counseled and kept tabs on by the qualified officer. Fine and dandy. Only it isn't a job many people want, sergeant. In practice. It gets monotonous. So we're spread so thin we might as well not be here at all. What it comes down to is a gesture in the right direction. . . . He's living in Culver City. You haven't got a warrant?"

"Not yet. Good evidence, but we just want to talk to him right now."

Nash sighed. "I'd better come with you. He lives with his mother. She's had five legal husbands and drinks like a fish."

"Actually," said Palliser, "I understand fish don't, much."

"I am not about to get into an argument on nature lore," said Nash. "Let's go."

The Kit-Kat Bar and Grille was surprisingly large for its type; most such places are holes-in-the-wall. It had a grinning cat's head neon sign above a narrow door; but inside it was one large square place with no windows, an L-shaped bar, and booths round two sides. There was the inevitable jukebox in one corner. At this hour it was quiet; the jukebox was mercifully silent. Four men sat at the bar, two alone, the other two talking in low voices.

The Kit-Kat Bar was emphatically not a place to intrude Luis Mendoza's elegant tailoring, gold cuff links and tie bar; Mendoza had taken off his tie, with a mental apology to his tailor, left his links in his desk, unbuttoned his jacket, and run a hand through his normally smooth black hair to tousle it: the best he could do on short notice. He had left the gold seal ring in his desk too; and he hadn't taken the Ferrari. A cab to the off-ramp of the San Berdu freeway, and then a bus. It was considerably more than half an hour since he'd spoken to Mike here.

He walked into the place after a covert survey, and up to the bar. There was only one bartender on duty, a clumsy-looking big man in a white apron. He glanced at Mendoza indifferently. "What'll it be, mister?"

"Straight rye. Is Mike here?"

"I'm Mike." The bartender poured rye.

"Is Harry here yet?"

The bartender looked at him closer. He had a heavy-jowled unshaven face; his eyes went up and down Mendoza, busy and curious. "Oh, you the—uh—guy called Harry here?"

"That's right."

"He's in the booth in the left corner. Last one." The bartender jerked his head.

Mendoza picked up his rye and carried it over to that booth. It was very dark in the corner of the room; he could see that the booth had an occupant, but that was all. He slid into the bare wooden bench-seat; the place smelled of stale beer, sweat, too much crowded humanity, whiskey, and it probably hadn't been so much as swept out in years. He

74

set his shot-glass down and got out a cigarette; striking a match he looked across the stained plastic-topped table.

The wary Harry looked very wary indeed. A man about forty, dark, going bald, a weak chin needing a shave, and a scar at the left corner of his mouth. A medium-sized man in nondescript clothes, blue shirt, no tie, trousers invisible. He was drinking beer.

"Hey," he said. "No call advertise. You the guy called?" His voice was thick and low.

"That's right," said Mendoza.

"Uh—where'd you get the number? I never seen you—don't know you. Mike said—"

"What's it matter? I'm here," said Mendoza. Talk about playing it by ear. It gave him a very little something that apparently Harry had been expecting a message—or a messenger?—of some kind, or the bartender wouldn't have so readily set up the appointment. Was that valid? Or was this just the normal way for Harry's friends to get in touch with him? Mendoza waited, playing for time. Harry didn't look very smart; he might give away a clue.

"Uh—" said Harry. The match flare dead, he was just a shape three feet away across the table. "What's your name?"

"What's the flag matter?" countered Mendoza, using the pro slang instinctively. "You think I'm fuzz maybe?"

"I dunno this damn burg," said Harry miserably. "I din' wanta stay around, when I get out. But where's the dough to go back east with? I dunno nobody here—just Mike, and he's just a pal of a guy I knew inside. A real ace, Johnny is, he told me Mike's O.K. Only damn name for anybody inna whole state I got, so I come down here, but I don't *know* the burg. An' Mike, he's no two-way guy, but he ain't on the bent neither, he don't know nothing tell me. And I wanna go back to Chi." He sounded wistful.

Mendoza waited.

Harry drank beer and set the glass down a little too hard. That hadn't been his first today; or, maybe, his fifth or tenth. He said, "Mike said he'd—kinda put the word around. Quiet. You gotta be careful. Jeez, back in Chi, places around, I'd *know*—'n' know fuzz when I seen it too, but out here it's all different—damn fool come out here inna first place, but Jim he kinda persuaded me. Nothin' but bad luck ever since. This damn place—I ain't no fall guy, but I don't know my way *around* here. Jeez, I—well, look. Look. You wanna do *business?*"

"That depends," said Mendoza.

"Well, you buying? Mike said he get Billy to put the word around quiet—you get the number like that? From somebody?"

"That's right."

"So all right. You wanna deal?"

"Depends," said Mendoza again. Deal? For what? What the hell were they talking about?

"Oh. You mean you gotta see it. Thass fair enough," said Harry. "O.K. Only listen, mister, I ain't no flat wheel, see. The P.A. thing to hell, I can lay hands on a equalizer an' you got any ideas in your head about havin' a strong-arm guy glom onto the stuff 'n' kick me out, you think twice, see. See?"

"Take it easy," said Mendoza. "On the level. O.K."

"Well, O.K.," said Harry, breathing heavily. "O.K. Just so we know. Where I bring it?"

Mendoza thought fast. Where, indeed? Whatever it was? He said, "Here."

"Oh, for Christ's sake," said Harry. "*You* a flat wheel? Here! With guys in 'n' out—"

"We don't have to stay here," said Mendoza. "I'll have a car waiting."

"Oh. Well, O.K. Nine o'clock maybe? An' you unnerstand, cash. Little bills."

"That's right," said Mendoza.

"So O.K. I don't *like* this burg," said Harry nervously. "Like a lost kid, I feel like. I wanna go home. Alla same, don't you think you take me, mister. It ain't my first time out, you ain't about to take me."

"So you know your way around," said Mendoza. "Nine o'clock." He got up, the rye untouched.

"I only hope I ain't bein' a damn fool again," said Harry gloomily. "Nine o'clock."

Mendoza got out of the place and started rapidly up the street, thinking furiously. Just what had that been all about? He wished he knew. A deal—for what? Dope, women, high-jacked liquor or—take your choice. Harry using the pro slang; Harry the pro—what? Nothing very slick, he thought. Implication, Harry just out of jail. The pen?

Look for him in Records. But just what the hell connection could Harry have with the nonpedigreed still-amateur con-man Carson-Conway-Blank? On what? A very unlikely combination.

Meet Harry at nine tonight. Something more would probably emerge. Yes, and meanwhile Harry might have found out that Billy—whoever he was—hadn't one damned thing to do with appearance of stranger-out-of-the-blue asking for Harry. Wait a minute, Mike had "put the word around." Yes. Mendoza stopped on a corner; there was a bus sighing out diesel fumes across the intersection, with *Civic Center* emblazoned on its front. He sprinted across the street on the amber for it, fished for change, found a seat. All right. Down here, a sort of half-world; the word would circulate on the grapevine, any criminal job, and pass by osmosis. Who had said that? Jase. *That* was an offbeat one, all right. . . . Anybody—any other pro of any kind—could have got wind of Harry. And his deal. Whatever. So, no matter about that.

But—maybe he was getting cautious in his old age—have one of the night men cover him. Just in case. Nick Galeano.

Only just what the hell the connection could be between Carson and Harry was the mystery of the month.

"What?" said Mrs. Leona Schuyler blankly.

"Your son William," said Palliser patiently. "Is he home?"

She looked at Palliser and the parole officer Nash a little blearily. This was one side of a shabby old duplex on a shabby block in an old section of town. Mrs. Schuyler was a raddled woman about fifty, bleached blonde, too much makeup slapped on over old makeup, and there had been too much gin and too few baths, too many parties and men and hangovers, to make her use what was left of her brain quick or easy. She was probably in the throes of a hangover now, wearing a soiled pink rayon bathrobe over sketchy underwear, and barefooted. "Oh, Bill," she said. "I dunno where he is. He borrowed my suitcase. I guess he's gone someplace."

"He's on parole, Mrs. Schuyler," said Nash. "He's not supposed to leave the city."

"Yeah, well, he's gone. Someplace."

"When did you see him last?" asked Palliser.

"Gee, I dunno." She yawned widely, showing dirty yellowed teeth. "What's today?"

"Wednesday," said Nash with a sigh.

"Yeah, well, I guess it coulda been Sunday. I woulden swear."

"He didn't say anything to you about his plans?" asked Palliser. To think, he remembered suddenly, that he'd once considered teaching English. The ivory tower—instead of dealing with the sludge at the bottom of things.

"What?" she said. "Oh, he never tells me nothing. Just like his father. I woulden know."

Back at Palliser's car, Nash said academically, "I wonder if she remembers who his father was. Put out an A.P.B. on him."

"That's just what," said Palliser. He looked at his watch. It would be good to get home to his Robin.

"A handful of nothing," said Hackett. He leaned back in the chair beside Mendoza's desk and it creaked under his weight; he ran a hand through his sandy hair. "See what George has to tell us tomorrow, but I've got nothing. That could say anything about the murder. A few former girl friends who hadn't seen Carson in awhile, and they all looked straight enough. *In* that sense only, you get me. Obviously recalled him with pleasant memories. Another few fond parents who'd enrolled their kiddies in the dancing school. And, if it says anything, one Mr. G. L. Whitehead. . . . That tale of Jase's is wild. What Matt said about it—"

"¿*Cómo*? Whitehead?"

Hackett stretched. "Address out toward Pomona. Turned out to be a refining and smelting company. I was passed around from hand to hand, finally got to a minor official who told me, all very haughty, that Mr. Whitehead was the owner of the company and not here today, I'd have to make an appointment—"

"Oh, you don't say," said Mendoza. "Same like Mr. Lamson. What does that say to me?" He pondered, lighting a cigarette. "A refining and—"

"But this Harry," said Hackett. "What the hell, Luis? What connection? The little rackets—the dancing school, the gullible females—my God, that Lamont woman, what people will swallow—I don't suppose though," he added suddenly, "that he could have *been* a—I mean, the spy stuff, they do get up to some incredible things these days."

"A real CIA agent? I would very strongly doubt it," said Mendoza dryly, "but if it'll ease your mind we can ask. As for Harry—"

"Look, Luis. That section of town—and Harry sounding

like a pro—whatever it turns out to be, you be careful," said Hackett seriously.

"*¡Qué disparate!*" said Mendoza. "I was not born yesterday, Arturo. Nick'll be standing by. In case."

"And what the hell Harry could have to do— No autopsy report yet? That *jewels* still bugs me," said Hackett. "I'd like to hear Bainbridge's opinion. Head injuries can be funny. Look, *amigo,* you wear the cannister tonight, *sí?*"

Mendoza laughed impatiently. "To please you, Arturo. Admit it, I'm damn curious about Harry."

Hackett yawned and stood up, his solid bulk looming over Mendoza. "You just be careful. Mixing with the pro hoods."

He went home, to the stable, sound, mundane place so far removed from the things and people he dealt with every day —the dirt and hate and random violence and malice and mindless destruction cops had to cope with. His brown-haired Angel was putting the last touches to dinner; Mark Christopher, nearly four, was prone on the kitchen floor coloring pictures solemnly; his darling Sheila staggered toward him drunkenly on still uncertain legs.

"Tough day, darling?" asked Angel.

"Fairly," said Hackett, picking up Sheila fondly. "The routine."

Mendoza, more conscious than usual of the routine that there hadn't been time to do today—the Delaney thing, and the liquor store shooting (the Identikit sketch maybe a waste of time)—interesting to see what, if anything, Jase turned up on the Snyder thing, an offbeat one but Jase was a very smart boy—Mendoza went home. Having briefed Nick Galeano. Still wondering about Harry. Went home to his hostages to fortune. And the livestock.

SIX

Mendoza came in through the kitchen, which was unoccupied; he glanced around, remembering the slightly forced atmosphere occasioned by Mairí's cake last night, but it all looked normal. Casserole in oven, a glimpse of the table set in the dining room beyond; in the service porch behind him, the cats' row of food and water dishes, the Cedric-sized dog bed and bowls opposite.

Alison appeared from the dining room and he kissed her. "You're late," she informed him. "As soon as I heard the car I started to get things on the table. Want a drink before dinner?"

"I don't think so—"

Mrs. MacTaggart came bustling in from the hall. "Now you two sit down and I'll fetch the rest, no trouble. The twins can wait five minutes for their baths."

Mendoza sat down, and Alison sat opposite, reaching for the coffeepot on its trivet. "Anything new turn up on the funny case, d—"

There sounded shrill and clear, somewhere close by, a piercing whistle—the first four bars of "Yankee Doodle." Mendoza jumped. "What—" Mrs. MacTaggart came back with the casserole and set it in the middle of the table. "I didn't know you could whistle, Mairí."

" 'Tis not an accomplishment I boast about," said Mrs. MacTaggart with aplomb. "I—" The whistle sounded again, shrill and clear, followed by the sudden saccharine *coroo-coroo* of a mourning dove.

"What the hell—?" Mendoza got up.

"Oh, dear," said Alison.

"Och, I do believe the creature's got out," said Mrs. Mac-Taggart, making for the door at a trot.

"May I ask what the devil you've inflicted on me this time in the way of livestock?" demanded Mendoza. "I will be damned—"

"Now don't get upset, Luis, it's just for a few days, and it's only—oh, damn," said Alison, making a sudden dive for Bast. "We had *such* a time with it yesterday, the cats—and I knew you'd find out sooner or later, but Mairí said—for heaven's sake catch Sheba!"

Automatically he bent and grabbed Sheba as she streaked past. "Why? What—"

"It *has* got out," said Alison. "Oh, damn." She snatched the loudly complaining Sheba from him, thrust both cats into the kitchen and shut the door. From the hall outside came a high loud whistle and then the rather sinister low notes of a barn owl. *Tu-whoo, tu-whoo. Yankee Doodle came to town Yankee Doodle came to town—*

"For the love of God," said Mendoza in horror, "you haven't got a *parrot?*"

"Don't be silly," said Alison crossly. She opened the hall door, which Mairí had precipitately shut against cats, to disclose an animated scene. Mairí was firmly clutching a yelling El Señor in her arms, adjuring Terry to catch Nefertite; the twins were hopping about in wild excitement, Cedric was an interested observer from the living room doorway, and—

"We was just lookin' at him an'— an'— the little flap door comed open an' he comed out," explained Johnny earnestly.

Alison scooped up Nefertite and thrust her in the hall door to the kitchen, and tossed El Señor after her. Loud and mingled Abyssinian and Siamese complaints rent the air. "You know you were *not* supposed to go into Mairí's room, Johnny!"

"I tol' him not to," said Terry complacently. "But now Daddy c'n meet *el pájaro lindo*—"

In the center of the hall stood the center of the controversy, some eight inches long, and announced in a shrill defiant whistle, *"Yankee Doodle came to town!"*

"¡Es el colmo!" said Mendoza.

"It's just a little while, Luis, all this fuss, it's only a—"

"What?"

"A mockingbird," said Alison at the top of her voice. "Johnny—Terry— *¡bastante!* Quiet! A poor innocent little mockingbird who can't fly. And—"

"I suppose it stowed away in Mairí's car this time," said Mendoza resignedly.

"Don't be an idiot. Bast brought it home, but she hadn't hurt it much. But if you'd look at it, you'd see that the poor thing must have got in the way of one of those spraying machines—you know they're blacktopping the next street —anyway, its wings are covered with the stuff, and it's stuck as fast as—as glue. I got it away from Bast—it seems quite tame, it knows we're only trying to help—and we tried nail polish remover at first but it didn't touch it, and we thought maybe solvent—and now Mairí's fixed a box for it all safe—"

"Doing fine on porridge and bread crumbs it is," Mrs. Mac-Taggart put in hastily, "though I am thinking I made a wee mistake in giving it a teaspoon of your rye against the shock— that cat. The creature seems to like it, and after the second dose it—"

The mockingbird teetered a few steps forward and uttered the one sound purely personal to mockingbirds. *"Yawk!"* it said in a loud raucous voice. Then, conversationally, *"Tu-*

whoo." It fixed a bright insolent eye on Mendoza's shoes and hopping nearer began to peck at his toes.

"*¡Vaya por Dios!* All we need around here is an alcoholic bird! And wouldn't Bast be the one cat for miles around to bring the damn thing here!"

"Now, Luis, it's just a few days until we can get all the tar off and it can fly again," said Alison reasonably. "We'd better get it back in the box, Mairí. And *you* two," she added to the twins, "into the bathroom with you—Mairí'll be along in a minute. We had an awful time with it yesterday—" Mrs. MacTaggart picked up the bird tenderly and bore it off, and Mendoza followed Alison after her. "But Mairí's fixed a box for it in her room—we had it in the kitchen last night—and we can shut it in there all safe. We've given it half a dozen baths of solvent—"

The box was a topless cardboard one lined with cedar shavings. A top of chicken wire had been tacked onto it, and a flap door cut out. There was a saucer of oatmeal, another of bread crumbs, a saucer of water. The mockingbird settled down in the cedar, his inquisitive bright eyes fixed on them. "Yawk!" he observed, and then proceeded to give them his best imitation of the sweet clear song of the meadowlark. He was mostly gray, with black tail feathers, flashes of white underneath. His normally gray-white wings were firmly glued down and darkened with dried tar, which covered his back as well.

"I think I'll just give him another teaspoon of whiskey, poor thing," said Mrs. MacTaggart.

"You do that," said Mendoza. "Give him the whole bottle— A mockingbird! It's not enough you saddle us with the shaggy dog, but a mockingbird—"

"It's just a few days," said Alison. "You needn't make such a fuss, Luis. As soon as it can fly—"

Mrs. MacTaggart came back with the bottle of rye and a teaspoon. The mockingbird's eyes flashed; it stood up and whistled, "*Yankee Doodle came to town,*" again and finished with a loud wolf whistle.

"Uncanny, how they pick things up, isn't it," said Mrs. MacTaggart.

"Including the human vices," said Mendoza. "All we *need* —my God. . . . And I have to go out again," he added as he and Alison headed back for the dining room.

"Oh? On what?"

"Now that," said Mendoza seriously, "I wish I knew myself."

He left the Ferrari in the headquarters lot; they took Galeano's car, an ordinary dark Ford, out to Boyle Heights. Galeano was curious and interested, but Mendoza told him he was just insurance. When they got to Brooklyn Avenue they had to hunt for a parking place, finally found one around the corner on Fickett. "I just want you to hang around," said Mendoza. "Keep an eye out." Galeano posted himself on the corner two car-lengths up, lounging against the side of the building there.

The street was more alive than it had been that afternoon. Crowds of people out, a pleasant night not yet turned chill— couples, little gaggles of teen-agers, older men mostly alone. Mendoza sauntered down to the door of the bar and went in, made through the dark big room, where now the jukebox was blaring, for the booth where he had met Harry before.

He slid into the seat and struck a match to light his cigarette, verifying the figure across the table. Harry. Still unshaven, still looking wary and unhappy. He said, "You ready to talk a deal?"

"Yeah—yeah, I said. We can't *here.*" They had to raise their voices to hear each other over the jukebox.

"O.K.," said Mendoza. "My car—outside." Harry got up and slid out of the booth. It crossed Mendoza's mind that for all his unprepossessing looks, Harry moved neatly and gracefully.

After even a few minutes in the fetid air of the bar the night air outside was sweet. "Around the corner," said Mendoza. Harry followed him down there, past Galeano's stocky unnoticeable figure, to the car. Mendoza opened the rear door and he got in. Mendoza got in after him. "So, cards on the table," he said, and waited for Harry to make the first move.

"Well—" Harry fumbled at the jacket he was now wearing. "Like I say, mister, I ain't no dummy, it ain't my first time. Don't think you rook me."

"Who wants to rook you? Come on, come on."

"All *right*." Harry produced a chamois drawstring bag. Slowly he untied the strings and, spreading a dirty handkerchief on the seat between them, emptied the bag onto it with care. "This ain't so good a spot to see—"

Mendoza snapped his lighter this time for steadier light, and light dawned on him. Scattered on the handkerchief was a miscellaneous lot of jewelry: rings, watches, bracelets, cuff links, earrings. "I know the loot," said Harry. "You don't rook me. It's worth a good eight C's—what I'd get from any honest fence in Chi, an' you don't tell me values any different out—"

"I don't suppose so," said Mendoza. He let the lighter go out. So, Harry. The pro burglar caught off home base, not knowing any fences here. A small stroke of luck for the L.A.P.D. "About a third of what it's really worth."

"You give me—"

Mendoza said, "It *is* a little dark here, Harry—too dark for you to see the badge. I'm taking you in on this—" And he got a good grasp on Harry's outstretched right arm and yelled out the window for Galeano.

"*Goddamn—you goddamn—*" Harry sobbed and jerked

away. A savage judo chop numbed Mendoza's wrist, and with surprising agility Harry had swept up the handkerchief, contents inside, and plunged forward. Mendoza swore and reached for him again, took a hard-fisted blow on one cheek, and then in the close confines of the car Harry's weight prevailed; he shoved Mendoza off the seat, had the door open, and was out, as Galeano came running.

"Take him!" gasped Mendoza, up again.

Galeano reached, and Harry half turned, and something zinged past Galeano's ear and hit the building behind. "He's got a gun—" Mendoza had his own out, and snapped off a shot. The next second Galeano was after Harry, gun out. Mendoza scrambled out of the car and chased after, but he could foresee the outcome of this. Down here, the crowds, and the dark side streets, and mostly people in this area not inclined to indicate helpfully to police, he went thataway. . . .

Ten minutes later they had lost him irretrievably, and came back to the car irritated but both intact. A little knot of interested spectators drifted along with them, mostly teenagers, making derogatory remarks about the fuzz.

"Hell and damnation!" said Mendoza. "Back to base, Nick. We'll get some light on the back seat and see if he left any of his loot behind."

All Harry hadn't managed to scoop up, however, was a small insignificant-looking gold ring with a single small diamond.

"So I see Goldberg in the morning," said Mendoza resignedly. "And as far as any connection to our mystery goes, the plot thickens. Just what the hell that gentlemanly amateur con-man had to do with Harry—"

He went home muttering to himself and told Alison all about it, disjointedly, over a drink.

At least the rye had apparently put the mockingbird to sleep: no unexpected outcries or patriotic outbursts of song disturbed the night.

Lieutenant Goldberg of Robbery looked at the insignificant diamond ring with interest. "Harry? Doesn't ring a bell. However, what you say he implied about just getting out—we can ask Quentin. And from the little look you got at the loot, it just could be—it just *could* be—from that celluloid artist's raid on the Biltmore. They had a little spate of it last week. The room-rifler while people are out to dinner and shows, you know. Hotel dicks got on the job after a couple of floors of guests had complained, but they never picked up anybody. He got away with a little haul—I've got a list, I'll have a look for this on it, and a look for Harry. Put out the word to the pigeons, we'll probably turn him up." Goldberg sneezed and reached for Kleenex. "Not much honor among thieves."

"And what the hell Harry had to do with my homicide—" But, Mendoza remembered suddenly, Carson had written down that *jewels* on his memo-pad. Whether or not it had been *in extremis*. And pro burglars quite often did steal jewels, ¿cómo no? Had Carson meant to indicate Harry? Then why not just write his name? Or had he thought he had the strength to get down a longer message? Or did the *jewels* have anything to do with his murder at all?

"Well, if and when we pick him up, Luis," said Goldberg, "you can ask him."

"You pick him up, Saul, and I'll break all records asking him," said Mendoza. He went up to his own office and looked at the overnight reports. It was Hackett's day off, and nobody else was in yet; five to eight. Goldberg was usually in early too. Just call us gluttons for work, thought Mendoza. It had been a quiet night—for Homicide, at least. One accident. Driver D.O.A., passenger in critical condition. Intersection of Hoover and Alvarado; two young men. Driver probably drunk, appended Galeano: car plowed into the side of a building, only one car involved. The senseless people: no regard for their own necks or anybody else's. I.D. on both men: the D.O.A. one Leon Lister, the passenger Peter Whiteley. The families had been informed.

"Morning, Luis," said Higgins. "You'll want to hear what I got on Carson Tuesday. A little something."

"Anything useful, George." Higgins sat down in the chair beside the desk. Mendoza thought that in the last six months Higgins had changed a little, subtly: still the same rough-hewn bulky cop, but— Maybe because he was happy, thought Mendoza. As simple as that. Higgins looking after Bert Dwyer's kids, married to Bert Dwyer's widow. He'd hoped that Mary Dwyer fully appreciated George, and evidently she did.

"One thing—I don't know it's important. I nearly called in yesterday and then—well, I—" Higgins looked as nearly embarrassed as he ever could look "—I had to take Mary somewhere and I didn't. I turned up a dozen people Carson knew, former girl friends and a few men—nothing very recent. One of the men, a clerk at Penney's, said Carson worked there, just a couple of months, about three years back—"

"Yes, he must have had to take a job once in a while, when he was down on his luck with the marks. Only as long as he had to."

"I expect. This fellow thought he was the greatest. Admired him like hell. He's a little weedy welterweight himself, probably the reason. Anyway, he said he'd sat in on a few poker sessions with Carson—oh, nothing big, he couldn't afford it, just friendly games—and Carson was hot with the cards."

"Mmh, yes. It does figure," said Mendoza. "They're all gamblers by nature, the con-men. Some of them lucky with cards, some unlucky. And the welterweight had stayed in Carson's address book because he thought Carson was the greatest. He'd probably be good for a twenty-buck loan at least if Carson got strapped. What's your one possibly important find? Oh, and what about Match-Mates, Incorporated?"

"That," said Higgins. "The latest gimmick. Find your soulmate through the all-seeing eye of the computer. They charge a fee for it. Quite a stiff fee. Carson was pushing it for the usual commission."

"*Así, así*. And?"

"And," said Higgins, "he was engaged. For real. He'd found a very sweet deal, and it just could be, Luis, that in some way it provided the trigger for the gun. Her name's Natalie Brookes. I had the hell of a time with her, she had hysterics all over me—kind who thinks nobody'll be convinced she's really grief-stricken unless she has hysterics—and then she calmed down and answered some questions. And at first I didn't think it was important, except that it could say he was about to close down his other gimmicks and live happily ever after. Natalie," said Higgins, "is scarcely the type to lavish so much true love on anybody but Natalie that she'd go killing him if she found he was two-timing her. Added to which, he wouldn't have. He was smart enough to know when he'd landed soft. You ask me, he was busy closing down all his other women, fading away. He—"

"He'd asked the Page woman to go to Vegas."

Higgins waved an impatient hand. "It'd never have come off. A guy like Carson, don't we know them, it's an earmark of the breed, Luis—one of the reasons they go on that lay, one of the reasons they're good at it. They really like people, if it's all on the surface—and they've got to be liked. They like to love 'em and leave 'em all easy and palsy-walsy. Leave Patti all misty-eyed at the idea of a weekend in Vegas— I'd take a bet, when he made that date with Rose Lamont, he was going to set it up that he was bound for one of his dangerous missions. Fade away, leave her to think the nasty Russian spy murdered him somewhere abroad. She'd have the great romance to remember the rest of her life. He—"

"Natalie," said Mendoza.

"Natalie. A very sweet deal for him. She's a looker, about thirty, divorced and got a settlement from the husband. Not alimony, to stop on a remarriage. Apparently a very substantial settlement. Lives in an apartment hotel on Sunset Boulevard—about two hundred per. Not," said Higgins, "a woman I'd want to spend much time with, but then I'm not Carson. All he'd have seen would've been the money. And all she saw," he added thoughtfully, "was the handsome Prince Charming, the fun times. She'll get over him very easy."

"So when did she see him last, according to her?"

"Last Sunday night. They had a date. She says she'd been worried, he usually phoned her once a day, and she'd been calling his apartment. They had a date set up for last night."

"I think I'd like to see Natalie," said Mendoza. Palliser looked in the door.

"Say, is it O.K. if I take an hour off? I'm meeting Robin at the realtor's. Clinch the deal for the house."

"The forty-grand one?" asked Higgins.

"You're only young once. Why not? It's a nice house," said Palliser airily.

"It should be, for that."

"Go, go, a fool in his folly," said Mendoza. "But don't forget we've got this and that on hand, and I'd take no bets that something new won't show up."

"She is," said Higgins as Palliser went out, "all very anxious to cooperate with the law on finding the fiend who shot her poor Rex. Shall I set up an appointment for you? Here? I get the feeling she won't be out of bed until around ten."

Mendoza laughed. "All right. Let the poor girl get her beauty sleep—Jimmy can call later. Send a car for her."

Higgins contemplated his cigarette. "That's about it, all I come up with. I did have to spend some time with Natalie. And it's possible she had something to do with it—provided the motive maybe. If another of his girl friends had found out about her—"

The door opened and Dr. Bainbridge marched in. "Don't rile me," he said at once, "by saying I should have got the report to you yesterday. We're *busy*, damn it. All the damn drunks and idiots and the fool drivers killing people and the old bums— As if we hadn't enough on our hands, another corpse down there now and a damn messy one too—drunk ramming a building." He sat down and slapped a manila envelope down on Mendoza's desk. "Carson. I sent the bullet to Ballistics, it wasn't much damaged, they'll be sending you a report. And I'm told you want to ask questions about Carson. Don't know what the hell you want to ask. Man was shot." He brought out a cigar.

"Doctor—" Higgins leaned forward eagerly.

"What we want to know—" began Mendoza.

"Looked like a small caliber," grunted Bainbridge. "Powder burns. Shot fired from no more than three feet, probably a lot closer. Bullet penetrated the—"

"Look," said Mendoza. "Could he have lived long enough to write something down?"

Bainbridge stared at him over the lighted match, puffing; with his bald head and round face he looked like an angry baby. "Write something down? With a bullet in his head?"

"Show him," said Higgins. "Doctor, you know all the case histories. People have lived for days with bullets in their heads. Head injuries—"

"Head injuries you can't predict," said Bainbridge shortly. "Is he supposed to have written down something?"

Mendoza produced the memo-pad. Bainbridge stared at it and shrugged. "Well, could he have?" persisted Higgins.

"He *could* have. Could not have. You're not going to pin me down because I don't *know*. How the hell could I know? No doctor alive could tell you anything else, damn it. Nobody could know. When I saw him first he was at least fifteen hours dead and possibly eighteen to twenty. I don't know when he died. To the minute or hour. I gave you the time limits—between six and nine on Monday night. That's all you get from me."

"But he could have lived long enough to do that?" insisted Higgins. "To realize he was dying—at least badly hurt—and make the effort to write that down?"

Bainbridge grunted and said unwillingly, "He could have. It's possible. He could also have died immediately."

"Well," said Higgins, unsatisfied.

"Was he drunk?" asked Mendoza.

"He was not. Not a smattering of alcohol in him. He had, I think, had a meal a couple of hours before. Beef, potatoes, peas, tomatoes and some kind of cake inside," said Bainbridge inelegantly.

"Which makes it look," said Mendoza, "as if it was nearer nine than six. Which figures. Because he had the date with Rose Lamont set up for nine, and it was only about three blocks away that—"

Lake looked in apologetically. "This woman. Manager of that apartment over on Alexandria. Carson's. She's creating about it. Rent was up the fifteenth and she's getting pressured by the owner, when can she get in to clean and what should she do with his things."

"Damnation," said Mendoza. "Pending anything from Newark, we don't know if he's got any family or— But I see her point. Tell her somebody'll be over to unseal the door. There's nothing there. And we can impound his belongings until we find out about the family. George, you can go do that, get it over with. And come back to sit in on the interview with Natalie."

"And I," said Bainbridge, "have got that messy corpse. And another one from over on the Row."

"You might leave me that address book," said Mendoza.

"Former girl friends—clerks from Penney's—¡caray!—flotsam and jetsam. Wasting time. I had a stray thought—"

"We can always use a hunch, Luis," said Higgins, and dropped the book on his desk.

At least, thought Mendoza, the all-point-bulletin was out on William Schuyler. For 99 per cent sure their boy on Milliken and Nordhammer. He wondered if Jase was getting anywhere on his witch woman. The word was out on that hot car the Arizona sheriff was interested in, and the squad cars would have an eye out for it. Whether anything definite would ever show up on the liquor store shooting—

He wondered how the mockingbird was doing. The tarred-and-feathered mockingbird. Guzzling his rye—

He opened the address book.

"He seemed like a nice quiet young man," said Mrs. Harper for the seventh time. "You could've knocked me *over*, I hear he's been murdered. Not that anybody here saw much of him, but times I did happen to see him—going or coming, you know—he was always cheerful and polite as could be. Once he did get behind on the rent, but only a month, and he apologized so—"

"Yes, we understand that, Mrs. Harper," said Higgins. He'd only rung her bell to hand back Carson's key to the apartment, and was trying to extricate himself politely. The front door of the building opened and a man came in past him, moving fast, and up the stairs. He didn't turn to look. In pulling the key off the plain ring Carson had carried, a couple of stray ideas had suddenly struck him.

"He was such a handsome young man—"

First, he thought, pursuant to Luis' complaint about the legwork turning up the flotsam and jetsam, that it might be a shortcut to get the press to run Carson's photograph. There had been only the noncommittal brief article, easily missed by the sketchy reader: man identified as Rex Carson found shot, etcetera. The photograph might bring in a few results, innocents who had known him, who could thus be weeded out.

His second thought, as he wrestled with the Yale key on the ring, was more specific. He was saying, "—apartment unsealed now, we're finished there, and somebody'll be around to collect his belongings, Mrs. Harper—" when the key snapped off, he offered it to her, and suddenly saw the other keys on the ring with more awareness. There weren't many. The apartment door key: two keys belonging to the car, ignition and trunk: the little key to the metal box where the jewelry had been—and the phone number for Harry. That was a thing. Pro burglar Harry in a strange town looking for a fence—and what possible connection with glamour-boy Carson? And a long slim key with no maker's name on it, a key that—

"Hey, you the superintendent here?" asked a voice behind him.

—that might very well be a safety-deposit key. To a safety vault in a bank. Somewhere.

"What?" said Mrs. Harper. Higgins turned.

The fattish young man in the blue post office uniform looked impatient. "I said, apartment eight don't answer. I gotta parcel. Can you take it in? I can leave it, you say you'll take it for him. Rex Carson."

"I'll take it," said Higgins. He produced his badge. A lead? "You Carson?"

"No, I—"

"Then you can't have it. I got to—"

"It could be evidence. This is police business. We—"

"No never mind," said the young man. "We got rules and regulations. Sorry." He turned away for the door.

"Hey!" said Higgins. "Come back here—"

"Rules and regulations," said the young man, and went out. Higgins went after him.

SEVEN

"Listen, I got to cover my route," said the post office man. "I get all behind. We got regulations, I can't let you take a parcel."

"All right," said Higgins, "then we go back to your base and see your superior. This is police business and it's important I see what's in that—" He had a little argument with the man, who kept wailing about being late on his route, but finally persuaded him; he tailed the post office truck to the main Hollywood station and, maintaining firm contact with the postman and the parcel, eventually was routed via minor authority to the superintendent.

"Police business or not, sergeant, we do have regulations, and I'm afraid that unless you get a warrant I cannot let you take away any parcel addressed to some—"

"The man's dead," said Higgins. "He's been murdered."

"Oh, really?" said the superintendent. "But it makes no difference. The principle of the—"

"Look," said Higgins, "I don't necessarily want to take the parcel. I just want to see what's in it. This is police business after all."

The superintendent pursed his lips. "Well, I expect we can get authority for that," he admitted grudgingly. "There are forms—" He looked some of them up, and Higgins filled them out, while the assistant postmaster was contacted. That worthy spoke with Higgins, took his badge number, and after an interval called back to authorize the opening of the parcel.

It was not a very big parcel, about six inches square all around, and the address label bore a printed return address: *Acme Printing and Offset,* an address on Vanowen in the valley. The superintendent opened the parcel neatly with his knife: it was fastened professionally with wide paper tape. An ordinary white cardboard box was disclosed; the superintendent removed the top, and there was revealed a neat stack of business cards with a folded invoice on top of them. In blurred carbon the invoice read laconically, *500 bus. cds.* $9.50, and a PAID stamp slanted across the sheet. Higgins picked up the top card. In neat squat modern print it announced:

UNITED STATES DEPARTMENT OF COMMERCE

and in the same print, lower left corner, *Mr. Walter Wheeler, Agent—Northwestern Regional Area, 522 Fifth Street, Portland, Oregon.*

Higgins stared at it. It meant nothing to him. The plot, he thought, thickened indeed.

The superintendent was being nobly incurious. "You understand, you can't take any of these—"

"That's all right," said Higgins hastily. He copied down the printer's address, the wording on the card, thanked the superintendent and left.

What the hell was this? Department of Commerce. Another gimmick? First a CIA agent and then— Higgins, if the truth were told, was not altogether operating on all cylinders today: he had a little something on his mind that he was deliberately trying not to think about, on the principle that if you wanted a thing too much you were bound not to get it. It wasn't until he had almost finished a cup of coffee at the nearest drugstore that he remembered the address book with the initials W. W. in it. Walter Wheeler? It could very well be.

He found a dime and called the office, relayed that to Mendoza. "*¿Qué es eso?*" said Mendoza thoughtfully. "We're getting disorganized around here, George. Just because we know his right name was Carson, concentrating on that address book. I'll have a look. I've got Natalie coming in, you want to sit in?"

"I don't think so. I'd better see these printers and then—" That key. A safety-deposit box?

"*Bueno.* I don't really expect too much from Natalie."

Carson hadn't had a bank account, checking or savings. At least, no books found. In any name. Had traveled light. No charge-account plates. Well, charge accounts left a trail. But, not much cash on him and none in his apartment. A safety vault somewhere? Higgins looked at the key. It was certainly that kind of key. And there were God only knew how many banks in L.A. County. Furthermore, there was no way of knowing, if Carson had had one, what name it was under.

Higgins sat in his car and thought. Like Luis was always saying, the idiot boy and the horse. Keep it simple. All right. No bank account. If he had had a safety vault the chances were he'd used it like a bank. For the cash. He must have had more than there was on him. So, most likely, he wouldn't have rented a safety vault at a bank miles away from where he lived. All right, he got around, but ten to one, if there was a vault, it'd be at a bank in Hollywood, either near the apartment or in downtown Hollywood. And if they could spot it, it would be a simple matter to get a warrant to open it.

There were a lot of banks in that area, but at least it narrowed the choice. However, the printer first. Higgins turned the ignition key and started the engine.

"Oh, I'd only met him last month," said Natalie Brookes. "Over at Vegas." She sniffed delicately into a scented handkerchief. "We only got engaged last week. It was a whirlwind romance."

"Is that so?" said Mendoza. He agreed with Higgins that Carson had had a stroke of luck with Natalie; at least Carson would have thought so. Natalie was a looker indeed: a statuesque brunette with all the right curves and a naturally amiable disposition. Nothing deep about Natalie; he'd sized her up in thirty seconds. She had big dark eyes and a magnificent olive complexion and she was slightly overdressed in a white sharkskin suit with a gold lamé blouse and stilt-heeled gold pumps. But she was too much the natural female to put on much veneer any other way.

"Just like my mama always told me, marry the first time for money, divorce is easy and you can marry for love the second time," she said to Mendoza. "But I guess I won't be right away. Poor Rex. Do you suppose it was some other woman shot him? I expect there'd be a lot who were jealous of him." She heaved a sigh. "He was so much fun to be with. We weren't going to stay here, you know. His idea, not mine. I like L.A. just fine, you got everything convenient around, but he said we might try Florida for awhile. We were getting the license this Wednesday, you know—going to be married Saturday. He said he had some things to sort of clear up— you know, like those two sales jobs he'd been working. He wouldn't have to do anything like that after—we wouldn't have any worry about money, you know. Oh, Rex wasn't very *steady*, it comes to money—I knew that—but it's my money, after all, I got a two million settlement from Chauncey. He could afford it. But Rex was such fun—such a darling." She sniffed again.

"Did he say anything on Sunday night—the last time you saw him—to make you think he'd—mmh—had a quarrel with anybody? Was afraid of anybody?"

She shook her head and her big drop earrings danced. "Goodness, no. And I don't *know* about any other women, who they might have been, but there'd've been bound to *be* some, wouldn't there? He wasn't any teen-ager and neither am I, after all. And women fell for him like mad. I didn't care, why should I? I had the money—he was marrying me."

She didn't know anything about his affairs, beyond the dancing school and the model agency: the on-the-surface respectable jobs. She'd taken him at face value, fun to be with, darling Rex. Natalie not at all deep.

Mendoza ruminated on Natalie when she'd left; he had the vague feeling that something she'd said had been significant, but he couldn't put a finger on it. Those business cards —very peculiar. Walter Wheeler. Why? Of course, by what they had turned up on Carson so far, unless he'd had a surer, steadier gimmick than they had come across, he wasn't getting rich at his little on-the-fringes con games.

And where did Harry tie in? Where indeed?

He swore to himself and reached for the W. W. address book and then got up suddenly and went out to the anteroom. He said to Lake, "Teletype up to the chief in Portland, Jimmy. Anything known of either Robert C. Conway or Walter Wheeler, in any connection? And is there a 522 Fifth Street in Portland?"

"O.K.," said Lake.

Piggott and Landers had gone back to the tiresome routine on the liquor store shooting. They were both finding it hard to keep their minds on, for different reasons. Piggott had a date with Prudence Russell tonight—they'd set it up at choir practice last night. And Landers's recently bullet-ridden shoulder was aching; he kept rubbing it. To make it more tiresome, the one witness to the shooting of the store owner was a flighty female who was not quite sure of any statement she made. He was kind of tall, well, maybe more like medium tall, and he had a crooked nose, no, it was more like flat. She hadn't made any of the mug shots they'd shown her.

Well, the citizenry—most of them tried to be helpful, and probably she was doing her best. But nobody was putting much faith in the provisional artist's sketch, and Piggott and Landers were back to doing it the hard way, looking through records for possible men with suggestive pedigrees, and finding them, and questioning them.

They had, at one o'clock this mild Thursday afternoon, just brought in another of the possibles, a big thug with a pedigree back to age twelve, who was eleven months out of Quentin from a three-to-ten on a very similar holdup job. Both of them were starving for lunch, and Landers had just said to Piggott, "Let him cool while we have something to eat, hah?" They had stashed him on the bench in the anteroom under Lake's eye; Lake, comfortably full of lunch but looking biliously at the cigarette he was smoking, picked up the phone as it shrilled at him and the next moment was beckoning them violently back.

"Oh, hell," said Landers.

"No rest for the wicked," said Piggott. "What now?"

"O.K. Somebody on the way," said Lake, and put down the phone. "Quite a dust-up in a bar out on Washington. Several corpses at least, and some wounded. The squad car's sent for ambulances." He added the address.

"My God," said Landers. "Do you want to bet we'll get no lunch at all? Come on, Matt."

It was, when they got there, quite a thing. Three ambulances, a squad of internes, two squad cars. Inside the bar, which was more coffee shop than bar, licensed for beer and wine only, about twenty people were sitting or standing around gabbling excitedly. Everybody there except the internes and three of the squad car men were Negro. The Negro squad car man was talking quietly to a dazed-looking girl seated at one of the little round tables. She was repeating over and over, "He just shot at anybody, like he didn't care— he just shot at—"

BURLINGAME
PUBLIC
LIBRARY

Piggott and Landers were greeted with relief by the uniformed men. The ambulances were just getting away. "Four dead and three people hurt," said one of the patrolmen. "My God, what a mess. By what we hear, he just pulled out a gun and started shooting in all directions. That's the proprietor over there, the elderly man—"

"All right—" Landers raised his voice. "Quiet down a minute here! Does anybody here know who the man was who did the shooting? Recognize him?"

There was an instant's silence, and then the girl with the Negro officer came out of her daze and said, "I know him, sir." Several confused voices cut across each other. "All right, nobody's to leave," said Landers. "We want to talk to all of you." Piggott went over to the girl, and Landers turned to the elderly man sitting, as if collapsed, at a table near the bar counter. He was a dignified-looking Negro, his kinky hair graying, dressed neatly in black slacks and a white shirt with a Western bolo string tie. He was being fussed over by a stout middle-aged woman in a flowered dress.

"Now it wasn't your fault, dad, you couldn't know nothing like that was goin' to happen—"

"You're the owner here, sir?" asked Landers. "You were here? Can you tell me exactly what happened, Mr.—"

"Bradwood," said the elderly man, "my name's Bradwood, sir. Yes, I own this place. I try to run a clean decent place, give the people a nice place to sit, and I get nice people comin' in, no riffraff. I don't tolerate riffraff here. I don't want the bums in my place, put the decent people off so they don't come no more. I run that fellow off before. That Freddy Seymour. He's a bum—trash." He wasn't exactly in a state of shock, but he wasn't being as careful about what he said to white men as he might have been otherwise. "He's a bad nigger, that one, the kind give people wrong ideas, no good to the rest of us. The decent people." He took a deep breath. "Gettin' drunk and fooling around with the yalla girls down back alleys and in cop trouble too, I heard. I don't want that kind in my place—even lookin' in my door—"

"It was my fault!" said the girl across the room, and burst into tears. She was a pretty brown girl, neatly and modestly dressed in navy blue; her eyes were still big with shock. "He came after me—and I only came in to get away from him, I knew Mr. Bradwood'd chase him off—" The Negro officer and Piggott bent over her.

"That's so, he come in after Nella—this time. And I did chase him off—I told him get out and stay out. I never knew he had a gun on him. I knew he was a bad one, but—" Bradwood drew another long breath and looked up at Landers numbly. "I figure he musta been doped up, though, to do that. Just start shootin' like that. Like he was crazy. I knew he's a bad one, and so many that kind gettin' doped up on something these days. Not even Freddy Seymour crazy enough to—but, oh, my God, poor Mrs. Freeman an' young Joey just gettin' a good start his new job an' Mr. Gates an'—"

"It was all my fault!" sobbed the girl.

The middle-aged woman rounded on them fiercely. "An' Nella's a good girl, she don't want nothin' to do with trash like that. Her with a good job in a lawyer's office, educated an' all, riffraff like that Freddy sniffin' around her! Just on her way back to work after lunch, wasn't you, Nella?" The girl sobbed. "An' Mr. Bradwood like a daddy to a lot o' young folks around here, she just run in when that no-good trash come pesterin' her. Ain't nobody's fault but his, his own self. He's the one shot off the gun, ain't he?"

"He surely did, ma'am," said the Negro officer. "He surely did." He looked at Landers. "We've got the names on the D.O.A.'s, sir. Would you like us to go round doing the notifying?"

"It'd be helpful," agreed Landers. "And the others. Let us have the names and addresses for the report." At least this one was not going to pose any mystery, only a lot of paper work. They took the girl Nella Hatfield and Bradwood in to make statements, and after sending them back in a squad car had a look in Records for Frederick Seymour. He was there big as life: pedigree of assault, robbery with violence, D.-and-D., and one count of rape. He was currently on parole.

Piggott said, "I seem to remember there's something in Isaiah about false leaders. What the courts are thinking of, turn one like this loose—"

Landers just said tiredly, "Let's go have some lunch before we start hunting him."

Jason Grace smoked an after-lunch cigarette placidly and listened to the twenty-year-old opinions of Jared Putman. He'd been listening to a lot of people around here yesterday and today. He was under no illusions that people in the neighborhood where Mrs. Sadie Snyder had lived would be willing to talk to him where they wouldn't to a white officer; there were people around, any neighborhood, who wouldn't talk to *any* fuzz, whatever his color. He had run into a few like that. He had run into a lot more of what he called to himself the borderline cases; and he didn't mean borderline between honest and dishonest. By the grace of God, the former usually outnumbered the latter by a great majority. It was something a good deal subtler.

"Typical, Mr. Grace," said Jared Putman, gesturing with his fork. This was a modest little short-order café, the food passable only. "Typical of the older generation. All the old shibboleths and outmoded ideas. Faithful churchwoman, what I heard. Like that. As for the other thing—" he laughed. "What you were asking about—oh, I'd heard something about her reputation that way—I remember my father laughing about it. Some of these people, Mr. Grace, you'll never prod them out of the nineteenth century. They don't *want* progress—" Young Mr. Putman waxed eloquent. Probably make a good lawyer, thought Grace; he was a law student at

L.A.C.C. Nice-looking boy, some white blood. He looked at young Mr. Putman benevolently, thinking about his borderline cases.

A lot of them. What it came down to, he reflected, was that for various reasons, though God knew the opportunity was there for anybody who wanted to use it, your average middle-class Negro was just a little bit more self-conscious about his education, and his middle-classness, than the average white man. A lot of them having achieved it only rather recently, and conscious too of some traditional traits attributed to them—for all Grace knew, rightly so. Luis Mendoza could joke about his superstitious grandmother, and that Italian fellow he'd known at the Academy freely admit his belief in the Evil Eye; but catch any respectable resident around here even admitting he'd heard rumors about Sadie Snyder. Even the ones who talked freely to him: as most did.

The grocer at the corner. The postman. The neighbors. The landlady. The druggist up on Washington. All respectable, decent people. Conscious also, thought Grace ruefully, that they were talking to somebody in an official position, and so maybe all the more anxious to make a good impression. *That* old nonsense—modern educated folk like us don't even think of things like that these days. Like so. Oh, those rumors, said the grocer, silly, you'd think in this day and age . . . and his wife's eyes expressive behind him before she looked away. A nice Christian old lady, said the druggist defiantly, and he never paid notice to gossip any kind. Oh, yes?

"My psychology teacher," said Mr. Putman, "says that all these old superstitions are just a way of sublimating guilt feelings by—"

"Psychology," said Grace mildly, unable to refrain—a promising boy if he ever grew up and started to think for himself—"just the latest fashionable mumbo-jumbo. You want to start taking a long close look at human nature, Mr. Putman. It doesn't change so much from generation to generation—more's the pity." He smiled, putting out his cigarette.

The kids, now, that was a little different. Grace might not know much about kids—Virginia still hoping for a family, all the tests and temperature-takings and so on—but he did know that by and large they weren't veneered over quite so heavily as adults. What was that one about children and fools speaking the truth? Yes. And he'd heard bits and pieces from the kids, on several blocks around the little apartment where Sadie Synder had lived. The natural reports, you could say. It was about all he had got. . . . Ol' lady Snyder was a real witch. Yah, my dad says there's no such thing. Well, my dad says there is *too*. She could put the eye on you—set the old Boogerman after you. Make spells— And, in answer to deft proddings, she didn't like Colly. She never *did* nothing to us kids—she never had trouble with anybody I heard of—'cept Colly. Called him a thief and said he'd come to a bad end. My ma heard her. She said Colly better look *out*, 'cause ol' lady Snyder—

That, with less embellishment, he had heard also from the landlady. That Mrs. Snyder had complained about Colly, who'd tried to snatch her purse once. Colly was Collingwood Brown, a drifter who lived with his mother—everybody said, hardworking Christian woman and she had a deal to put up with—up the block. Grace had heard reports that Colly had done a little time.

Colly sounded possible to Grace. Colly just the sort, by all reports, to take Sadie Snyder's reputation for granted, as per the kids. He had been to Colly's address twice, hadn't raised anybody there. Now he thought he'd try again, and if nobody was home, go back to headquarters and look for Colly in Records.

"If you'd just hold it still, *achara*," said Mrs. MacTaggart.

"I'm *trying*," said Alison. She grasped the mockingbird by feet and tail feathers, over the large dishpan on the kitchen table; Mrs. MacTaggart applied solvent liberally to the dried tar. The mockingbird exclaimed *Wheeee-yoo!* in its lewd wolf whistle, and struggled. "Honestly!" said Alison. "Why it had to be Bast who came across you first—be quiet, idiot, we're only trying to help you!"

"I wonder now if paraffin would do it?"

"Para—oh, you mean kerosene. I don't know," said Alison doubtfully. "Or turpentine?"

"*Mamacíta, Mamacíta!* Do *el pájaro* be all better now?"

"*Mamacíta, el pájaro* goin' to *fly?* Daddy said—"

Lined in a row outside the kitchen door were the four cats all talking to each other indignantly about the unwelcome intruder, the twins, and Cedric. Cedric was not interested in the intruder; he was there only because everybody else was there, and Cedric was the complete extrovert.

"*Wheeeee-yoo!*" exclaimed the bird. "*Yankee Doodle came to town—Wheeeee-yoo! YAWK!*"

"The creature must have been tamed before by somebody," said Mrs. MacTaggart. "'Tis so bold, and a wild bird to let a body lay a hand on it—"

"Oh, mockers are terribly curious and aggressive," said Alison. "All of them."

"*Mamacíta—*"

"Woof," said Cedric amiably, to join in the chorus.

The mockingbird suddenly began to buzz like a staccato bee. "What on earth would that be meant for, now?"

"I think he must have heard a pneumatic drill someplace," said Alison. "They pick up everything, you know. I wonder if paint remover— Is it coming at all?"

Mrs. MacTaggart squeezed another half-pint of solvent from her cloth over the mockingbird. "I do think 'tis beginning to soften a bit."

"Wheeeeee-yoo!" said the bird, fluttering in Alison's hands. *"Yankee Doodle came to town, Yankee Doodle—"*

"The things," said Alison, "those cats get us into!"

Disorganized, thought Mendoza, brooding at his desk. Going senile. But if he hadn't seen it, Art or George should have. Minds dulled by all the legwork, that was it. The three address books. Damn it, because the corpse was Rex Carson, they had gone all out looking at Carson *as* Carson. They had evidence (the Oregon driver's license) that he had used the Conway alias—on what? And now, Walter Wheeler.

He thought, separate compartments. The con-man. Hearty hail-fellow-well-met on the surface, inclined to be calculating and tidy-minded underneath. Natalie hadn't known much about him really: hadn't really cared. Just that he was fun to be with. His other marks—the women—probably the same. And some of them at least, the aces-in-the-hole. Like Rose Lamont. Keeping her sweet, on the string—his absences explained by all those dangerous missions—and if he suddenly wanted a couple of hundred, the sad story about the greedy ex-wife, back alimony. The patriotic hardworking servant of his country—*¡Dios!* Mendoza laughed, but with irony. And the different plausible stories for other females. All sorts of gimmicks. But, what about the aliases? Mendoza was suddenly seized with impatient curiosity as to what he had been up to in Oregon. Wait for it. The dismal fact being that possibly no one but Carson had known.

But, he thought. Conway. Wheeler. Carson had had a date with Rose Lamont the night he was shot, and he had been shot—that car hadn't been driven a foot after he was shot behind the wheel, according to George—a scant three blocks away from where Rose Lamont lived. Had he been on his way there? But—with a passenger? Why? And Carson had got around places and known a lot of people. It occurred to Mendoza, suddenly and belatedly, had he been shot *as*

Carson? Or as another man, for some reason not connected to Carson at all?

The address books. A lot of names in them. Mendoza had now looked through all three, page by page, and he was wondering rather hard, not about any of the names, but about a few that had been crisscrossed out in firm ballpoint—X-ed out so thoroughly that they couldn't be deciphered. They were all in the book marked R. R. C. The Carson book. Opposite one of them, under the B's, Carson had scrawled *bad medicine.* Opposite another, under the Y's, appeared a cynical *nice girl,* with the *nice* heavily underlined. That one self-explanatory. The others? He was wondering if the lab could do anything with infra-red photography when Lake came in with a manila envelope.

"Ballistics report."

Mendoza took the sheet from the envelope. On Carson, and about time. They hadn't made the gun absolutely, but they couldn't always; most gunsmith manufacturers produced some similar models that left much the same markings on bullets. The bullet that had killed Rex Carson (immediately or after an unspecified time?) had been fired by an Iver-Johnson .22 revolver, either the Supershot, the target-design model made in three barrel lengths, or the I-J Target made in two barrel lengths. All three were eight-shot double-action revolvers.

And the only thing that said to him at the moment was that, that being so, Carson's shooting might have been the impulsive, even the unintended thing. With a single-action revolver, you had consciously to intend to fire it to get a shot off, bring the hammer back; with an automatic, unless you were dangerously carrying it with a load in the chamber, ditto. But a double-action revolver, fully loaded, could be fired in a fraction of a second—a moment's passion, as it were. And a .22—any .22—didn't as a rule have a very stiff trigger-pull.

He was still brooding on that when Palliser looked in and said he'd let himself in for the time-payments all official. And the new call had been a suicide, note left, and Glasser was typing up the report. "That wholesale shooting out on Washington was something. They've just booked him—Matt was telling me."

"What wholesale— Nobody tells me anything," said Mendoza.

"About one o'clock. All-Negro place. Guy with quite a pedigree, Matt said. And quoted Isaiah." Palliser grinned. "He was on P.A., they found him at home—a flea-ridden hotel down on Main—high on something. H or reefers or take your choice. He's in the General and there's a warrant in the works. About thirty witnesses. Four people dead and a few more shot up."

"*¡Santa María!*" said Mendoza.

"And," said Palliser, looking thoughtful, "Robin now talking about furniture. Only the necessities, keep the expense down, but at today's prices, my God—"

"In for a penny," began Mendoza inattentively; and Dr. Bainbridge marched in, his tubby teddy-bear figure erect and belligerent.

"Thought you'd better hear about your new mystery," he said, grinning like a ferocious baby.

"What now?" asked Mendoza.

"That traffic D.O.A." Bainbridge plumped himself down in the other chair beside the desk and got out a cigar. "Looked like the typical drunk-driver thing, no other car involved so I understood, driver losing control and ramming into a building. About half-past midnight last night. Passenger critically injured, driver killed. Messy, as I said. One Leon Lister the D.O.A."

"So?"

"So," said Bainbridge, striking a match, "I come to take a close look at the corpse—as per rules and regulations, and just as well too—in some places where the rules aren't so stiff he'd have got buried as the accident victim pure and simple. I come to take a look, he's been shot. In the head. You won't get any make on the gun, the bullet was all to pieces. But, a bullet. Without much doubt, reason the car went out of control."

"¡Válgame Dios!" said Mendoza. "Shot? You're—"

"You'd better ask the passenger about it," said Bainbridge dryly, "if and when he's ever conscious again."

EIGHT

By the time Mendoza and Palliser got over to Central Receiving Hospital on Loma Drive, it was after five. The car—Leon Lister's two-door Ford—had been towed into the police garage; no examination had been made of it, but now there would be. There hadn't been a gun in the car. And just what any examination might turn up on that mangled mass of metal was anybody's guess; probably nothing. But the gesture had to be made.

They found the family at the hospital; both families in a sense. The D.O.A. Lister and his passenger Peter Whiteley had been brothers-in-law; and the young widowed Mrs. Lister was there with her parents. Whiteley was still in critical condition.

It was Gloria Lister who first grasped what they were saying. "Sh-shot?" she said. "Leon—*shot?* But I don't— It wasn't an accident? But who—" She turned to her mother and father, starting to cry all over again. "Leon, *shot.* They've just found out—"

"I always said there was something wrong, it couldn't be an accident, Leon a good careful driver—" Mrs. Whiteley's voice was monotonous, as if most emotion had been shaken out of her. "It didn't make sense—an accident—not much traffic that time of night—" She stared up at them from the upholstered bench in the drab waiting room, a thin middle-aged woman, dry-eyed but only because tears had long been shed. "And maybe Peter going to die too—"

"Now, Mother." Her thin gray husband laid a hand on her arm. "It's God's will. He's hung on this long."

"Mrs. Lister," said Mendoza. "We're sorry to bother you at a time like this, but now we know your husband was shot, you understand we have to ask questions. Do you know anyone your husband had quarreled with lately? Any enemies he may have had? Or your brother, for that matter?"

She stared up at him, a pretty blonde girl no more than twenty. "Enemies?" she repeated. "Leon? Peter? Why, that's just crazy. Just crazy. Leon—"

"Ordinary quiet young fellow, working steady—going to church Sundays—I never heard Leon speak a cross word to anybody," said her mother dully. "And my Peter—a better son nobody ever had—nobody had any reason not to like Peter, he's not the quarrelsome sort—he and Leon all through school together, and they never—"

"But, Mother," said the girl. "An accident—we couldn't believe that either, because Leon's such a careful—"

Mendoza got what he could from them, while Palliser hunted up the doctor. The two brothers-in-law had, last Tuesday night, attended a stag party for a friend getting married the next day. But they hadn't meant to stay late, as they both had to be at work in the morning; the wedding was scheduled for Wednesday evening. Lister, who was twenty-four, worked at a Bank of America branch; Whiteley, twenty-five, was a C.P.A. in an office downtown. The upright citizens. But the stag party—at all events, they had evidently been heading home when they came to grief. Both the Whiteleys and the young Listers lived on Thirty-ninth Place.

See the other men at the stag party, find out what state

both men were in when they left. If necessary, prod at the family some more.

He met Palliser at the end of the hall. "They're not saying yes or no about Whiteley," said Palliser. "Just our luck if he dies without coming to. And his, of course. But I did get it out of the doctor that he wasn't drunk, so far as showed. No smell of liquor on him when he was brought in, and he reacted normally to drugs."

"But a stag party," said Mendoza. "The people who called us—"

"Just found the accident, I don't think they saw it."

"Mmh, yes. But they'd better be talked to."

"All right, I'll do the overtime," said Palliser. "This is a funny one."

"Funny is not the word," said Mendoza.

He went home to a house for once quiet and seemingly normal. He kissed Alison, got himself a glass of rye in the kitchen, and told her about the newest funny one. He was a little early tonight, and Mrs. MacTaggart was setting the table, having told Alison brusquely to pay the man a little wifely attention, she'd put things to rights. The twins, somewhere, were quiet as mice. Bast came to settle on Mendoza's lap, Cedric was asleep beside Alison's chair with Nefertite between his front paws, and Sheba on Alison's lap, while El Señor slurped down his half-ounce of rye from a saucer.

"Of course you don't really know much about it yet," said Alison encouragingly.

"True," said Mendoza somnolently. "But—"

A sudden raucous squawk sounded down the hall, and then a piercing, *"Yankee Doodle came to town, Yankee Doodle—YAWK!"* Mendoza jumped, Bast's ears shot up like twin exclamation points, and El Señor stopped lapping to hiss loudly. Cedric lifted his head in annoyance and flopped down again. Mrs. MacTaggart trotted out of the dining room agitatedly.

"That creature," said Alison.

"And how is our little feathered friend? Coming untarred?"

"We got about half of it off today, but his wings are still stuck. And," said Alison as Bast spat at a renewed chorus of *Yawks* in the middle distance, "you're the one brought him home after all."

Mrs. MacTaggart appeared at the door and said, looking distrait, that everything was on and the coffee just on the perk and she'd be seeing to the twins. "And I was only feeling sorry for the creature, what with the tar and Bast biting it and all—the poor thing in a state of shock—but it was a mistake ever to put that whiskey down its throat. Just the few times the first day or so. It's got to expect it now and it takes on no end if I don't bring it. And fixing me with *such* looks if I offer it bread crumbs instead."

Mendoza burst out laughing. "Corrupting the wildlife now. My God, Mairí, when you do turn it loose it'll be bringing every mocker in Southern California to demand our—mmh—hospitality." He finished his rye and started for the dining room.

They were just starting on Alison's special apple pudding, after the roast, when the phone rang; he put his spoon down resignedly as he got up to answer it. "Might as well be a doctor. . . . Mendoza."

"Just thought you'd like to be brought up-to-date," said Galeano. "There's a teletype in from Newark. On Carson. Shall I give you the gist of it?"

"*Por favor.*"

"Carson was the only child of Edward and Erma Carson. Edward deceased nineteen sixty, Erma nineteen sixty-four. Edward was a jeweler, had his own shop in Newark. Retired when he died. Rex Carson was the sole legatee when his mother died—she was sole legatee of husband. The lawyer's name is here—one Glen Knight. But there wasn't much of an estate. They don't say why, either the elder Carson didn't make much or the widow blued it. Anyway, no car or real property. Carson—Rex Carson—went back for his mother's funeral. Lawyer settled the estate for him, just personal possessions, and that was that. Nothing further known of Carson in Newark."

"Well," said Mendoza. "That says a lot."

"Doesn't it? George called in just before Jimmy went off. Said he'd been hunting through banks—didn't say why—and he'd see you in the morning."

"Well, thanks very much," said Mendoza, and went back to his dessert. "That Carson. There's no way to backtrack him, damn it—elusive as an eel. Not as if he kept regular hours, had any regular routine. Typical of the breed, of course. The different irons in the fire. Nobody at the apartment will even swear to seeing him the last couple of weeks. What he might have been up to—besides pursuing the fair Natalie—"

"What really got me," said Alison, bending to a light for her cigarette, "was the CIA-agent bit. How anybody could be so gullible—"

"I don't know, cara," he said seriously. "Fantastic things are going on all around. And he was probably a damn good actor, you know. Put it over with a flair. And probably got quite a kick out of it."

"But even so—"

And Mendoza paused in the act of lighting his own cigarette and said suddenly, "¿Pues qué? Now I do wonder. A jeweler. And—mmh—personal possessions . . ."

"It was awful," said Mrs. Myra Pickett earnestly. "Just awful. So bad for Oliver. My husband."

"Now," he said mildly.

The Picketts, a couple in the sixties, faced Palliser in the comfortable living room of their apartment on La Cienega Boulevard. They were well-dressed, respectable citizens in substantial circumstances by appearances, and very eager to be helpful to the law.

"You see, Oliver's had one coronary, he has to be careful," said Mrs. Pickett. "We never go on the freeways. Just in case. We'd been downtown, you see. These very old friends from our old home town, Kansas City, Mr. and Mrs. Wedemeyer, they're staying at the Biltmore downtown, and we'd been to dinner with them there. We were on our way home."

"Now I don't suppose the sergeant's interested in that," said Mr. Pickett.

"It's all background, sir," said Palliser. "Did you see the crash?"

"Oh, goodness, no," she said. "We *heard* it. Awful. There wasn't any traffic at all, and the street lights weren't working." Most places in town, the automatic signals stopped working at midnight. "No, the car hadn't passed us. At least I don't remember—"

"Nothing had passed me for blocks," said Pickett firmly. "Business district along there, all deserted at that hour. I was on Alvarado. We heard this crash somewhere up ahead, it was fairly quiet, you know—what?—yes, the windows were all closed, chilly night. And I said to Myra, that sounds like an accident. And a couple of blocks up we came on it. No, sir, I didn't see any other car there at all. What?"

"Did you hear a shot, sir? Before the crash?"

"A *shot?* No, certainly not. These fool drunks," said Pickett, looking disgusted. "It was a mess. An unholy mess. And we had to hunt round quite awhile for a public telephone—"

Palliser asked more questions, but that was it. He thanked them and went home to his Robin, who was poring over furniture catalogs and cannily calculating the lowest possible expenditures.

Mendoza got to the office at five of eight on Friday morning, and Hackett made the same elevator. "Anything new?" he asked. Mendoza brought him up-to-date as the elevator bore them upward. "But what a thing," said Hackett. "The stag party—a fight? Everybody full of booze?"

"We'll see. You'd better sit in and hear what George has to say about Carson." But he'd just hung up his hat when Lake buzzed him.

"Goldberg."

"Right," and Mendoza picked up the inside phone. "Morning, Saul. Have you picked up Harry for me?"

"Not," said Goldberg, "in the material sense. But does this ring any bells in your head? Harry Schumacher, age now forty-seven, five eight, a hundred and sixty, hair graying from black, eyes blue, complexion medium, scar left corner of mouth?"

"The places I met him, I wasn't noticing eye color," said Mendoza, "but that could be him all right."

"I thought so. He's out of Quentin about three weeks, from a one-to-three for a burglary he pulled with another guy, who died inside. It was his only count in California—Washington's got a pedigree on him mostly from around the Middle West. Same sort of stuff, mostly burglary. He's done time in the Illinois pen."

"Yes. Homesick Harry," said Mendoza.

"Well, we've got feelers out for him. If he's broke he's probably still here. See if any of the pigeons turn him in. I'll be in touch," said Goldberg.

Mendoza put the phone down, brushed his moustache the wrong way and back again, and said, "Personal possessions," in a dissatisfied tone.

"What?" said Hackett.

Higgins came in, said good morning, and sat down. "I had a little brainstorm yesterday afternoon, Luis. When I was handing back that key to the landlady it just occurred to me—"

"Belatedly I got there too," said Mendoza. "When Nick said you'd been canvassing banks. He hadn't any account that we found a record of. I take it you didn't find anything?"

"Not so far. I went to see the printer first—" Higgins looked a little abstracted over something but was automatically making the concise verbal report. "It's a big outfit, and they do a lot of business by mail. They had quite a time finding the original order. And I can see that, you know—a big busy business like that, who takes much notice of the copy on an order sent in? I sort of got the impression that nobody'd turn a hair if an order came in for a stack of business cards printed *His Satanic Majesty, Address Hell.* Just automatically set the print and fill the order, as long as cash on the line came with it."

"*Dineros son calidad*," agreed Mendoza.

"They did finally find the record of payment. It came with the order, a bank money order."

"Which bank?"

"Security-First branch on Vermont. I—"

"Then we look there first for any safety-deposit box."

"It was the first place I went after I saw the printer, naturally," said Higgins. "I've been a detective awhile, Luis."

"*Mea culpa.* No go?"

"Not a thing. No safety-deposit box for Carson, Conway or Wheeler."

"Mmh," said Mendoza.

"I thought Art and I could go looking some more. Take all the banks in downtown Hollywood, likeliest, split 'em up. If he did have a box—"

"I think so too," said Mendoza. "We'd like to know."

"And damn it, that *is* a safety-deposit key," said Higgins. "Mine looks just like it."

He and Hackett went out on that, Hackett groaning at the legwork and Higgins telling him the exercise would do him good. Mendoza found Piggott and Glasser in the sergeants' office and brought them up-to-date on the new and peculiar Lister-Whiteley thing. "We want a list of all the men at that stag party, you can see that. I got a couple of names out of the Whiteleys—a Bill Christiansen on Rampart, and a Steve Reinfeld, Cypress Avenue in the Atwater section. Suppose you go do some legwork on it."

"I left the report on that shooting yesterday on your desk," said Piggott. "You ought to get a medical report on Seymour some time today. But what a thing. And now this. The devil's keeping busy lately."

"He usually is, Matt," said Mendoza.

He went back to his desk and looked over the accumulated reports. Another suicide. The unidentified body had now been identified, and claimed by a son, one Juan Gomez. There was the report on the mass shooting. It was Landers's day off. It was a little early to expect anything in from Oregon on Carson—if there was anything there to be got. On Lister, the most likely thing was that a quarrel had developed at the stag party—and, with the liquor flowing, somebody had had a gun handy.

There was no smell of William Schuyler from anywhere. Well, he hadn't vanished off the face of the earth. He hadn't made much of a haul at the Milliken house—Mendoza didn't think Mrs. Milliken had had a drawerful of diamonds there —and he hadn't been working, he wouldn't have much money. He ought to show somewhere, with the all-points-bulletin out.

Diamonds, he thought. *Jewels.* Personal possessions. Oh, yes? The address books . . .

He got up, told Lake he'd be right back, and went down

to the lab with the R. R. C. address book. Scarne looked at the X-ed out names as he pointed them out. "I just wondered if you could bring them up. Infra-red? Some chemical—"

"A couple of things to try," said Scarne, looking interested. "We'll have a stab at it. Let you know. Matter if we ruin these pages for you?"

"No—you made us photostats, remember? See what you can do anyway," said Mendoza.

Mr. Gilbert Goldstein was at that moment lounging in the doorway of his Plymouth-Chrysler agency out on Rosemead Boulevard. It was a nice day and he'd just made a good sale; he was feeling pleased with life. At the same time he was wondering whether he ought to call in about that thing, because Mr. Goldstein was a conscientious citizen and not averse to being involved. Hell, he was always telling people, whether you want or not you *are* involved, you're breathing, aren't you? And so when he saw the black-and-white patrol car nosing down the street, his expression lightened and he hurried out to the curb to hail it.

"Hi, Gil, anything up?" asked Bob Polanowsky, getting out of the squad car.

"Bob," said Mr. Goldstein. They knew each other from the circumstance that they both dropped into Gertie's Café up the block for coffee breaks and lunch; and Mr. Goldstein had sold Polanowsky a new Plymouth last year. "Bob, I think a guy just tried to sell me a hot car."

"That so? What makes you think so?"

"Well, he came in with it, he says he wants to sell. No, he doesn't want to trade it on anything new, just wants to sell. Not a thing like I usually get for the used lot, Bob. A thing you'd hold for a special customer, see. A foreign job, a very beautiful piece of engineering, Bob, if you know it—a Maserati. You don't see one just so often. I take a look at it, it's a 1963 Vignale 3500 model, only seventy thousand on it, my God. I tell him I'll offer eighteen hundred for it, and he jumps at it. My God, I was ashamed of myself, Bob. I could ask thirty-five for it easy, it looks in pretty good shape. Only when I ask for the pink slip, the papers, whatever, the guy backs off. Doesn't have any to show. Hems and haws and says they're at home. And off he goes. In the Maserati. And the more I think of it, Bob, the more I think that could be a hot car. In fact, I—"

"Did you notice the plate number?" asked Polanowsky interestedly.

"I did. I may not be any big brain, Bob, but the first he starts stalling about the papers, I take a look and memorize the plate number. A foreigner—just like the Maserati. An Iowa license. It was IS-5777," said Mr. Goldstein.

"Lemme take a look," said Polanowsky. "We got a hot list." He turned back to the squad car. Three minutes later he emerged and said, "You're absolutely right, Gil—that *is* a hot car. Call out on it from Central. I'd better call in. There'll likely be a plainclothesman out to talk to you."

"Any time," said Mr. Goldstein amiably. "Glad I spotted it." He liked to feel he was a good citizen.

Matthew Piggott reflected that this was the first time he could recall that he'd been sorry to hear about somebody being a good upright Christian. It was a funny thing. Part of him, Piggott the fundamentalist believer, should have been happy to hear it; but Matt Piggott, plainclothes detective attached to Central Homicide, was disappointed at the setback in the case. He thought it was a funny little thing to mention to Prudence when he saw her at church on Sunday.

"Drinking?" said Frank Hodges. "At the party? For Bob? You mean like, the fellows getting drunk? Oh, there wasn't anything like that! I mean, you know—well, I guess you *don't* know—it was Bill Christiansen gave the party. For Bob Gerard. The night before the wedding. They nearly postponed the wedding—that terrible thing, Leon and Peter—we just couldn't figure it. You know, Leon's a real cautious driver. Never even had a ticket, any kind. We couldn't figure it. But the minister, the Reverend Bell, he said Leon and Pete'd be all upset, think they'd disturbed things, and so they went on and had the wedding after all. We're all getting together about flowers for the funeral and— But what I meant to say, you got all the wrong idea. About the party. I mean, you know, Leon and I and Bob and Bill, we're all members of the Foursquare Gospel Church and we're all teetotallers. And the other five-six fellows were there, old friends of Bob's, well, they brought a case of beer, but they knew the rest of us wouldn't touch it, and they weren't any of them *drunk*. They maybe had a couple of bottles each, I don't know, wasn't noticing. I don't *approve* of it, but it's their business. They're all nice enough fellows, fellows knew Bob from school and work, it wasn't that kind of party like you make out—"

"I wasn't making it out anything," said Piggott mildly. "Just asking. So nobody was tight?"

"No, *sir*. Just a party. Kidding Bob, and jokes, and Bill's wife left sandwiches and cake and cookies and soft drinks— like that."

"All right," said Piggott. "Were you still there when Lister and Whiteley left?" Frank Hodges was the first stag party guest he'd seen, from a list supplied by Bill Christiansen. Who had told him much the same thing Hodges was telling him.

"Yes, sir, we left about the same time," said Hodges promptly. "I suppose you got to have all this for the record. There'll be an inquest, we heard. Terrible thing. Just terrible. Yes, most of us had to be at work next morning, you know. It was about ten minutes past midnight. Leon and Pete and Steve and I came out together, and I saw Leon and Pete drive off. In Leon's Ford. Up toward Sixth Street."

Making for the main drag Hoover Boulevard, thought Piggott, heading home toward Thirty-ninth, all kosher. "And neither of them had had anything to drink during the evening?"

"I told you," said Hodges. "Why cops have always got to think— Cokes. That's all. They didn't *drink*. Ever. And I just can't figure how Leon came to have an accident. What? Any arguments with anybody? At the party? Well, of course not. We were all friends. Well, as I say Bob was so cut up, he wanted to put off the wedding, one of his best friends, but the Reverend said—"

Piggott walked up the street to his car, thinking pessimistically that the way this one was shaping, they'd never get anything on it. The natural assumption to make, once they knew it hadn't been an accident, and hearing about the stag party, was the drunken quarrel. Now—

He wondered what Henry was getting. More of the same. And that intersection where it had happened, a busy corner daytimes, but at that time of night deserted. All business there as he recalled, no apartments above stores. So?

So, the anonymous thing. Sniper? The juvenile roaming the streets with a gun? Firing it off just for kicks? It could be just as anonymous as that. And no hope of dropping on who.

The violence, he thought. The random evil. Right back, these latter days, to Sodom and Gomorrah. The things that went on. Satan going up and down the world. Ultimately the Lord would lose patience, and not before it was time.

At twelve fifty Hackett, plodding on at the legwork, hit the jackpot. At a Security-First bank on Hollywood Boulevard up toward La Brea. Asking for the manager, showing the badge. Their records showed a Rex Carson as renting a safety-deposit box from June of 1962, a box renting for eleven dollars a year. The next-to-cheapest box.

"You understand, of course, you can't—"

"Yes, yes," said Hackett. "And—" it was a fairly common name "—let's just check the signature to be sure it's the Carson we're interested in." He had a photostat of Carson's California driver's license. The signature checked. "So, you'll be putting a seal on it anyway. He's dead. And we'll be getting a warrant to open it."

"Dead?" said the bank manager. "That means a bank officer to witness—oh, dear. Monday?"

"With any luck we should get the warrant through late today," said Hackett. "I'm sorry, police business, we'll probably want to get at it sometime tomorrow."

"Oh, hell," said the bank manager. He looked at Hackett unkindly. "Stevens is off sick and O'Brien's doing overtime on that special audit. I *was* going to get in some golf."

"Very sorry, sir," said Hackett insincerely. He wondered just what they would find in the safety-deposit box. He wondered if Goldberg had picked up Harry yet. And what *that* connection had been.

He called in to headquarters, and set the machinery going on the warrant. And then—they had split the list of downtown Hollywood banks, before trying the outlying ones, and most of those were along the main drags—he cruised up Hollywood Boulevard and then on Sunset looking for Higgins's car. He spotted it in a red zone along Sunset near Cahuenga, and slid into the yellow zone behind it. In five minutes Higgins came up the block from the bank on the corner, and Hackett hailed him.

"I've got it—we can knock off. You had any lunch?"

"I have not," said Higgins. "There was one? Where?"

Hackett told him. "Back to base. Lunch first. Around here, or could you use a drink?"

"I could," said Higgins. "Meet you at Federico's in twenty minutes."

Hackett agreed. . . . Ensconced at a table there, awaiting

drinks, he said, "I wonder what's in it. Just suddenly occurs to me, George—he was on the con, if just the legal fringes—could he have been blackmailing somebody? With the evidence locked away in the—"

"You've been reading the sensational fiction," said Higgins, yawning. "How's the diet coming?"

Hackett scowled. "Damn doctors. The insurance tables say I can go to two hundred and ten." The drinks arrived and he took a long swallow.

"Calories," said Higgins, and sampled his.

"You go to hell. How's Stevie?"

"Fine. Doctors say the brace can come off next month," said Higgins, smiling.

"Good. Rest of the family?" asked Hackett idly. He was astonished to see a distinct, if faint, blush spread over Higgins's face. Higgins looked embarrassed and defiant at once, and then nothing at all but the familiar George, and Hackett wondered if he'd imagined that.

"Oh, fine," said Higgins. "Fine. I'll have the steak sandwich, Adam."

"Yes, sir. Sergeant Hackett?"

"The low-calorie plate," said Hackett automatically.

"What?" said Mendoza into the phone. "What? That— ¡vuaya!— Talk about the millionth chance. You don't say. Of all the— Yes, thanks so much." He'd been just about to go out to lunch. He picked up the phone again and said, "Jimmy, get me a long-distance call. The sheriff of Mohave County over in Arizona."

NINE

"Well, I'll be damned," said the sheriff, whose name was Quackenbush. "The car's showed over there, hah? Just today?"

"Only a couple of hours ago, I gather," said Mendoza. "The reason I'm calling you—" And a very long chance that was too, that car turning up here. The call on Hollister's car had gone out to every force in California, on the very tentative identification of part of a license plate by that border guard two weeks ago. But here apparently the car was, and if there was no firm legal connection between whoever had killed Hollister and whoever was now driving his car, still they'd like to find him and talk to him. "Have you got any kind of description yet—of who you're looking for? The man who brought it across the border, or—"

"I've got quite a bit," said Quackenbush. "This Hollister had one of these BankAmericards, and we've been busy tracin' it all over—up in Utah and Colorado and back here. Lots of people seen the guy by now, and we've got a good description pieced together, the same fellow. About twenty-five, dark, stocky, maybe five eight, sideburns, and pockmarks."

"*Bueno*," said Mendoza. "I wanted to know before I send somebody out to see this fellow he tried to sell the car to. We'll get the plate number on the priority list, and should pick him up, only a few hours behind him. I'll let you know."

"You do that. You pick up a guy meets that description and I'll be over *pronto* to question him. Good luck, *amigo*."

Mendoza went to see who was in and found Palliser typing a report. He chased him over to Rosemead Boulevard to see Mr. Goldstein and went out to lunch.

When he came back at one o'clock he found Grace talking to Lake in the anteroom. A big fattish brown young man, looking nervous, sat on the bench. "Well, somebody in at last," said Grace. "We are so conscious of witnesses to our genteel behavior these days, aren't we? You like to sit in on some questioning?"

"Who've you got?"

"That Colly Brown." They drifted over to the doorway of Mendoza's office, out of earshot. Grace stroked his neat moustache thoughtfully in unconscious echo of Mendoza. "He's the only possible I've turned up. It's very likely he's far from the only one there is, but you've got to start somewhere."

"Well, let's see what comes out of him," said Mendoza.

They took Colly Brown into an interrogation room and began to ask him questions. There wasn't any trouble getting him to talk. He wasn't a pro; he was a little scared of cops, but there was no smart-aleck stuff. When Grace mentioned Mrs. Snyder he shied back and rolled his eyes emphatically.

"Oh, now, man, you don't think I had nothin' to do with that one! With her gettin' killed? Oh, man, I never did! I wouldn't have no truck—"

"But she didn't like you, Colly? You tried to steal her purse once, and she—"

"Oh, my God, man," said Colly fervently. "I did sure—I didn't know who she *was*, that time. Not then I didn't. Jimmy, he tol' me, my God, man, don't mess with that one— she a witch woman. Got the power for sure, put her eye on you an' you jus' shrivel away, she want to. Put ol' Boogerman atter you, jus' snap her finger like that. Man, was I scared! Better go tell her you sorry, he say, be real polite to her. I didn't like even go to her door, man, but I don't want her eye on me— No, sir. I 'pologize real nice, an' I stay clear o' that one atterward, I tell you, man. Once-twice I see her like laughin' to herself at me, but long as that all she do— Man, you don't catch me in a mile o' her, I help it! You think I'm crazy? Take it in her head put somethin' on me, no tellin' what—"

"Did you think she had, Colly? Put the eye on you?" asked Grace.

Colly thought a minute, painfully. He was the kind, black or white, who in the end often made more trouble for the cops than the consciously dishonest pro criminals: the drifter, the irresponsible loafer who so often drifted into crime because he was weak, lazy, and greedy. "I don't reckon she had," he said. "She couldn't've, 'cause I got lucky at craps just t'other day, an' ain't nothin' real bad happen awhile. So she couldn't've. Man, I find out about her, I never go near, can I help it."

"Well," said Grace. "Last Monday, Colly. You remember Monday? Where you were, Monday night?"

Colly looked vague. "I dunno. I guess I was just foolin' around, like usual, up on Washin'ton. With some o' the boys."

"Who, Colly?"

"Uh—Mikie an' Boo-Boo an' Piggy—I dunno, a lot o' fellas I pal with, I don't remember—"

"When'd you get home that night, Colly?"

"I dunno. Maybe Ma could say."

They talked to him some more, but all they got was a repetition of that. "The funny thing is," said Grace out in the hall, "that Mrs. Brown's a nice hard-working woman, and she's got two other boys working steady in good jobs. What do you think?"

Mendoza lit a cigarette. "If he's the one, you'll never prove it. Never get a definite alibi for him. Hunt up his pals, they all say, sure he was with us. But all that about being scared of the real witch sounds as if it came from the heart. Colly fairly simple-minded, Jase. Kind to run from trouble, not meet it head on."

"There is that. I don't really think it was Colly. But I wonder now," said Grace, "if he knows somebody else who was scared of the real witch? Maybe thought she'd laid a spell on him."

"We can ask him." But as they started back to tackle Colly again, Lake said, "Lieutenant. Long-distance call from Portland."

Mendoza shot into his office and picked up the phone. "Lieutenant Mendoza, Homicide."

"Sergeant Basil here," said a cheerful voice. "We had your query about this Conway. Robert Conway. I want out on it myself. Our D.M.V.'s got a license registered to him here, you know that?"

"Yes, we knew that. What about that address, a phony?"

"Nope. All kosher. Conway rented an apartment at that address about four and a half weeks ago. Paid two months' rent in advance—a hundred and thirty bucks. In cash. He told the landlady, a Mrs. Smythe, he wouldn't be moving in for a week or so, he had business affairs to clear up in San Francisco."

"In San—"

"Said he was moving up here from 'Frisco, had a new job here."

"Oh. Did he say what?"

"Nope. She took him for a salesman of some sort, said he was a nice polite good-looking young man, dressed well. It was O.K. with her, his not moving in right away, because she wanted to paint the place after the last tenants. Now she's wondering where he is—he hasn't showed."

"Mmh, yes. Did he—" Mendoza paused, thinking of Natalie "—say anything about bringing a wife with him?"

"Nope. It's just a little single apartment. Cheap place, old. Sort of place a fellow without much money'd rent, have a place to sleep. He's not in our records, by the way. You want him? Think he'll show here? We can stake out the place—"

"I've got him," said Mendoza. "Somebody shot him down here, and we're still wondering who."

"Well, be damned," said Basil. "Anything else we can do for you?"

"I don't think so, thanks very much."

"Always glad to cooperate, Lieutenant."

Mendoza put the phone down, brushed his moustache the wrong way and back again, and said to himself, "*¿Qué es esto?*" Hackett came in with Higgins, the two of them suddenly dwarfing the office.

"We found the—"

"Bank. *Sí.* I know. Jimmy set the machinery going for a warrant. Twist some arms and get them to open the safety-deposit for us tomorrow."

"Yeah. But—" Higgins sat down opposite Hackett on the other side of the desk, lit a cigarette, and contemplated it. "We've been kicking this thing around, and I think we'd better look at it again, Luis. I don't know why we didn't see it before—too busy running around on the legwork—it's really damn simple. What—"

"Before I listen to your brilliant deduction, listen to mine." Mendoza snapped the gold table-lighter, leaned back in his chair and relayed the information he'd just had from Oregon. "So, first, we can deduce he really did mean to move up there. Why? Take your choice among guesses, but my first guess could say something significant. It might be he'd found a new gimmick, but con games are con games, L.A. or Portland—why move? What it could say, boys, is that one of his marks around here was making trouble for him. Tumbled that he was being taken—"

"She," said Hackett.

"—Maybe was threatening him. Maybe actively. And the ones like Carson usually fairly cowardly. They—slide out from under," said Mendoza, remembering Patti Page. "And just maybe it was the X who took him off before he could—mmh—clear up his business affairs and run."

"All right," said Hackett. "Why did he hang around here a month, if that was so? He hadn't any ties. All he had to do was pick up and go."

"Ah, but he had, Arturo," said Mendoza. "And if it was like that—some real or imagined danger for him here—how very awkward for him. You're forgetting Natalie. Let's see, four and a half weeks. That puts us back to the beginning of February. He was intending to change his base of operations, and whatever the gimmick was he wanted those business cards for—new or old gimmick—he'd made his arrangements, because he knew the address, he'd already got that apartment up there. He had— ¡Dios!—why the hell didn't we see that before?"

"What?" asked Hackett and Higgins together.

"The date on his Oregon license! Look at it—it was issued February twelfth this year. That just confirms it. He was getting out period, changing name and place. And that says all the louder to me, something here had blown up on him, and he was afraid of repercussions. But then, amigos, then he went over to Vegas—last little fling at the tables before he went north?—and he met Natalie. Such a sweet deal for him —all that nice easy money and Natalie too. But he had to woo her a little, after all. Follow her back here and play the suitor."

"Oh," said Hackett. "Yes, I see that, and it just could tie in. I mean, Luis, you are always talking about the lost horse and the— And what that really means is, keep it simple. I know you like things complicated, which is why you imagine things that aren't there. Sometimes. But when you stop to think about it, isn't it kind of significant that Carson was found—was shot—just about three blocks from where he'd said he'd be at nine that night?"

"Well, he could have—"

"He *could* have anything," put in Higgins, "but we've got to look at probabilities, Luis. The likeliest thing. And we said, or you said, that the ones like Carson tend to keep the different marks in separate compartments."

"*Obvio.*"

"Yeah. So, it doesn't strike me as very likely that he'd have had a passenger with him when he started out to keep his date with this Rose Lamont. Why? Who? Somebody with a reason to kill him, and he stopped the car all obliging so X could make with the gun? Just three blocks from Lamont's apartment? Are you going to say it's likely that X also lived in that area, and Carson maybe stopped to call on his way, kill two birds with—? When you think about it—"

Mendoza put out his cigarette impatiently. "I know what you're going to say, George. Not being a fool, I saw it too. But you haven't met that woman. She's—"

"I can read plain facts," said Higgins. "Art agrees with me."

"Look, he said he'd come to see her that night," said Hackett. "Isn't it the easiest thing to suppose he did? And suppose she'd realized that he was conning her, getting money out of her with his plausible—or implausible—little tales. She's not a rich woman, you said. That little coffee shop. And suppose she was good and mad. Hell having no fury like—well, a woman conned. Realizing she'd fallen for the sweet talk. Maybe she'd found out about his other women—or one of 'em. Anyway, she was mad. Enough to kill him. He comes, she says let's take a ride, go here or there. She doesn't want a corpse cluttering up her place. So they start out in his car, and she gets him to stop when they're away from her street, and *kaput*. She gets out and walks home."

"You haven't met her," said Mendoza. "She's not Sarah Bernhardt, Art. Very simple woman. Believed absolutely in her big James Bond hero. The patriotic government servant. She really did. She never suspected him."

"She made you think so. Women," said Hackett cynically, "are all good actresses."

"Now I have been around, Arturo. You think I'm as easy fooled as all that? I saw it too, naturally. The easiest thing to think. And it could just be, my Arturo," said Mendoza thoughtfully, "that somebody else saw that too. It could just be that he had—despite the separate compartment bit—got such a kick out of his theatricals with Rose Lamont that he'd told somebody about it. And the somebody—"

"Planted him at her door? How wild can you get?" Higgins shook his head. "We all know, how often have we said it, what it looks like is usually just what it is. He was *there*. Three blocks away from a mark he'd taken for a respectable profit. If she'd realized that—"

"Which I very strongly doubt, George." Mendoza drew on a new cigarette. "For one thing, what we've just deduced about Oregon. You're not telling me Carson was afraid of Rose Lamont? That little dreep of a woman? And when there was—we can deduce—some X he *was* enough nervous about to be clearing out, it'd be a long coincidence if— But all right. Bring her in, lean on her. See for yourself. She's— transparent. She's not covering up anything." He was silent, and then said, "His other women—even Natalie who was going to marry him because he was fun—saw halfway through him. The women we've found, at least, were just his occasional marks. I think, second string when he got strapped for cash. I still say he had some steadier game that brought in more loot. Those women liked him, he gave them some-

thing—'made you feel on top of the world,' Patti Page said
—even while they knew, without really admitting it to themselves, that he was no good. But Rose Lamont didn't. She
honestly believed he was all he said."

Hackett made a disbelieving sound. "Looked pitiful and
said she was awfully worried when he didn't show up that
night, and you—"

"Have been a cop some twenty-three years," said Mendoza
dryly. "And by the age of ten, Arturo, I had come to grips
with human nature."

"Well, I don't say you're—but—" Hackett rubbed the back
of his neck.

Sergeant Lake looked in. "Sorry, Lieutenant—I didn't want
to disturb you, said I'd pass it on. That Mrs. Lamont just
called in. On Carson. She said she'd thought of something
she wanted to ask you about. When you've got the time,
she said. Actually it wasn't anything important. She was sort
of dithering. I gave her the polite brush-off—"

"All right," said Mendoza promptly. "There's an excuse,
boys. We'll all go round to see her right now. You can judge
for yourselves." He got up.

On the way down the hall Hackett said, "There is just one
thing makes me hold back on this, George. It looks so likely
—except for that *jewels*. What the hell does that mean? Because I'm with you there— I think he lived long enough to
make the effort to—"

"Well," said Higgins, "considering who we're saying he
was with—he'd conned her with that fool tale of being a
CIA agent. It could be he was feeding her some story along
that line and made up something about jewel thieves or—
Well, it was just a *thought*. We don't know—"

The little café on Beverly Boulevard in the middle of the
afternoon had only one customer, an elderly man drinking

coffee and reading a newspaper at the far end of the counter. Rose Lamont was polishing the formica counter top with a wet cloth, and her lank daughter, in a white apron, was clearing some dirty plates and glasses from the counter. Mrs. Lamont looked up as they came in, recognized Mendoza, and gave him a small smile.

"You called in and said you wanted to see me about something, Mrs. Lamont?"

"Oh, I didn't mean you to put yourself out—it isn't anything much." She gave fleeting glances at the other two men, the big solid men looming over Mendoza. Her dark eyes were anxious, her thin figure bowed a little as she faced authority, apologetic. "It's just—just, Rex never spoke much about his family, sir. I know his mother and father were gone, but he never said about any brothers or sisters, and if he did have— You see, he gave me a—a ring. As a sort of— Well, when we did get sort of engaged. Not a real engagement ring, but it'd belonged to his mother, he said." She was tugging at one finger. "And I got to thinking, maybe it isn't right I should keep it—not now. A family ring. And if there was anybody it ought to go back to—" She got it off at last and proffered it to Mendoza. He looked at it. An old-fashioned ring, a cluster of small garnets set in gold.

"I don't think you need worry about it, Mrs. Lamont. There wasn't any family," he told her.

"Oh—"

The girl moved up to them. "My daughter Mary," said Rose Lamont automatically. "She helps out after school, earn her allowance."

Fourteen, she'd said: a gangling fourteen, maybe be pretty later on but right now the half-child, half-adult fourteen usually was. A coltish figure, the neat Dutch bob at least different from most teen-agers these days. She had rather fine dark eyes in a pale thin face. She said a little timidly in a reedy voice, "I said I didn't think you ought to give it back, Mama. He meant you to have it."

"Well, I only want to do what's right," she said. "I didn't know but what there was family. If you think it's all right to keep it, sir—"

"I'm sure it's all right, Mrs. Lamont. Don't worry about it." As they came out, she was standing there turning the old ring around in her fingers, the gawky girl silent beside her.

"Convinced?" asked Mendoza.

Both Hackett and Higgins were silent. "I don't know, Luis," said Hackett at last, "we ought to *look* at her anyway. Ask around at her apartment. Did anybody see him come? Go? See her that night? And by the way, now I think of it, how come nobody heard the shot? That's a residential neighborhood—"

"Yes, but a .22," said Higgins, "doesn't make all that much noise, and it's still chilly at night, windows shut."

"All right, boys," said Mendoza. "Go and look. Ask around. One thing I'll give you. She told me the little girl—well, I don't suppose they think of themselves as little at fourteen —had gone to see a girl friend that night, but it was a school night, Mrs. Lamont strikes me as a conscientious mother, and I shouldn't think the kid was home later than nine thirty. On instructions from Mama. Maybe even earlier. And I will also remind you that the autopsy report gave us a leeway between six and nine. He could have been shot at six—it'd be dark by then—and it could be simple coincidence that it was anywhere within ten miles of Mrs. Lamont."

"That ring," said Hackett suddenly, "looked very much like the rest of that collection he had. Old-fashioned."

Mendoza took out his lighter. "I wouldn't doubt," he said, "that it did belong to his mother. Yes. Personal possessions You want to go look for any evidence on Rose?"

"I just think we might," said Higgins slowly. "For fun. You never know."

Mendoza left them there and went back to the office. He found Palliser on the phone in his office, eagerly saying, "Yes? Yes, we do—yes, he is—oh. Well, somebody'll be up to get him, sergeant, thanks. He's wanted for P.A. violation at least and probably—thanks very much." He put the phone down and vacated Mendoza's desk chair. "Fresno. They've just picked up Bill Schuyler for us."

"*Qué bien.* Progress. What'd you get from the agency fellow?"

"Oh—that," said Palliser. "From what he said about the fellow tried to sell him the Maserati, it matches the description Arizona's got."

"Good. I'd better call the sheriff. How'd Fresno come to pick up Schuyler?"

"Patrol car spotted him trying to break in a liquor store last night. They've just identified him. I'd better call Nash— he's the one to go after him, or somebody in the parole office. We don't know he's our boy on Milliken-Nordham-mer—"

"Ninety-nine per cent sure," said Mendoza, and asked Lake to get him the parole office.

"But I can't possibly," said Nash when he reached him. "Not *possibly*, Lieutenant. I've got an official meeting to-night, and I've got to be in court tomorrow morning."

"So you take a little plane ride up to Fresno and ferry him back, John," said Mendoza to Palliser. "He is our boy for al-most sure, and somebody's got to go get him."

"Oh, hell," said Palliser. "I suppose. I'd better call Robin—"

Mendoza went home, to the brief bedlam of greeting from the twins before they were shepherded off by Mrs. MacTaggart. Alison said, "Dinner in ten minutes," and brought him a preprandial drink he didn't especially want.

"And how is our little feathered friend?" he asked, wandering out to the kitchen after her.

"I think the turpentine's doing the trick. We've got one wing nearly loose," said Alison. "But it's a madhouse trying to keep Johnny and Terry away from him, not to mention the cats. The poor thing needs some peace and quiet, after—"

"To sleep off his hangovers," said Mendoza. "If Bast had had any sense, she'd never have brought him home, and you'd never have known anything about it. What the eye doesn't see—"

"But once we did, we had to rescue him. And—" Alison was interrupted by a piercing wolf whistle from down the hall, and a series of loud *Yawks*. Mrs. MacTaggart appeared, muttering to herself, took down the bottle of rye and went out.

"If you ask me," said Mendoza, "there's not much to choose between you and Bast. Corrupting the morals of an innocent wild creature—"

"Oh, you! Go and sit down," said Alison.

But after dinner, with Bast on his lap and El Señor in Alison's, Sheba and Nefertite curled together against Cedric's hairy back at Alison's feet, he was suddenly smitten with a rare spasm of self-doubt. "Could I be losing my touch?" he wondered aloud.

"With what, *amante?*"

"Females. After all, I have been a respectable married man for some time now. The day was, *cara*, I saw through females like glass."

Alison laughed. "In one way, yes. In another—fortunately for females, no man ever does, quite."

"You've ruined my poker game," said Mendoza. "I don't get to practice often enough. Have you ruined my sense of the nuances?"

"I don't think anything could. Sometimes," said Alison, "you see too much. Why?"

"That Lamont woman. Damn it, she's not that good an actress. And yet he was that near her— But equally, just as I said, it could have been as early as six. Damn it, it could even be simpler than that. On his way to her apartment, and he picked up the casual ride-thumber. People do that in town who'd never dream of it on a lonely country road. And the ride-thumber held him up for his wallet, and then got nervous—"

"This is Carson?" said Alison. "But if so, Luis, what about that *jewels* note?"

"We don't know that has a single thing to do with the murder."

"Well, I think it had," said Alison. "It's too—too peculiar *not* to have had something to do with it."

"And who am I to laugh at female intuition?" said Mendoza.

"You must have known," said Grace gently to Betty and Albert Snyder, "the kind of reputation she had. I don't mean to say you believed in it. But it sort of leaped to the eye—"

Albert Snyder merely looked embarrassed. He was a big slow-moving man, chocolate brown, clean-shaven, nearly bald. He rumbled something inarticulate. His wife looked at Grace quietly. She was a neat birdlike little woman, lighter-skinned than her husband, and her speech betrayed her West Indian origin: the faintly British intonation.

This was a comfortable, if old, apartment over the Snyders' little grocery store on Sixtieth Street. Old but well-kept furniture, a piano, a rather gaudy flowered carpet, a dime-store landscape on the wall over the couch. Mrs. Snyder had apologized for Willy's absence—out on a date with his girl. "A nice girl, Eleanor, we'd be happy see him settled down with her."

140

Now Grace just waited, trying to exude sympathy and goodwill; and Sadie Snyder's son rumbled embarrassment and looked away from him, but his wife cocked her head and seemed to study Grace seriously.

"Willy said something," she said at last. "It was an awful shock to him, finding her like that. He was awful fond of her. And her of him too. Mr. Grace, I don't know how you believe—if you go to church or—"

"I was brought up in the Episcopal Church, Mrs. Snyder."

"Oh," she said. "I don't suppose I'm what you'd call superstitious, Mr. Grace. Leastways, I graduated from high school and I don't believe everything I hear tell about—"

"Betty," rumbled her husband. He looked agonized.

"You let me do the talking, Bert," she said imperturbably. "I don't reckon Mr. Grace is a fool either." Grace smiled at her. "You know, Mr. Grace, there are things we can't account for in life. Queer things. There's scientists looking into them now, I've heard. What they call this ESP and all."

"That's so," said Grace.

"Well—" She took a deep breath. "Maybe you'll think I'm crazy, but I've got to say it. Get it straight. My mother-in-law—Bert's mother—she was a—an unusual woman, Mr. Grace. She had a power to her. Something ordinary people don't have. I don't know what it was, but I've seen her heal hurts—cuts and burns and such—the way a doctor couldn't. And maybe some worry on us, she'd say—she hadn't any education, you know—say, no mind, daughter, I take it to the Master and it all come out right. And it would. Maybe— I wouldn't like to say—it was just her power of faith. I don't know. But she had—a something."

"Is that so?" said Grace. "There are a lot of things we still don't know, Mrs. Snyder."

"But—what I'd like to say," she said, with a quick little dip of her head, "all those stories about her being a—silly! She—she couldn't read or write, Mr. Grace, and she was full of a lot of old fancies and funny old-fashioned notions, but she was a *good* woman. A good Christian woman. She'd never have done any harm to anybody."

"Well, I had gathered—"

"You've got to believe that," she said earnestly. "What Willy said—when he found her like that— Just a terrible wicked thing, poor old Mother Snyder killed like that. Some wicked ignorant person—I said it to Bert, I said, some silly fool believing all the tales. About her. Thinking— But it wasn't *so*," said Mrs. Snyder. "She was a good woman."

"But somebody didn't think so," said Grace.

"I guess," she said miserably. "I guess it was that way. Somebody—all those silly tales. I—I used to try to keep Willy away from her, all the old stories she filled him with, and him believing every word—but I come to see, her being such a good loving woman, for all her old-fashioned ways, it wasn't any harm."

"Betty," said her husband.

"Now, Bert, I just want them to understand."

"And that's very interesting, ma'am," said Grace gently.

TEN

"So all right," said Higgins on Saturday morning, coming into the office just as Mendoza was hanging up his hat. "Your hunches are still working and Art and I were woolgathering."

"On what? Lamont? What did you get?"

"A nice solid alibi. The other three families in that apartment building aren't visiting back and forth all the time, or with the landlady, but they all know each other. Not very big apartments, and I've seen solider-built places. Two of the women, in the front apartments, saw Mrs. Lamont come home on Monday night. Remember because she was early. Usually came home about seven, this was about six-fifteen. Maybe she was going to pretty herself up for Rex. Anyway, both of 'em say she didn't go out again. One of 'em, downstairs, had her apartment door open onto the front hall, and the front door has a creak in it when it moves. And the woman across the hall from Lamont dropped over to borrow something about eight thirty, and stayed chatting." Hackett had drifted in silently and taken the other chair. "She was there till nine fifteen. Says Lamont mentioned she was expecting a friend to drop in. The only visitor to the building that night, says the woman with her door open, was Mr. Stewart from the next block over, and his kid. The Lamont girl was going to her girl friend's—the Stewart kid—to do her home-work, and Stewart doesn't believe in kids being out alone af-ter dark. That was at six thirty." Higgins looked discouraged.

"Well, so that's that," said Mendoza. "Just a coincidence that Carson was— Or had he been moved? The car moved?"

"I don't think so," said Hackett. "The lab didn't think so."

"All right. It could still have been the planned thing—or even simpler, the ride-thumber. Maybe a juvenile, if so. Life's little ironies. But one thing we have deduced—can we say?— is that Carson must have been damn nervous about some-thing or somebody here, to be arranging to clear out. That's clear enough. Nobody we've come across, from his local ad-dress book, had seen him recently—except the Page woman, and I'm inclined to agree with George, that little visit was hail and farewell. And he was pressuring Natalie to move away when they were married—so it wasn't any trouble money would cure. He'd suggested Florida, you notice, not Oregon. He'd dropped the Oregon scheme after he'd captured Nat-alie. He had some pressing reason for cutting his losses here, and to me that says either he'd been up to something defi-nitely illegal and was afraid somebody was going to talk, or he was afraid of somebody personally. I'll take a little bet— he hadn't been seen recently at the Alexandria Street place either—that when he had to follow Natalie back here to woo her, he found temporary—mmh—lodging elsewhere. A motel or— The Alexandria Street address is in the phone book, un-der his own name. And the Conway and Wheeler books are exclusively connected to Oregon, by the contents."

"Why two aliases?" asked Hackett. "In Oregon?"

"No sé," said Mendoza, "but at a blind guess—he'd been up there before, on vacation or business, and used the Con-way name. When he decided to relocate, it was as Conway first and then, maybe to give himself a better cover, as Wheeler. It doesn't much matter."

"What matters to me," said Higgins stubbornly, "is that

I don't much believe in coincidence. I don't much like your ride-thumber either. When a lot of people might have had what they thought was reason for revenge on Carson."

"We haven't been through all the addresses yet, George." Mendoza lit a new cigarette and brought out the photostated pages of Carson's local address book. "Anybody in that general area we haven't looked at? Virgil Avenue—Rampart Boulevard—Vermont—Ninth Street—he got around and met people, didn't he? And seems to have listed every address he ever knew. Who's to say whether these were old friends, marks, or restaurants he liked?"

"Rampart," said Higgins. "That's the closest of those to where he was found."

"Yes. A Miss Peggy Hobbs. And what you said about the innocent Mrs. Lamont of course applies to everybody else —nobody wants a corpse cluttering up the living room. Anybody would take steps to—"

"So let's have those addresses," said Higgins. "We've got all the legwork to finish anyway, I might as well start on those."

"*Buena suerte*," said Mendoza. He commenced to glance through the reports on his desk, to see if anything new was in. A new body, shabby but respectable hotel on Fourth. They had thrown the liquor store shooting into Pending as of yesterday; that was a dead one. Medical report on that mass shooter, Frederick Seymour. They had a patrolman stationed at Central Receiving in case Peter Whiteley came to and said anything, but so far he hadn't. The hospital was now saying he was much improved and would eventually recover. Lake was off today, and Sergeant Rory Farrell was on the switchboard.

Mendoza opened his mouth to say that Hackett had better go check out the new body—the call had come in fifteen minutes ago before the day shift was due—and the inside phone rang. He picked it up. "Mendoza."

"You like to talk to Harry?" asked Goldberg.

"Don't tell me you've got him?"

"Just now. We put a stakeout on that bar, of course, and watched Mike the bartender, but no go. After, naturally, questioning him. He just played dumb. Didn't know nothing about nothing. Finally we got a tip from one of the pigeons, just an hour ago, and Betts went and picked him up. At a flophouse calls itself a hotel on Main. He's right here, big as life, *and* he had the Biltmore loot on him. Except for—"

"*Bueno*— I'll be right down. Come on, Art—Goldberg's got Harry. Matt can go see the new corpse."

Four of them stood around Harry at the questioning in depth—Goldberg, Sergeant Betts, Mendoza, and Hackett—and he didn't like it; but it was nothing new to him and he sat there stolidly, answering or not. He looked resigned to his fate: a month out, already in violation of parole, and still homesick for Chi, he'd just run into some more bad luck. It probably didn't occur to him that it was of his own making.

Goldberg went after him first about the Biltmore Hotel burglaries, and seeing he'd been caught with the loot still on him, Harry admitted that. He'd just wanted dough to get home with. Railroad fare. "I earned some while I was in, not much, and they give me back what I had on me when I got dropped on, but it wasn't much. And a guy's gotta eat." He kept shooting Mendoza puzzled, angry looks. "I can't figure out how anybody dropped on me—"

So Mendoza said easily, "Through Carson, Harry. You remember Carson?"

Harry blinked. His scarred, rather stupid face wore only bewilderment. "I don't know nobody named Carson."

"He give you a different name? He had your phone number, Harry. At least the number of that bar where you could be contacted. Through Mike. That's how we got onto you. Carson had it written down."

146

"I still don't know nobody named Carson."

Mendoza produced a photostat of Rex Carson's California license, with its photograph of the handsome smiling black-haired man. "This ring any bells, Harry?"

Apparently it did. "Oh, *him!*" said Harry. "The guy I give the di'mond ring. Oh, sure. Well, I be damned. I kinda thought he might be on the bent some way—he sure cleaned me out. So you drop on him too, and— Of all the goddamned luck!" He said it mournfully.

"The diamond—what diamond ring?" asked Mendoza.

"So that's why it was missing from the Biltmore loot," said Goldberg, sniffing and feeling for Kleenex. "Why'd you give it to Carson, Harry?"

"I *told* you. He—"

"*¡Diez millones de demonios!*" exclaimed Mendoza suddenly. "I am going senile! And this long at the job, I should know enough to do the routine thoroughly. Duke said, when he brought that jewelry back—and I never read the lab's evaluation! Art, chase up to the office and bring it all down—second left drawer." Hackett went out quickly.

"What's all this?" asked Goldberg.

"The jewelry in Carson's possession. We did check out the name in the one box—a big cut-rate place on Vermont, they couldn't tell us anything. That ring was a cheap synthetic aquamarine. Bought as a present for Natalie? Or somebody else? He wasn't wasting much money on it—I doubt if it was for Natalie. But— Why *did* you give Carson the diamond ring, Harry?"

"I *said.* I thought maybe I could make a little bit sitting in at poker. I ain't no flash man myself—" a crooked gambler, he meant "—but I'm not so bad. Mike told me it ain't legal here. A hell of a place, California. But he said about this one town it was. Some name like a flower—"

"Gardena. So you went down there to find a game?"

"Yeah. Just the once. Last Saturday, week ago. I had nothin'
but bad luck ever since I got out," said Harry. "I swear it's—
Well, that's where I run into that guy. That handsome guy
there. I wound up owin' him about five C's. Never had such a
run o' bad luck, I dint hold no cards at all. But he wasn't a
real flash man, I don't think, see. Is he?" As nobody said
anything, he went on, "Well, anyways, I asked to talk private
and I offer him the di'mond, see. Settle up what he's into me
for. I had t' do *somethin'*. Mike says these places are pretty
strict, see. Well, he—Carson's the monicker, you said? He just
tol' me Rex—he looks at it, and I get the idea he knows
a little about that kind o' thing." The father had been a jeweler, Mendoza remembered; had Carson picked up some
knowledge of the trade? "An' he takes it, an' then—this is
where I get the idea he's on the bent some way, see?—nor
I ain't no two-way guy, ordinary pals I don't split on, but this
guy's no pal o' mine. Anything but. Anyways, I tell you about
it. He asks me, have I maybe got anything else that line to
sell? And like I guess you know—" he looked at Mendoza
bitterly "—I been lookin' for a fence, an' I see he ain't about
to run to the fuzz." Nuances to these things, thought Mendoza,
that even the Harrys would get. "So I says yes, and shows him.
The rest o' the loot. We was there in the men's room at
that place. And he looks it over, and says maybe he can help
me sell it. See, for a cover story I tell him it's family stuff
I got left."

And Carson, thought Mendoza, would have believed that
just about as easily as he'd have believed Harry was a Har-
vard graduate. But why should— Hackett came back with
the bag and handed him Willis's evaluation list while Goldberg pounced on the ring, pawing aside the bits and pieces
of Victorian antiques. And there of course it was, in Willis's
neat typing: "Diamond solitaire, .91 points, white gold
mount, value approximately $900." "*Loco*," murmured Men-
doza, "me. Overlooking—"

"So I give him the number where he could call me," said Harry, "but he never did. I suppose you dropped on him."

"No," said Mendoza absently, "the other way ar—" And then he exclaimed loudly, "*¡Santa María y Jesús!* Of course—"

"What's hit you?" asked Goldberg. Mendoza took him by one arm and Hackett by the other and steered them out to the hall.

"Look, *amigos*. That loot of Harry's—minus the big diamond worth nearly a grand—he offered to me for eight hundred. Fence's price—about a third of the real value, *¿cómo no?*"

"Sure," said Goldberg. "Why?"

"And that, Carson would know. Even if he didn't know the ways of fences, he knew enough about jewelry to know that that was one hell of a bargain. Harry must have named a price. And while Carson might not have had the money to buy it himself, he knew somebody who—"

"Natalie," said Hackett. "By God, yes. And another thing, Luis, while he must have suspected it was hot, if it was in private hands and never came on the market, who'd know? He'd be perfectly safe."

"*Pues, sí.* Where's a phone?" Mendoza snatched up the one in Robbery's anteroom, demanded his own office. "Rory, go into my office and look on the current phone index. Natalie Brookes. What's the number? . . . O.K., thanks." He dialed quickly and waited, furiously rubbing his moustache the wrong way. He waited quite awhile, and then the monotonous buzzing stopped, a sleepy voice answered, and he put all his charm into his voice. "Mrs. Brookes? Lieutenant Mendoza. I'm so very sorry to disturb you at this hour, but something new has come up on Mr. Carson, and I wanted to know at once whether—"

"Oh, anything I can do to help," she said, mollified, through a yawn.

"—whether he ever told you he could get you some jewelry, diamonds and so on, at a great bargain? Recently?"

"Why, however did you know that?" she asked. She sounded astonished, recovered herself quickly. "Why, yes, he did. Just on Sunday night. He said this friend of his wanted to sell some family jewelry, but nothing old, nice new things, and it was wonderful value for the money. He knew about things like that, Rex did—his father'd been a jeweler and he used to work in the store, he got to know— And I just love jewelry of course, and besides it's a good investment, especially diamonds. Chauncey taught me that. So I told Rex—"

"Was any price mentioned?"

"Yes, he said his friend would take fifteen hundred dollars. He said it was a terrific bargain, it was worth twice that."

Pues, sí, thought Mendoza; approximate market value. But Harry satisfied, everybody satisfied— "Had you decided to buy it, Mrs. Brookes?"

"Well, I had," she said. "I told Rex Sunday night I would. I told you—I knew that—he wasn't just so steady over money, but he did know about jewelry. That he did know. I knew, because I've read up a lot on it myself. Chauncey taught me quite a lot. And once when I showed Rex some of my diamonds, he told me nearly to a cent what they were worth. And so when he said about this stuff his friend wanted to sell, I knew he'd be right. I told him I'd give him the money. He said the man was ashamed of selling family stuff and he'd clinch the deal for me, when I got my check the first of the month."

"Mmh," said Mendoza. He didn't think it was worthwhile asking if she'd suspected the deal even fleetingly. Natalie wouldn't be any too scrupulous about it, any more than Carson. "Well, thanks very much."

"Was there something wrong about it?" she asked anxiously. "I never thought—I believed what Rex said—" Yes, now covering up. Mendoza thanked her again and put down the phone. He was thinking furiously.

"Carson," he said, getting out a cigarette, "was going to earn a nice little commission on the deal, unknown to Natalie. Clinch the deal with Harry for eight hundred, get fifteen from Natalie. He couldn't resist it. And Natalie'd be getting more than full value. *De veras.* But he wouldn't see Natalie's money until the first of the month. By which time Harry might have found a fence. Maybe—just maybe—Carson tried to clinch the deal with his own money, a down payment, if he hadn't that much on hand. I don't think Harry'd have gone for that. Maybe Carson tried to dicker with him. And—"

"You're tagging Harry," said Hackett. He rubbed his jaw. "How, Luis?"

"I don't think Harry's any stranger to violence." Mendoza snapped his lighter. "And the old pros usually like to have a gun around. He had one the other night. Maybe a stolen one. Just possibly, the gun was part of the Biltmore loot that didn't get reported to you, Saul." Goldberg looked thoughtful. "Build it. He meets Harry in that bar—or somewhere— Monday evening. Early, maybe. He dickers with him. They argue a little. And Carson says, well, I've got a date, we can talk as we go and I'll let you out somewhere you can get a bus back downtown. They get to arguing some more, and he stops the car when Harry flashes the gun. And—"

"A little bit forced, but not much," said Hackett. "Funnier things have happened. It could be, Luis. It could. And the reason I like it—with reservations—is that it makes that *jewels* more or less reasonable. More plausible. After all, the man was dying. Whether he realized it or not. And what would be uppermost in his mind was, Harry shot me over the jewels. Or even jewelry. It was a scrawl—"

"*Exacto.* I think we go back and ask Harry," said Mendoza.

"Easy enough for him to get rid of the gun. See what he has to say."

"No gun on him," said Goldberg. "Or in his room."

"So he got rid of it afterward," said Mendoza.

Higgins stood by his car smoking and wondering just exactly what he thought about Mr. Calvin Gibson. He had found Mr. Gibson, unexpectedly, at the Rampart Boulevard address of Miss Peggy Hobbs. Mr. Gibson, it seemed, had married Miss Hobbs six months previously and moved into her apartment with her. And he was a man of few words—pugnacious, ex-Navy, well muscled. When Higgins had mentioned Carson's name, he had barked a short laugh.

"That one. Glamour-puss. Knew Peg before we got hitched. I found him here tryin' to sweet-talk her into lendin' him some dough. Hard-luck story. Peg's a sucker. I kicked him out—told him we didn't need his kind around here."

"Oh. When?"

"Couple o' months back. First *and* last time I saw him. He take some other sucker, police want him?"

"No," said Higgins. "Not exactly. He hasn't been here since? You didn't—"

"Not likely! Knew what he'd get. All I can tell you about the bastard," said Gibson. "Excuse me. Due at work half an hour." And that was that.

Possible? wondered Higgins. Belligerent, touchy Mr. Gibson. The crude customer. Was Peg possibly regretting getting hitched to him? Hankering back after suave gentlemanly Rex? And if Mr. Gibson found out—

But gentlemanly Rex had captured Natalie. The very sweet deal. He wouldn't be looking elsewhere for awhile, would he?

Higgins sighed. He let his mind wander toward personal matters, and his rough-hewn face softened to something near fatuousness. He got into the car and looked at the other ad-dresses he wanted to check.

Piggott had been out on the new call, the body in the ho-tel on Fourth. It depressed him considerably. The hotel a cheap, shabby place and the body an old, tired, frail body. The old fellow on pension, no family, and finding he had cancer, so he'd written a careful note to be sure nobody else would get blamed and turned on the gas.

It wasn't anything to work, just the report to type up, but it was depressing. Old fellow with nothing, no relatives at all. Taking his own way out, and Piggott couldn't really feel the Lord would blame him much.

He only had a couple of second cousins himself. No real family. He wondered if it was too soon to ask Prudence to marry him. And if she would, anyway.

When he got back to the office, he typed the report at once, and just as he was sorting out the copies and stapling them, Sergeant Farrell summoned him.

"The hospital just called on Whiteley. He's conscious. You'd better go over there, see what you can get."

Probably nothing, thought Piggott, but he went.

At the hospital, a nurse conducted him to the single room: critical-condition patients warranted such, evidently. The uniformed man was standing by the window; he shook his head silently to Piggott's raised brows. Whiteley hadn't come out with anything yet. There was another nurse, a trim young one, at the bed. Whiteley was tossing and moaning.

"He's been conscious off and on, sir," said the nurse. "I think he can understand you, but please—we realize you want to talk to him, but you mustn't talk much or tire him."

Piggott bent over the bed. "Mr. Whiteley," he said. "Peter. Peter. Can you hear me?" Sometimes they answered better to a first name.

Whiteley opened his eyes, very blue eyes. They hadn't shaved him, and he had a wild sandy growth of beard: a young man, he looked drawn and gray. "Leon," he muttered. "Leon. Yes?" His eyes focused on Piggott.

"Mr. Whiteley. I'm police. We want to know about the accident. Can you remember anything?"

Whiteley swallowed painfully. He whispered weakly, "Leon. *Not* accident. You—you find them—arrest—" One hand reached to clasp Piggott's arm urgently, weakly. The nurse rustled up disapprovingly. "Two—beatnik kids—nearly sideswiped us—crazy—'n' Leon yelled at—they—chased us—crazy—"

"All right, that's fine," said Piggott. "Don't get upset, Mr. Whiteley."

"Leon. Leon. *Shot*. They *shot*—I thought—"

"All right," said Piggott. Whiteley closed his eyes again. The nurse put a hand on his wrist and gave Piggott a frosty look.

"No," said Whiteley. "No. Don't." He opened his eyes and looked at the nurse, pleading, stubborn. "Where's—policeman? I want—"

"Here, Mr. Whiteley."

"You'd better leave now," said the nurse.

"*No!*" said Whiteley, and made a great effort to sit up. The nurse gently pushed him back on the pillows. "Got to tell—policeman—don't you try stop—" he mumbled. "My wallet. *Wallet*. Look." Sudden strength seemed to flow into him, and he said more rationally, in a clear whisper, "First time—nearly hit us—said to Leon, crazy fools—ought report to police—'n' I—I—there was light from drugstore—got good eyesight, I—in my *wallet*." He fell back and shut his eyes. "Police—get 'em. Leon. I—"

"You'll have to go now, sir," said the nurse firmly. She nearly shoved him out. Piggott went down to the desk and asked what had been done with Whiteley's clothes. After a little wait he was informed that all the patient's belongings had been returned to the family.

He drove up to Thirty-ninth Place and found the two women together at the Whiteleys' apartment, Gloria Lister and her mother. They looked surprised, but found Whiteley's wallet for him. They hadn't looked at it at all. It was just as it had come out of his jacket, the jacket cut off him at the hospital. Under their eyes, Piggott went through it.

A lot of cards in the slots. Photographs. Five one-dollar bills in the money compartment. And along with them—he stared at it—a scrap of paper, a scrap Whiteley had had in his pocket by chance? On one side a shopping list in a careless female hand, *bread, milk, gr. round, cat food, matches,* and on the other side a hastily scrawled set of figures and numbers. A license-plate number: FJB-699.

"My dear Lord," said Piggott reverently. Could it be—the beatniks' plate number? Glimpsed, memorized in that one indignant moment after the near collision?

It could be. By the grace of God, they might catch up on this one after all. Piggott made tracks for the office.

"Well, it's nothing," said Hackett. "*Absolutamente.* Which leaves it up in the air."

"Chapter and verse," said Mendoza.

"It's a flophouse calls itself a hotel," said Hackett, sitting down and lighting a cigarette, "just as Goldberg said."

What they had got from Harry, once he understood that Carson was dead and they were wondering if he was the X on that, was vehement and frightened denial. Of course. He'd never laid eyes on Carson again after last Saturday, hadn't heard from him. And last Monday, well, he hadn't felt so hot, he'd had a cold or something, he hadn't gone out all day, and there was a guy in that place could see the door, he could say. And he wasn't talking about the gun at all: just clammed up on that.

"It doesn't mean a damn thing," said Hackett. "Walkup hotel. Little lobby about twelve by four, and a clerk, sure. A fellow about sixty sound asleep with his head on the counter and you could smell the *vino* six feet off. He says, when I wake him up, sure he was there Monday, from noon to midnight. Anybody could've walked out past him—he admits it."

"Yes. I wonder," said Mendoza. "If it was Harry, Art—and damn it, Carson no loss but I'd like to know—it's going to be impossible to prove it. Charge him. We'd probably never get hold of the gun." They had to think about that too—the admissible evidence. Hackett sighed. There'd been an inquest on Sadie Snyder yesterday morning. Inquests on Carson and Lister on Monday; Tuesday, on Milliken-Nordhammer. And so on. Unless they got Bill Schuyler to break down and make a confession to that, they probably couldn't get the evidence pieced together in time to charge him at the inquest. The open verdicts on all of them. "Well—" Mendoza looked at his watch "—come on. Take a look at Carson's lock-box. And John's due back any time after one with Schuyler."

The safety-deposit box held ten thousand, seven hundred and seventy dollars in cash, and the pink slip on the Chrysler.

"*Que hermano*," said Mendoza. "I wonder what little effort—or combined efforts—this represented. Just as we said —he was using it as a checking account, you could say. Not leaving a trail behind. Just in case. I do wonder what the main gimmick was."

"We don't encourage the practice of keeping cash," said the bank manager remotely.

"I'm sure you don't, but banks," said Mendoza, "are very new on the scene compared with human nature. Mmh, yes." A photograph of Rex Carson had been run in the *Times* yesterday, at his request. "Police are still seeking information on . . ." Would it turn up anything new? "I'll tell you one thing," he said. "He wasn't reporting all the nice cash to the I.R.S. boys. Not nohow."

The bank manager looked shocked as Hackett laughed.

"But it doesn't tell us anything, Luis."

"Not one thing." Mendoza shrugged and rose from the long table in the room outside the bank vault.

And Hackett said to the manager, "So you can get in your round of golf after all." The manager smiled thinly.

"And where is everybody?" Mendoza asked Farrell when they got back to the office after lunch. "Isn't John here yet?"

"No sign of him. I don't know what Higgins is on—"

"I do."

"Oh. Jase called in and said he's still wandering around on the Snyder thing. Matt came in looking as if somebody'd handed him a thousand-dollar bill or," said Sergeant Farrell, "a free pass into heaven, and said he'd be down in Communications. I don't know what that's all about. And can either of you think of a seven-letter word for a North American marsupial?"

"Raccoon," said Hackett.

"Opossum," said Mendoza. "A raccoon is not a marsupial, Art."

"You sure?" asked Farrell.

"I am an expert on wildlife," said Mendoza. "Just lately."

The corridor door opened and John Palliser came in behind an unshaven, sullen-looking young man in a gray suit slightly too large for him. "Well, welcome home," said Hackett. "We expected you earlier."

Palliser looked slightly bilious. He said briefly, "Weather. The flight got delayed, twice. When we finally got off—" he coughed "—in a six-seater Cessna, my God, we hit every air pocket and down draft between here and Fresno."

"Have you had lunch?" asked Hackett.

Palliser looked more bilious and said, "Don't mention it. *Au contraire,* as the channel passenger put it."

The prisoner said unexpectedly, "I kind of liked it. I never been in an airplane before. It was exciting, sort of."

They looked at him. Bill Schuyler. With the pedigree. For pretty sure their boy on the Milliken-Nordhammer thing.

"My God," said Palliser.

"We'd like to ask you some questions, Bill," said Mendoza gently. "About Mrs. Milliken and Mr. Nordhammer."

"Who?" asked Schuyler blankly.

"The house," said Mendoza, eyeing that baggy gray suit Schuyler was wearing, "where you picked up those clothes, Bill."

"Oh, that place," said Schuyler casually.

Palliser sat down on the bench and said, "If you don't mind, you can go at him without me. I need some Alka-Seltzer."

ELEVEN

They took him into an interrogation room and Mendoza meticulously recited all his rights to him. Schuyler just sat, head down, silent. "Would you like to answer some questions, Bill?" asked Hackett. "We can guess some of it. But how'd you come to pick Mrs. Milliken's place?"

After a long pause Schuyler asked, "How'd you know it was me there?"

"You left a nice set of fingerprints," said Mendoza dryly.

"Oh," said Schuyler. "Oh. Could I have a cigarette?" Hackett gave him one. "I guess that's—I'd forgot what she said her name was till you said it. The old lady. It was in the paper, an ad. Room for rent. I got awful tired livin' with Ma alla time, all her boy friends and all. So I—just thought— and I had about forty bucks I'd won in a crap game. I didn't know that place was so far downtown—address in the ad —but it was O.K. I never thought about doing nothing till I give the old lady twenty bucks and she put it in her purse and I see she's got quite a little wad. So then I thought. What the hell, you know? Only she come in from the kitchen and found me in her room and let out a squawk. So I hadda shut her up. And then I found that guy upstairs when I—she'd said something about somebody home sick but I— And, so, well, I didn't think it'd take much to shut him up, but just

159

like her he put up a fight. Then I—" he dragged on the cigarette, as if thinking, and it was easy to see why Mrs. Milliken hadn't hesitated about renting him a room. He had an immature face, narrow at the jaw, curiously innocent-looking; and the sweep of black hair, the long-lashed blue eyes, made him nearly handsome. "Well," he said, "that's all. I didn't get much except the cash, and two suits that fit pretty good." He shrugged and stopped. Mendoza and Hackett looked at each other.

"You do know they're both dead, Bill?" said Hackett. "That you killed them?"

Schuyler swallowed, looking at the floor. "I—I figured. I never meant do that. But they were both kind of old, and—" he shrugged again. "I guess that's all there is, tell you. I looked around that house awhile, an' then— I was in the old lady's room, door shut. I hear somebody come in an' go upstairs—" Jarvis "—so I figure, better get out. I guess that's all I got to say."

"What were you doing up in Fresno?" asked Mendoza.

Another long pause. "Well, I'd never been to Fresno," said Schuyler. That seemed to be that. He stopped talking. And the chances were, of course, he'd recant the confession or claim it was made under duress, at his trial. Hackett took him over to the facility on Alameda to book him in temporarily for parole violation, pending the homicide warrant. Mendoza was just going back to his office when Piggott came in, looking as angry and excited as Mendoza had ever seen him.

"You'll never believe it," he said. "I swear I don't believe it, but we've got—or are going to get, if the D.M.V. ever gets around to answering my teletype—a make on the sniper's car." He told Mendoza about that. "Just God's own luck, Whiteley keeping his head and memorizing the plate number, managing to get it jotted down before— I've been hanging around down there waiting for the D.M.V. to answer—"

"I'll be damned," said Mendoza. "That is a piece of luck—Saturday afternoon, Matt, they're bound to be slow. We might not get anything from them until tomorrow."

Piggott looked morose. "I know, I know."

Sergeant Farrell thrust his head in the door. "Call in from Traffic, Lieutenant. Squad car's spotted that hot Maserati, the Iowa plate, over in South Pasadena. Raymond Street. It's sitting in front of a house there. Squad car's up at the corner keeping an eye out where they aren't noticeable. They want some orders."

"You chase over there, Matt—*pronto*," said Mendoza. "Ask all the indicated questions and if you find whoever left it there fetch him in. *¡Vamos!* Rory, tell Traffic to tell the squad car, if it moves, tail it and call in." Palliser had gone down to First Aid.

"Listen, the D.M.V.—"

"Is probably not going to be handing us a make for at least another couple of hours, if today at all," said Mendoza. "You know as well as me. Go, go!"

Piggott went out, grumbling, passing Jason Grace on the way in. "What's all the excitement?" asked Grace.

Mendoza told him. "Well, I'm glad to see something coming unstuck," said Grace. He sat down, looking dissatisfied, and brought out a cigarette. "I haven't got one smell on Mrs. Snyder. Once we'd figured out what the basic setup was—"

"Once you figured it, Jase."

"—it should have been easy. Just one more step. Who thought she'd put a hex on him? But—nothing. I want to see Willy again. I get the impression he was a lot closer to the old lady than either of his parents. She may have said something to him he hasn't realized has a bearing. But—" Grace looked at his cigarette.

"At least we haven't any new mysteries on hand. Yet. The old ones doing us nicely," said Mendoza. "I'll try Harry on you—see what you think." He brought Grace up-to-date on that, and Grace listened, head cocked.

"It could have been that way. I like the idea of the gun being part of the loot—that's very likely, sure. But best of all I like the way Harry might tie up to that funny note. The jewels," said Grace. "But as far as evidence—"

Mendoza laughed. "I know. Damn all."

The house on Raymond Street in South Pasadena was an old white frame house. The scarlet Maserati with the Iowa license plate was still sitting in front of it; Piggott had passed the squad car up at the corner. He parked ahead of the Maserati, walked back and looked it over. It might have been abandoned here. Or it might not. Considering that whoever was driving it had apparently thought he could sell it without any papers.

Piggott walked up to the front porch of the house and pushed the doorbell. After a minute he pushed it again. He was just about to turn away when the door opened. "Yah?" said the man standing there, and to someone in another room, "I got it, Lolly!"

Piggott looked at him and felt tired, illogically. You felt discouraged when the chase was difficult and tedious, or so much the anonymous thing that you knew you'd never get anywhere on it; and then, quite often, you felt just as discouraged—over the state of humanity, which surely to God didn't seem to have improved much since the Garden of Eden—when they were so stupid you caught up right away, as soon as you started looking. For here was the young fellow Sheriff Quackenbush was looking for, all right: dark, stocky, pockmarks, sideburns.

"Afternoon," said Piggott. "You own that little foreign job?" He gestured.

"Yeah, I do, why?"

"You interested in selling it?"

162

The young fellow looked interested. "I might be, at that. You wanna deal?" He opened the screen door and came out. "Uh—my name's Wall, Arnie Wall."

"Piggott." They went out to the Maserati and Piggott started to look it over thoroughly. He peered at the registration slip in the visor. Howard Hollister, Dubuque, Iowa. "How come it's registered to a Howard Hollister?" he said. "I thought you said—"

Wall looked taken aback. "Well," he said, "uh—well—my real name's Hollister, I just—"

"Now is that so?" said Piggott. "Very interesting. Somebody must have identified the wrong body over in Arizona last week." He produced the badge. "Come on, Wall. I'm taking you in on suspicion of harboring stolen property— for the start. Later on that sheriff'll probably do better than that."

"You can't do that—goddamn it, why the damn fuzz has always got to—"

"Break up all the fun and games?" sighed Piggott. "I know, we're the world's worst spoilsports, Arnie." He had Wall by the arm. The squad car came nosing down the street.

"Like some help, sir?" asked one of the uniformed men, leaning out the window.

Piggott finished frisking Wall; he was clean, no gun. "You might as well take him in, I'm alone. Down to Central. Now, Arnie—" Wall was struggling; the two men handcuffed him and loaded him in. A man and a woman came out of the house and down the front walk, staring.

"Who the hell are you? Fuzz? Where're they takin' Arnie?" demanded the man, a big dark man in dirty work clothes.

"You any relation, sir?"

"I'm his brother, damn it! What you taking him in for?"

Piggott said laconically, "Not us. Arizona eventually. Murder. You can see him at the jail on Alameda. And there'll be a police truck up to tow in that Maserati—leave it alone."

He went back to his own car, wondering if the D.M.V. had sent down the make on that plate number yet. Even if it was Saturday afternoon.

When he got back to the office, it was the first thing he asked. "Don't ask foolish questions," said Mendoza. "I don't know the latest statistics on how many cars there are in California, but it'll come to a good round number. Even with computers— Did you pick up the driver?"

"Oh, yes. There he was, no trouble. As per the description that hick sheriff gave you. Squad car's bringing him in. Gave his name as Arnie Wall. Staying with his brother."

"*Bien*," said Mendoza, and picked up the phone. "Rory, get me Sheriff Quackenbush in Kingman. . . ."

"Well, now, isn't that gratifying," said Quackenbush in his slow drawl. "Matches our description, hah? That's very nice. I think I'll break the Sabbath and come over and have a look at him. And fetch him back for some witnesses to look at."

"He'll be waiting for you," said Mendoza.

"Take a look at that plant you got over there too. I understand you got quite a system."

"We like it, sheriff. Wire us your flight time and somebody'll meet you." Mendoza put the phone down, grinning. "Matt, you'd better take Wall over to the pokey and book him in. He'll cool overnight."

"See if there's anything in from the D.M.V. first," said Piggott.

At four minutes to six the main complaint desk at Central Headquarters had a call from a puzzled good citizen. The desk sergeant listened, automatically taking notes in shorthand, asked a few questions.

"It just seemed funny," said the citizen. "I thought you ought to know, even if—"

"Yes, sir." The sergeant debated. It was as funny a little thing as had ever come his way in several years of sitting on the complaint desk, and he wasn't quite sure what to do about it. On the one hand, it wasn't anything much; on the other, you never knew. He compromised. He said, "I'll pass it on, sir, thank you for calling in." He noted the time on the note; it was just six o'clock, and his relief man just coming in. He got up and stretched. "Say, Tom—a funny thing just now—" He told him about it. "Who the hell do I pass it on *to*? Why?"

Tom said, "That *is* a funny one all right. I wouldn't like to say, Bill." But after a moment he brightened. "Send it up to Robbery," he suggested. "It's a burglary in a sort of way. Pass the buck up there, if there's anything to it you'll be off the hook, you did pass it on."

"You may have something there, Tom. I'll do that. Or rather you'll do it." Bill chuckled, preparing to leave. "Have a nice quiet night."

"That's a hope, Saturday night!" Tom took his vacated chair. "At Central? My God. Now out at the Valley station—" He'd just been transferred a couple of months ago, and everybody here was sick and tired of hearing about all the benefits of Valley versus Central.

"I'll see you," said Bill hastily, and started for the lot and his car.

Tom lit a cigarette, eyeing the switchboard with apprehension, and read Bill's shorthand again. "Damn funny," he said to himself. Pass the buck to Robbery: they were used to mysteries in the plainclothes divisions. He was only an ordinary man in blue, graduated from riding squad cars last year.

Mendoza came in the back door of the house on Rayo Grande, and found his way blocked by Cedric slurping water from his bowl. "Don't let me disturb you, *bufón*," he said. Cedric looked up, his hairy jowls dripping, and offered a polite paw. Mendoza shook it gravely; Cedric liked his formalities acknowledged. He preceded Mendoza into the kitchen and Alison looked up from the stove. "Hello, darling—let him out the *hall* door, *don't* let any cats in, and shut it, *por favor.*"

"*Qué demonios*—" Mendoza opened the door to the hall, Cedric marched sedately through it, and Mendoza shut it just as El Señor appeared at a gallop from the living room.

"That *damned* bird," said Alison. "Please heaven we can let it loose tomorrow or next day! This is bedlam." She was flushed from the stove. "We've got it in here—the twins were forever going into Mairí's room to see if *el pájaro lindo* had got his wings unstuck yet—and of course they left the door open. The next thing the cats would be in there—El Señor trying to bite the chicken wire open and Bast chattering away like a pair of castanets and *el pájaro* swearing at her a blue streak—at least you can't say he's lacking in courage—"

"YAWK!" confirmed *el pájaro*. The box covered with chicken wire was on the counter top, in the far corner, shoved against the wall. Mendoza went over and inspected their feathered friend. One wing was untarred and free, and it was spread proudly as if to illustrate the fact, its flashy white underside gleaming. With the other one still stuck at the tip to the lean sleek gray body, the mockingbird looked lopsided. It hopped on one leg toward Mendoza, remarking, "Tu-whoooo. Yankee Doodle came to town, Yankee Doodle came to—Tu-WHOOO." Its bright eyes followed him, insolent and curious.

"And Mairí has decided that since the poor thing's not getting its usual exercise, the whiskey is keeping up its strength and it's just the creature's natural sense makes it want it. I think it's half drunk now," said Alison, going back to the stove with the butter dish in one hand. "And remembering to keep the doors shut—with the cats' dishes *and* their tray in the service porch—"

"You see what kindness to dumb animals gets you into,

carried too far," said Mendoza. He got out a shot-glass and the bottle of rye. The mockingbird began to shriek loudly, hopping up and down on one leg and rattling at the chicken wire. The one useful wing flapped hysterically.

"There!" said Alison. "He thinks you're stealing his very own whiskey. Bedlam, I tell you. Pray heaven we get the rest of the tar off tomorrow."

With the bottle out of sight, their feathered friend settled down and seemed happier, muttering dove cries to himself. But it was to a repeated chorus of the first four bars of "Yankee Doodle" that Alison—with the door from the dining room to the hall shut—got dinner on the table. Mrs. Mac-Taggart, looking in benevolently to report that the twins wanted Daddy to read them a *Just-So* story when he'd finished dinner, said, "It's wonderful how that bird can imitate things. Smart, they are. Picking up—"

"If he's so brilliant," said Alison a trifle bitterly, "why didn't he stay around long enough to learn the whole thing, from whoever was whistling it? It's like waiting for somebody to drop the other shoe."

"If you keep it around long enough, *cara*, maybe you can complete its education."

"Heaven forbid! I only hope it has sense enough to go away—"

"And forget the daily dose of rye? Deliberately corrupting an innocent creature of nature, I call it."

"YAWK!" came the raucous shriek from the kitchen. "Yankee Doodle came to town, Yankee—"

"Heavens above!" said Alison.

Hackett went home to his Angel, who said briskly as he kissed her, "Dinner in five minutes." She was making salad dressing. He sniffed hopefully at the pan on the stove. "That's *not* for you. Too many calories. Ground round steak and no hollandaise sauce for you."

"Oh, hell," said Hackett. "Why I had to marry a good cook—" Sheila came staggering toward him, arms held up, and he bent to pick her up. Mark Christopher came tearing in, discovering belatedly that Daddy was home. The great silver Persian stalked in, tail high, and demanded instant attention.

But after dinner, with Sheila in bed and Mark also demanding last-minute attention before consenting to have the light turned out, Hackett's concentration wandered from his newspaper and he sat staring thoughtfully into space. When Angel finally came in, sat down and picked up her sewing, he said, ruminating aloud, "But they aren't much, really."

"Who aren't what?" asked Angel.

"The old pro burglars. Given to the violence. Random or otherwise. In fact, they tend on the general average to be kind of shy. Object of the whole exercise," said Hackett, "is to get in and get out with the loot. Without disturbing anybody. I grant you that these days, that doesn't always hold true. Burglars apt to be not so much pros as just hoods eager for the loot—and lots of times, with a habit to support for which they need the loot. That kind very often given to violence. But Harry's not that kind. Pro burglar, old-fashioned type." He thought some more. "So he did have a gun. And hasn't now. And there are the jewels. Certainly Harry would be connected in Carson's mind with the jewels. And the man was dying. And on the other hand—well, as Luis says, we can deduce that something or somebody was scaring Carson out of town. And that could have been X. It seems, even with one like Carson, a little farfetched to imagine two X's gunning for him at the same time. Doesn't it?"

"Does it?" murmured Angel. "This is your con man?" She held a needle up to the light to thread it. "If you ask me, all of that breed would find it a lot simpler and safer just to go into politics. That's legal."

Hackett laughed. "God knows there are enough of them there already."

Palliser went home and told Roberta he'd never been subject to motion sickenss before, but that flight today— "And of all the stupid little louts, that Schuyler! It makes you wonder, Robin. Wonder about people. He started out at thirteen. Well, sure, a bad background—bad home. But that isn't always the answer either. I tell you, all the j.d.'s we see, it makes me feel nervous about even trying to bring a kid up. All the outside pressures, and the damn-fool things the schools are up to—"

"You're just feeling pessimistic," said Roberta. "Well-known aftermath of indigestion. I did have some veal steaks. No?"

"I guess I could get down some scrambled eggs," said Palliser gloomily.

Piggott went home, impatient with the D.M.V., and while he fried himself a hamburger in his apartment kitchen he thought about that poor old man again. All alone. Nobody to care—take care of him. He thought about that offbeat one the lieutenant had turned up a couple of months ago, all the helpless old people. It made you think.

He was on tomorrow, but unless there was a press of work the lieutenant didn't mind him taking off to go to church. He'd see that nice girl Prudence Russell; they were both in the choir. See if she'd have dinner with him Monday or Tuesday. But any nice girl wanting a permanent husband and family might not want to gamble on a cop—not these days.

Higgins went home, and went straight to Mary standing at the stove, his eyes questioning, for once impervious to Stevie's greeting and Laura running in from the living room.

Mary smiled at him. "Monday," she said. "Monday we'll know for sure."

"It's just," said Higgins humbly, "I don't quite believe it. Hi, Stevie."

"George—" Laura was insistent. "George, I've got a new piece to play for you—"

Jason Grace went home, and after dinner said to Virginia, "You don't mind if I go out again, honey?"

"If you want to do the overtime, go," said Virginia, smiling. "This one's got you bugged, Jase. Why?"

"I don't know," said Grace. "Offbeat in a way. The motive only. Once I saw it, it should have been easy to spot who. Gossip around the neighborhood. But—"

"Secretive," said Virginia. "Do we tend, Jase?"

"I don't know. Stands to reason, logical there should be racial tendencies. Like with families. Still, individuals—" he shook his head. "As well as—um—tendencies of human nature." He shoved back his chair, absently brushing his precise moustache in Mendoza's gesture.

It was eight o'clock when he knocked on the door of the Snyders' apartment above the little grocery store. And he thought suddenly that he was a fool: Saturday night, and Willy had a girl; ten to one he'd be out with her. Still, they hadn't had a funeral yet for old Sadie Snyder, body released just yesterday, and maybe—

When the door opened, it was Willy Snyder standing there. He just looked at Grace for a second and then silently stepped back.

Grace came into the rather stiffly furnished but comfortable old apartment, with its upright golden-oak piano, flowered carpet, old couch and chairs and crocheted antimacassars on the backs of all the furniture. "I'm sorry to disturb you again," he said, "but there were just a couple of things I wanted to ask you."

"Yes, sir," said Willy dully. "It's all right, Mr. Grace." He sat down on the couch.

"Your mother and father not here?" Grace sat down without invitation and offered him a cigarette. Willy took it with a nod and bent to a light.

"No, sir, they—" He drew a long breath and said belatedly, "Thanks. I don't smoke much, regular—I'm saving my money to—I'm—"

"You've been upset about your grandmother," said Grace gently. The Snyders the upright citizens: Willy a good young fellow, good record. Work permit at sixteen, and he'd been a regular employee of Sears ever since. And the respectable Willy, from nuances gathered, closer to his grandmother than the rest of the family. Willy, going to see her as he frequently did on his day off, finding her like that—and a little something might have been said. "I just wanted to ask you—"

"Upset!" said Willy. He looked at Grace wildly. He dropped the lighted cigarette; it smoldered on the gaudy carpet. "Oh, my God. Oh, my God, it's like a sign—you comin'—I'd been sitting here try get up my nerve, go and tell —and you come and you say, *upset!* Oh, my God, my God." Suddenly he bowed his thin figure, head on knees, and moaned. "My God. Ma and Pa over to the funeral home— pay last respects—but I couldn't. I couldn't. I don't know what they thought—why I—but Grandma, I just got to hope she understands—I couldn't, when it was *all my fault!*" He began to cry.

Grace stared at him in astonishment. The good boy Willy Snyder. He got up and picked up the smoldering cigarette and put it in the dime-store ashtray on the table. He sat on the couch beside Willy, a hand on the shaking shoulders. "Now how's that, Willy?" he asked quietly. "How was it your fault?"

"Oh, I got to tell. I got to tell! I been tryin' to get up my nerve to tell—even Eleanor don't know—but I got to—" Willy

171

sat up, fumbling for a handkerchief, wiping his eyes un-ashamed. He was shaking all over. "Mr. Grace, I don't know if the law says I oughta be punished too. I reckon I ought. I knew he's a bad man. I knew—but Grandma—"

"Tell me from the beginning, Willy. Maybe you've got some whiskey, brandy around? A little drink'll steady you some—"

"Oh, no, sir! We're teetotal. But I got to—"

"All right. From the beginning. You just take it easy, now." But what the hell was this?

"Yes, sir." Willy gulped. "I try. It was Eleanor, Mr. Grace. My girl Eleanor Adams. A—a nice girl, and smart. She graduated from high school, she's a file clerk at the head office, this big market chain. Uptown. We're engaged, when I get enough money saved—and she's saving too. And this guy, this real bad one, he comes after her. She's scared of him and—and so am I. I oughta be ashamed say that, but I am." Willy wiped his eyes. "Eleanor, she's a real pretty girl, Mr. Grace. And—nice. She goes to the same church we do, Southern Baptist. This guy—"

"Who, Willy? You know his name?"

"A lot of people know Davy Diller," said Willy. "Oh, my God. He's real bad medicine. Real bad. I don't know where he lives, he hangs around—but I know he's been in jail. For cutting people. And other things, I guess. He's a bad man, Mr. Grace. He doesn't care what he does. And he's pestering Eleanor—go with him. You know. I—I heard him. I'm shamed to be scared of him. I don't want any trouble with anybody. But he's all the time pestering Eleanor, like saying he's goin' to get her, he'll get hold of her some night and teach her whose girl she is—says he'll—" Willy stopped. "I've heard he's raped girls before. And made them scared to say—you know—oh, he's a wicked man, Mr. Grace. And—and we were both scared of him."

"I don't blame you," said Grace seriously. "Why didn't

you call us, Willy? If he'd threatened to rape Miss Adams?"

Willy sat up and gave him a pitifully scornful glance. "Mr. Grace, I got every respect for you fellows, like my ma and pa taught me. Law 'n' order. But you know as well as me all you could've done. You'd've sent a man tell Davy Diller, you better be a good boy and not do noth—anything wrong! You aren't goin' to put a man watchin' him all day and night. And just sayin' that to him, Mr. Grace, that'd be about like —like tellin' an earthquake not to go and happen."

"O.K.," said Grace. "What did you do?"

"Oh, my God," said Willy. "I—I went to my Grandma. Just the best Christian woman there ever was, Mr. Grace. And she had the power in her. And I—I knew Davy Diller, he's just awful superstitious about things like that. That kind —no schooling, they mostly are. You know. He believe anything in that line. But it was for Eleanor! She was scared —and it's dark now, when she comes home, I'm at work and can't meet her bus, and she's got no brothers, her pa's dead—" He pounded his knees in impotent agony. "If I'd-a *guessed* what he might do—! I took it to Grandma. And she said, the funny laugh-y way she had, she said, 'Willy, we gonna fool this bad man.' She said, 'I don't meddle with the wrong power, but he don't know that, Willy.' She—she hadn't any schooling, Mr. Grace, that was how she said. She said, 'We fool that bad man with the good power. We don't make a spell out of hate for the bad man, but for God's love and blessing for Eleanor an' you, you be protected.' But she said, 'You know, Willy, the power's a mighty funny thing, and it works a myster'ous way. Even if that bad man thinks I a real witch, and put a cursin' on him, it could be it don't work right, lessen there's a real thing done about it an' that bad man knows.' That's what she said, Mr. Grace, and that's why she got that sheep's heart and—and made a real spell like. I—I don't believe all that, Mr. Grace, Grandma said it was real sometimes only the wrong kind of power, but I don't know. But, she said, 'Willy, we don't use the black kind, we do it in love an' askin' God's protection. But if he believe in his black heart there's a cursin' on him, he's afraid.' That's how she said, Mr. Grace. I shouldn't've *let* her! I—"

"So it was like that," said Grace softly. "The trappings, not the intent." The good Christian woman. But—

"I *shouldn't've!*" said Willy. "She said—all laughing-like she was, Grandma—she said, 'Willy, you tell about this around, your Grandma she's called down the power against Davy Diller, that he's a wicked man due for judgment, an' you hark to me, he'll not be harmin' your Eleanor or you.'" Willy pounded his knee again. "But Davy Diller—oh, he must've heard and believed it all right—I did like Grandma said—but —but—! I never thought what he might *do!* Because it must've been him—oh, Mr. Grace, I been through hell thinkin' about it—all my fault! I—"

"No, Willy," said Grace sadly. "Davy Diller's." In the long run.

"I never thought—but I should've—"

Contributing circumstances? There were always those, thought Grace.

TWELVE

"The devil of it is," said Grace the next morning in Mendoza's office, "I don't think we can pin it on him. There's no technical evidence at all, no nice prints or footprints. As you see, I got Schenke to check out Diller's record last night. He's a mean one, all right. Counts of assault, D.-and-D., and what not, all the way back to age twelve. We can bring him in and lean on him, but—" he shrugged. "That kind doesn't break down for a few questions."

"Another moral certainty where we can't charge him," said Hackett, and Higgins grunted beside him. Mendoza smoked moodily.

"It's a damn shame," said Grace musingly, "that we're so hampered by all the rules. Oh, not that I think Davy Diller'd break under the third degree—no hankering in that line, no —but what I would like to do is maybe make him attend a séance and fetch Grandma's dead voice back to accuse him. That probably would set him confessing. Of course—"

"Well, what can we do?" asked Higgins impatiently.

"Well," said Grace slowly, "he was convinced Grandma had laid a spell on him. He might not be too sure the spell's lifted just because Grandma's dead. I'm going out to look for him, anyway, bring him in. We can at least try to put the fear of God into him about Eleanor and Willy, so he'll leave 'em alone. I've got a couple of ideas about where he might hang out—"

"You'd better not go hunting him alone, Jase," said Mendoza. "If you're going to be bringing him in. That kind have pals."

"You are so right." Grace got up. "Tom's going along. See what we can do on Davy, anyway." He went out, and Hackett swore.

"He's right, of course. How I hate these things, you know who but you can't do anything about it."

"I'd settle for that on Carson, personally," said Mendoza. "Just so we *knew*. Harry or whoever. By your expression, George, you didn't get much yesterday on those addresses."

"I don't *know*, damn it," said Higgins. "That's the hell of it, how can we know? ESP?" He told them about Calvin Gibson. "Then there was a fellow—he met Carson at a poker palace in Gardena—who bought a car secondhand from him. A Ford. About the time we know Carson bought the Chrysler, seven months ago. Fellow thought Carson was a swell guy, innocently took his word about the Ford being in prime state, paid him six hundred bucks for it. Now he's calling Carson that damned chiseler—Ford needed practically everything done to it."

"*Caveat emptor*," said Hackett.

"Yeah. And the other address was a School of Voice. He once worked there—not very long—selling the courses, on commission. This was two years and more back, they barely remembered him."

"They said," said Mendoza. "Which is the point. We don't know he didn't get all chummy with somebody there, maybe still was, or—well, what? It's up in the air."

"He paid a thousand for the Chrysler," said Higgins. "He had a little windfall then?"

"Probably," said Hackett. "Or a profit off a mark."

176

"But not a smell of a lead, where to look further," said Higgins.

"Harry," said Hackett. "Though I had a thought—"

"That bartender. Mike." Mendoza sat up. "Goldberg's not bothering to rope him in on the charge. Too much trouble to collect all the evidence, for a very small charge. But he seems to have been at least halfway in Harry's confidence. Let's fetch him in and lean on him. If we do find out, for instance, that a gun—an Iver-Johnson revolver—was part of Harry's loot, that would tell us yes or no right there."

"True. Only direction to look, that I can see," said Hackett.

"There are still addresses we haven't checked—" but Higgins shrugged.

"If the lab comes up with any make on those crossed-out items—" began Mendoza, and stopped as Piggott came in.

"At long last the D.M.V. came through. Here's the make on the plate number Whiteley gave us. It's—"

"Well, progress," said Mendoza, and Sergeant Lake looked in.

"New one—funny one—body on a woman's front porch, over on Crosby Place. The squad car just—"

"Oh, hell," said Hackett. "I'll go." He got up.

"It is, if you'll believe it, a Beverly Hills address," said Piggott. "One Roderick Dover."

"I'll be damned," said Hackett.

Mendoza stood up, pulling down his cuffs automatically. "So let's go look at the sniper, Matt. George, you can go and pick up the bartender."

"I suppose. Next obvious direction."

"And don't look so pessimistic. Things sometimes come unstuck all at once," said Mendoza. "You never know."

"Go look at the sniper, Pollyanna," said Higgins.

The Beverly Hills address was one of the older places, a

very substantial old Spanish stucco, spacious on a half-acre, with lush planting and probably a pool and a three-car garage somewhere behind the house. Piggott looked at it doubtfully as they went up the curving front walk between clipped rose trees. "It just doesn't look likely," he said. "I took it for granted, a j.d. from east L.A."

"A lot of them," said Mendoza, "come from places like this now, Matt." He stopped. Piggott followed his glance. There was an open Lincoln convertible, a couple of years old, standing in the driveway, and it wore the plate number Whiteley had scrawled down. They went up to the square porch and Mendoza pushed the bell; chimes sounded faintly. "Satan finding work for idle hands, Matt."

"And that is so true," said Piggott.

After a pause the door opened. "Yes?" said the middle-aged man confronting them. He was about fifty, and at this hour on a Sunday morning wearing a tailored silk navy dressing gown; but he was shaved and very neat and clean.

"Mr. Roderick Dover?" asked Mendoza. He and Piggott simultaneously produced their badges. "L.A.P.D., sir."

The man was silent for a moment, and suddenly looked much older. He said, "Come in." He opened the door wider. "I'm Derek Dover. You want my son. I have been meeting quite a few of you peace officers the last few years. You have my every sympathy, gentlemen." It was a richly furnished house, by what they could see from the large square entrance hall: old, good furniture, the house of a substantially wealthy man. In the strong sunlight streaming in the open door Dover looked ravaged: a heavily lined face, strong nose and jaw, a firm mouth, but a man life had not dealt with kindly. "Why," he asked calmly, "are you interested in Roderick?"

Mendoza said, "It seems he was concerned in a homicide last Wednesday night. A sniping. At least his car was."

Dover shut his eyes and opened them. "Which is," he said, "the last straw. I'm finished—let him go. I expect you hear

178

a good deal from the parents of these—" he lifted his shoulders and let them drop. "Where did I fail, I tried to do right, what went wrong? That you won't hear from me. It's true his mother died when he was fifteen, but doesn't the Catholic Church say it's the first seven years that are important? In the last few years, gentlemen, I've begun to wonder whether our superstitious ancestors who believed in changelings were so superstitious after all."

"Is your son at home, Mr.—"

"He is, or was, in the bedroom to your right at the top of the stairs," said Dover precisely. "One of the rare occasions when he is here. He comes now and then, chiefly to annoy me —and filch my liquor. Unfortunately he has money of his own from his mother now—he's just turned twenty-one. I don't wish to see him again, now. As far as I'm concerned, he has ceased to be my son—I don't know who he is—nobody of mine. You can tell him that—not that he'll be interested." Dover went into the living room to the right of the entrance hall and stood at the windows, hands in pockets, back turned.

They went up the stairs. A landing curved to make two corridors on which the front bedrooms faced. The door they wanted was open, and they looked in.

"Good Lord almighty," said Piggott mildly.

The room, a large square bedroom with solid old furniture, was a shambles. Clothes, papers, magazines, were strewn carelessly. The bedclothes were tumbled half off the bed. Sitting in the middle of the bed, staring into space, was a young man smoking a cigarette. He had shoulder-length hair, brown and greasy, and a scruffy beard. He was stark naked. "What the hell you want?" he demanded, jerking around.

"Roderick Dover?" said Mendoza.

"So what? You're fuzz," said Dover acutely, and giggled. "Spot you ever' time. Fuzz." He started to get off the bed.

In one corner of the room a light rifle stood against the

wall. Mendoza went over and looked at it. It was a Marlin model 81-DL, a twenty-five-shot repeater. Something: though Bainbridge had said the bullet in Leon Lister's head was smashed, there'd be no positive ballistics evidence. "Is this your gun?" he asked.

"Lieutenant, he's high on something," said Piggott. "The rules—"

"Well?" Mendoza walked over to the bed. Dover stood up unsteadily.

"Fuzz," he said again. "So what?"

"So you killed a man with it last Wednesday night. Do you remember that? You nearly sideswiped a car along Hoover, and the other driver yelled at you. And you—"

"Nobody yells at *me*. *I* do whatever I want 'n' be damned to you. *All* o' you." He grinned insolently at Mendoza. "I wanna smoke pot, thass nobody else's business. *Nobody*. See?"

"Until you kill somebody," said Mendoza. "Do you remember any of that, Dover? At all? Do you remember nearly hitting—"

"Wasn't me. Wasn't drivin'. Colin. *I* had the gun. Wow— that was a crash! Bing-bing, Roderick gets his man. Pretty. Oh, wow, that was a fun thing." He stood swaying, staring dreamily.

Piggott said something under his breath, and then, "And that's just no good at all in court."

"Not worth a damn," said Mendoza. He took the cigarette from Dover and looked at it. "I think this may interest Pat Callaghan. We want a squad car to take Roderick in anyway. Keep an eye on him while I find a phone."

"Man," said Roderick in a thick voice, "that was a fun thing. Yell at *me*. Nobody tells me—what t' do or—"

He didn't fight the squad car men; he was in a pleasant haze by then, and couldn't have cared less what was happening. They got some clothes on him and took him away, down to Central Receiving to be looked at by the doctors. Lieutenant Callaghan of Narco arrived with a couple of men and poked around; they found quite a stack of reefers, a little hoard of heroin. That was a solid temporary charge to book him on, anyway.

None of them exchanged a word with Derek Dover while that was going on; he still stood there in the living room, back turned. But when Mendoza and Piggott came down the stairs for the last time, Mendoza went into the living room and said, "Excuse me, Mr. Dover."

"I don't want—"

"He mentioned a Colin. Would you know who that is?"

Dover said in a remote tone, "I believe a Colin Donovan is an—acquaintance of his. They were at military academy together."

"Thanks very much, sir."

He didn't answer. He was still standing there when they left the house.

"But what is the answer?" asked Piggott. "Besides Satan tempting idle hands?"

"I wouldn't know, Matt." Mendoza was silent on the drive back, the Ferrari purring smoothly. Maybe, thought Piggott, he was thinking about his own family. Do the best you could, what you thought was right, and then— As they turned into the lot, Piggott looked at his watch. It was ten to eleven.

"My Lord," he said, "I'll be late for church—see you," and he bolted for his car.

Palliser had come in late; he and Higgins had had a little session with Mike before Mendoza came back. Mike had been easily picked up, cozily having Sunday breakfast with a plump wife and three kids at an apartment on Marietta Street. They had abandoned him temporarily when Mendoza came in and told them about Roderick Dover.

"How nice," said Palliser. "And so what happens? It's only a manslaughter charge. He gets a three-to-ten, serves two, gets out on P.A. and the next thing we know maybe he's killed somebody else. Another innocent citizen."

"Well, at least we've got him now," said Mendoza. He sat down at his desk and lit a cigarette; they came in after him. "So what have you heard from Mike?"

"A loud chorus of no's," said Higgins wearily. "He never laid eyes on Harry until a couple of weeks ago. He was nice to him, tried to help him out, on account Harry'd known a pal of his who was in Quentin. Not that Mike runs with hoods, oh, no, he's nice and clean, never done anything wrong, etcetera. But the gist is, he never knew Harry was up to anything, let him use the phone in the bar just being friendly, doesn't know nothing about the gun, and so on."

"Mmh, yes. Who, me? Expectable. What do you think?"

"Well, Luis, I'm kind of inclined to think he's telling most of the truth," said Higgins. "He knew Harry was hunting a fence, sure—that he's not admitting. He probably didn't know where the loot came from. Come to think, why should Harry confide in him? Evidently their only link was the pal up in Quentin—and that you heard from Harry too, after all. Before he found out who you were."

"*Seguro que sí.* Which again leaves it all up in the air," said Mendoza irritably, snapping his lighter. "I like Harry, George. Or I did. Principally because of the jewels, I will admit to you."

"Well, that could be a very wild goose indeed," said Higgins. "Look. Look, I've just had an idea. You said that Carson had the wind up about something, reason he'd planned to leave town, and had maybe, because of the Alexandria Street address being in the phone book, been staying away from there. Though there were clothes—but one like Carson, they usually are natty dressers and have a sizable wardrobe, of course. But all right, say he was. And all of a sudden, some-time on Monday, say, he remembers that box with his mother's jewelry in it—and the ring he got from Harry—and wrote himself a little note to remind himself to pick them up. And—"

"But," said Mendoza suddenly, "but, George, he'd only got the diamond ring from Harry last Saturday night—a week ago last night, that is. If he—or if he hadn't— *¡Aguarda un momento!*—he did come back in pursuit of Natalie, and—that was, after all, a month ago—"

"You've had a sudden hunch?" asked Higgins hopefully.

"*No sé,*" said Mendoza slowly, "but—" He ground out his cigarette and very deliberately lit a new one. Palliser looked at his watch.

"I've got to go out to the airport, meet that sheriff and bring him in to talk to Schuyler. I'd better—" He made for the door, and passed Hackett on the way in.

"Another little anonymous bit for us to go round and round on," said Hackett. "Just thought you'd like to know. And what a shock for the innocent citizen. Nice old lady, a widow, living alone. She opens her front door to take in the Sunday paper, and there's a dead man on her porch."

"How come?" asked Higgins.

"I don't think anything mysterious. Only of course he had some money on him— Man about fifty, looked as if he'd been beaten. Mugged on the street, and the mugger clobbered him a little too hard—they will do it. He staggers toward the near-est house, looking for help, collapses, and dies on the porch. See what the autopsy says. I'll get out a report." Hackett went on down the hall.

Another unidentified corpse. To be hoped he'd be identi-fied eventually.

"A hunch?" repeated Higgins. "On Carson, Luis?"

Mendoza didn't answer, stared at his cigarette. Then he said, "I wonder . . ."

Jason Grace turned his back on Dave Diller and looked out the one tall window of the interrogation room. It showed him the line of the Hollywood Hills smudged on the horizon across the city; even in March, a March warm and sunny as usual, a little haze of smog. Grace was tired of Diller; of all the Dillers, of every color and accent, they saw so many of. He heard Landers strike a match for another cigarette.

They had found Dave Diller at one of his known hangouts, a pool hall on Jefferson Boulevard. Diller was a big hunk of a lout, all but illiterate and with a naturally mean disposition. Which his pedigree had told them even before they'd seen him.

They had gone to work on Diller, pounding at him with all the questions, and as Grace had foreseen they hadn't got anywhere at all. He was used to the questioning-in-depth; he hadn't many brains or any sensitivity at all, in any sense, and they hadn't shaken his smart-aleck attitude one iota.

"Come on," said Landers toughly, "you know you did it, Diller—you killed that poor old woman, beat her and strangled—"

Grace turned and shook his head very slightly at Landers, who turned away and shut up. Diller just sat, vaguely sneering. The big crude lout. And you'd never change him, that kind. Grace looked at him. A lot of adjectives for him. Besides the obvious ones—mean, greedy, lazy, violent, dumb, wantonly cruel and destructive, aimless—and superstitious. Yes.

He walked over to Diller. He said in a soft voice, "She put a thing on you, Dave, you know that. That was why you took her off. You were scared. We've been beating round the bushes on this. The white man's laws. But you know and

I know there's more to it than that—than maybe other folk ever know. Isn't that so, Dave? Did you ever stop to think, Dave, that now she's dead—she can't take it off you? You ever hear that, only the one put it on can take it off."

Diller growled. "What the hell you—" He was a big gross man, shaven-headed, soft with fulfilled greed. He hadn't held a job in years; when he wasn't in jail he was on welfare.

"You made a little mistake taking her off," said Grace. "Now the thing's on you forevermore. For good. All sorts of things might happen to you, you don't know." He laughed.

Diller's eyes moved whitely. "I dunno what you—" But that thought had, indeed, been in his mind; Grace saw that. Good. Long let it stay there. But it might be reinforced by something more practical, at that.

He stood close above Diller, conscious of the stale dirty smell of him, and bent to look him in the eyes. "But whether that's so or not, I am here to tell you that there'll be an eye on you, Dave. You'd better mind where you walk and what you do and what you say. And you'd better forget all about a girl named Eleanor Adams, and Willy Snyder. You get that through your thick skull, Dave. Because if anything should happen to Eleanor or Willy—or if you put one foot on the wrong side of the law, any time from now on, Dave—we'll get you so fast and hard you won't know what's hit you till you're in a cell with the key thrown away. You understand me, Dave?"

Diller's eyes dropped. He made a sullen growl.

Grace felt a lot more tired. He went out to the corridor and Landers followed.

"Let him loose?"

"We'll never get anything concrete on him," said Grace. "Let's just hope we've scared him. And somehow—" he smiled briefly "—I kind of think Dave is worried about that spell Grandma cast on him. I hope he is. Maybe—in a funny kind of way, Tom—it really was a spell and it is still working. Not that I believe in—" And he broke off to laugh at himself.

At two thirty that afternoon, a quiet Sunday with no more new calls so far, Sergeant Lake came into Mendoza's office where Mendoza, Hackett, and Higgins were still arguing about Carson, and said there was somebody asking for whoever was in charge of the Carson thing.

"Oh?" said Mendoza interestedly. He glanced at the wall clock. "John will be bringing that sheriff over, guided tour through headquarters. What's this one look like, Jimmy? A nut?" They so often got those.

"He gave me a card."

Mendoza took it. In raised engraving it said, *Mr. Rodney Pike-Carter,* and in the left lower corner, *Pike-Carter, Whalen and Browser Engineering, Ltd., Birmingham, Worcs.*

"*¡Porvida!*" said Mendoza. "What's he look like, Jimmy?"

Lake considered and said, "That fellow who used to play English butlers in the movies. Only younger."

"I doubt he'd be flattered. Shoot him in."

The resemblance was a family one only, chiefly in the accent. Rodney Pike-Carter was tall, broad-shouldered, impeccably tailored, very blond, very tanned, about thirty-five, and nobody could have mistaken him for anything but British. But his behavior was less impeccable. He came in, and Mendoza introduced himself, Hackett, and Higgins. Pike-Carter said polite things correctly. "You have something to tell us about Rex Carson, sir? About the—"

And Pike-Carter suddenly commenced to laugh. He laughed heartily, gaspingly, and sank into a chair still convulsed, groping for a handkerchief. They stared at him.

"Do apologize," he gasped. "Couldn't help—all of you so damn serious—and all I could think of was that bloody little nit running like a scared rabbit—funniest damn thing I ever saw! Sorry." He put the handkerchief away. He was still grinning.

"Carson?" said Mendoza. "You knew Carson? What—"

"Saw that photograph in the *Times*. Police asking help. I thought about coming to see you—have to help the police, naturally—didn't see that I could," said Pike-Carter, clipped and British. "I don't know a damn thing about how he came to get shot. But I also thought, if I did tell you about it, Agnes might think twice again. Begging me all tearful not to come in, she'd die of shame. My wife, you know. Dear little soul, but flighty—I've got to say that. Have to keep an eye on her. Oh, she'd never actually play me up, not *that* kind, good Lord, no, but she's just got a soft heart. And rather a soft head, if you take me. Should have explained, I'm over here for six months as a consultant—hush-hush deal—one of your aircraft plants. Can't tell you any more about that, but it doesn't matter. Brought Agnes with me—we've got a very nice little place, Sunset Towers in Hollywood."

"But where did you—"

"Carson," said Pike-Carter. He started to laugh again. "That bloody little glamour-boy. Not an ounce of harm in Agnes, but she's a damned flirt. Half-Irish, of course. And what you call a sucker for the poor-mouth story. Couldn't count the times she's been taken by some scoundrel kissing her hand and making up pretty things about her beautiful eyes, and tells her some damned sad tale about his mother. Thing is, she gets bored, poor girl, and she's got a generous allowance. And I swear that type can smell her out—and unfortunately, I do have to leave her alone now and then. Business. The hush-hush bit. I thought the shops and restaurants might keep her satisfied, but bless me, she finds the same type—or he finds her. While I'm—hum—over at one of your nuclear proving grounds. Forget it—doesn't signify about that."

"Yes?" Mendoza was still at a loss.

"So, I come back unexpected—to the apartment, you know —as I say, all this hasn't one damn thing to do with his murder, but you did say you wanted any information on him, and there it is, I can tell you this. I come back and find this smooth bastard *with* my wife, *in* our flat, cool as be damned making love to her—oh, not the real thing," he assured them, grinning, "Agnes isn't that kind, just a damn fool where men and money are concerned—and I am fed up. I—um—gave him a good hiding. I spend my spare time mostly at tennis and squash, I'm in pretty good condition, and I let him have it, as you say."

"Oh, really?" said Mendoza. "When was this?"

"Oh, last month. Call it five weeks. I bloodied his handsome nose for him," said Pike-Carter in satisfaction, "and gave him a beautiful black eye, and banged him around some. And talk about rabbits—that kind always are—oh, please don't hit me—didn't even try to fight back, he got away and ran. Like a rabbit. I was really fed to the teeth with Agnes's idiocy, you know, and I got his name and address out of her—she'd met him, you might know, at a cocktail lounge. She never learns, same old gambit, weren't we introduced at Mrs. Smith's—attracted by all her jewelry, I expect—and I went to the trouble of following him up. Bastards like that are a menace," said Pike-Carter. "I rang him up next day and—chiefly for Agnes's benefit, maybe scare her a little that I meant it—I told him, by God, I was out for his blood. Fellows like him ought to be castrated for the good of society, and I'd be only too pleased to take care of the job myself. That kind—cowards from the word go. Oh, dear, oh, dear," said Pike-Carter, and started laughing again. "The fellow was terrified—it was all very amusing. Luckily he hadn't got anything out of Agnes yet."

"I see," said Mendoza gravely, his mouth twitching. "That's very interesting, sir."

"Not an earthly to do with his getting shot," said Pike-

Carter. "The paper said, last Monday night? Well, in case you're harboring any suspicions that I did follow it up, we were at a formal dinner party last Monday night from about seven on, at Newport Beach. I just thought all this might give you some bearing, if you didn't know the type he was. Snotty little glamour-boy on the make, after the women. I should think—you know your own business best, of course—but I should think it was something like that, reason somebody shot him. Some female he'd played loose with, or a husband." He got up. "That's all I could tell you. No idea whether it's any use to you."

"I think," said Mendoza, "it could be a lot of use, sir. Thanks very much for coming in."

"No trouble. But when I think of his expression when I went for him—" Pike-Carter was still chuckling as he went out.

"The intrepid Britisher," said Mendoza, and laughed too. "But there's our answer. To some of the puzzle at least."

"How do you make that out?" asked Hackett. "I see it was the intrepid Britisher who scared him—"

"*De veras*. The X who scared Carson—to impress Agnes and—mmh—just for fun," said Mendoza. "And Carson believed him. The scared rabbit—yes, your typical con-man usually is that way. He believed Pike-Carter's threats. Believed him enough—our Britisher a big strong fellow, and Carson'd know he had money to hire the private dicks—that he was going to make tracks away. Cut his losses, start new in Oregon. Where apparently he'd been before. So he started to make all his arrangements. But, *amigos*, Carson was no fool. Likely he stayed away from Alexandria Street for awhile, afraid Pike-Carter was lying in wait, or some minion of Pike-Carter's—but by the time he met Natalie in Vegas and followed her back here to press his suit, he'd realized that the threat was an empty one. That Pike-Carter couldn't be bothered setting the private dicks on him, or lying in wait. So, by the time he met Harry and took that diamond solitaire for the poker debt, he was back at Alexandria Street. Though pressuring Natalie to move to Florida—just to see pastures new."

"But," said Higgins, "but we said—"

"I know, I know," said Mendoza ruefully. "That the X who had scared Carson into planning to clear out was probably the answer. So this leaves us even farther up in the air again. Pike-Carter was that X. But Pike-Carter didn't shoot Carson. And by the time somebody did, Carson knew Pike-Carter wasn't any serious threat. And—I just put it in for us to think about—Pike-Carter has no connection with any jewels."

"Oh, hell," said Hackett. "Up in the air you could say. And I'm not thinking so much of Harry now."

"It was a woman," said Higgins with conviction. "It has to be a woman. Look, that Patti Page—"

"There!" said Alison. "See, he's all well again and we can let him loose to fly away and find his own food."

"*Bueno*," said Johnny, hopping up and down. "*El pájaro* fly all nice. *¡Muy bien!*"

"*El pájaro* fly *away*," said Terry mournfully.

"Of course, my dearies," said Mrs. MacTaggart cheerfully. "He flies off the way the good Lord meant birdies to fly, look to themselves and their families—"

They had the box with the chicken-wire top out in the back yard, and everybody was there. Cedric stood by, wagging his tailless rump rhythmically. Bast ambled toward them; the other three sat on the back porch, eyes fastened on the box. Alison unfastened the flap door and tilted the box. The mockingbird, now completely untarred and healed, hopped out onto the lawn. He spread his wings wide but didn't take off immediately. He remarked, "YAWK! *Yankee Doodle came to—Tu-whooooo.*"

"So fly, *estúpido*," said Alison. "Shoo."

The mockingbird fluttered up to light on the rim of a redwood tub containing a pillar rose. Bast crouched four feet away, chattering, her hind end swaying, gauging her leap. "YAWK!" said the bird.

"For heaven's sake go away, idiot!" said Alison.

"*El pájaro* want to stay with us," said Terry happily.

"Heaven forbid," said Alison. "Shoo, *estúpido!*"

The mockingbird regarded them with bright insolent eyes, head on one side, and said, "*Tu-whooooo. Yankee Doodle came to town, Yankee Doodle—*" Bast flattened herself for the final pounce.

"It's not had its whiskey," said Mrs. MacTaggart. "If the creature hasna the strength to fly higher—"

The other three cats started for them on the run, seeing the game so inviting.

"You said *el pájaro* fly away, *Mamacita—*"

"Oh, he will!" said Alison, making a grab for Bast. "For good, if—shoo! *¡Vamos!*" She gestured violently at their feathered friend.

The mockingbird took wing, elegantly, the underside of him flashing white as he curved in the air. He lit on the lowest limb of the big alder tree and began to swear raucously at the cats.

"Honestly!" said Alison.

THIRTEEN

By nine o'clock on Monday morning Sheriff Quacken-bush had had his guided tour around headquarters and had departed for home with Arnie Wall. They'd probably never hear the outcome of that unless it got in the local papers; but the sheriff seemed to think he had some good evidence on Wall. Who had, said Palliser, admitted being in Hollister's car but said he hadn't killed him, that had been another hitchhiker who had threatened to kill Wall too if he interfered. The other hitchhiker had conveniently vanished into limbo to let Wall escape with the Maserati and Hollister's wallet and BankAmericard.

It was Piggott's day off. Overnight, there had been a brawl in a bar and one man stabbed to death. Galeano's report contained the names of several witnesses who had to be brought in to make formal statements today: Higgins and Grace had gone out to do that. Hackett would be attending the inquest on Lister. An inquest in another court on Milliken-Nordhammer: Landers was covering that. They had shoved the Delaney thing in Pending on Thursday; very long odds they'd ever get anything on that. But at nine five that morning Lieutenant Andrews of Vice called Mendoza to relay the news that they'd just picked up a dame on that lay, through a tip; it could be she'd been the one Delaney went to. Mendoza sent Palliser down to see Andrews and look at the abortionist.

So far there hadn't been a new call today. That Colin Donovan, thought Mendoza. Locate him through the private-school record: he had Lake calling on that, probably never raise anybody before nine anyhow. Carson—well, just where else was there to look on Carson? The legwork—the rest of the address book. They could, of course, ask Chicago if there was any violence showing on Harry Schumacher's record.

He had just lit a cigarette, ruminating on Harry—if that "jewels" meant anything, well, the only jewels Carson had been connected with recently were those of Harry's loot—when Scarne came in.

"Interesting little exercise," he said, and laid some five-by-seven glossy prints on Mendoza's desk. "The infra-red bit. We got some middling results for you."

They had. The three crossed-out addresses in Carson's local address book. Mendoza looked at them. Two girls' names, Hollywood addresses. One of those had had the cynical "nice girl" comment attached; it could be presumed that the other one had been X-ed out for the same reason. Though they'd look. But the third read, discernible even with the inked marking-out showing faintly, *George Drucker, Drucker-Kraus Engineering Corp.*, and an address on Chandler in the valley. Oh, really? There had been other addresses vaguely like that, business places—that small-aircraft-parts place, and —and on one of those, what the hell was the name, Lamson, Art had said he'd been scared at the mention of Carson's name. *Scared.* Why?

"Thanks very much," he said to Scarne. "Nice job."

"We always do nice jobs," said Scarne.

Mendoza got his hat and started out. Lake told him he hadn't got hold of anybody at that military academy yet who was any help, but had been told the headmaster would be available at nine thirty. "Yes," said Mendoza. "I'll be back sometime, Jimmy." He headed the Ferrari for the valley.

It was warmer out there, of course. The address was in North Hollywood. A lot of large and small manufacturing plants out here, almost anything you could name. A vaguely titled engineering corporation might make almost anything. It was, when he found it, one of the middling-sized ones: smart modern-looking buildings on a couple of acres, the main office embellished with synthetic-stone panels on the front, a large parking lot, a guard. The badge got him through the gate. The badge brought awed surprise from a blond receptionist, who sent a minion scurrying. Eventually, some fifteen minutes later the badge brought him into the private office of Mr. George Drucker. It was a modestly affluent office, carpeted in beige, with a vast walnut desk and quite a good reproduction Renoir on one wall.

"And what can we do to help out the L.A.P.D.?" asked Drucker genially. "Got an appointment later but anything I can do—er—?"

"Lieutenant Mendoza."

"Sure. What's up?" Drucker was a large square man with a head of wild gray hair, curly. His gray herringbone suit had undoubtedly been tailored for him, but he was the kind of man who'd always look as if he slept in his clothes; and his hands were originally a laboring man's hands, scarred and large and knuckly. Self-made man, thought Mendoza; probably he and Kraus had started this place on a shoestring, maybe a quarter of a century ago during the war—a lot of such places had had their beginnings then.

"Do you know a Rex Carson, Mr. Drucker?"

The smile vanished from Drucker's mouth. "Why?" he asked baldly.

This one you'd better not beat around the bush with, thought Mendoza. "Quite simple. Your name and address was in his address book. He was murdered a week ago. Shot."

"I'll be damned," said Drucker. "I will be eternally

194

damned. No, I didn't see it in the papers. We've been pretty busy over a special order." He ran a hand through his wild hair. "Siddown," he said. "Why the L.A.P.D. and not the FBI?"

"What?" said Mendoza.

"I don't know about all that jazz," said Drucker, "but I should think a civil service employee—well, maybe not. I don't know. Just occurred to me."

"Civil service—"

"Well, he did work for the Department of Commerce," said Drucker. "You must know that much about him."

Mendoza sat down and lit a cigarette. Drucker lounged on the corner of the vast desk. "Suppose you just tell me, Mr. Drucker, how and when you met Carson," said Mendoza gently, "and what dealings you had with him."

"Dealings!" said Drucker. "Goddamn it, I didn't have any deals with him! By God, I'm an honest man and anybody says I'm not'll answer to me pretty damn straight! Anything Drucker-Kraus gets, it gets on its own merits, and if anybody thinks different—"

"Take it easy," said Mendoza. "I wasn't implying anything. Carson. You knew him?"

"No, I didn't *know* him," growled Drucker. "He showed up here one day and sent in his card. My God, Department of Commerce, first thing I think is, what've we done wrong now? Not hired enough Communists maybe, according to the Supreme Court. Anyway, I tell Nelly to shoot him in. And he sits there and gives me a lot of damn four-syllable doubletalk, and winds up—oh, he wrapped it up, but that's what it amounted to—by offering to get us a government contract for a thousand-buck payoff. That was the sense of it. And damn it—"

"I *will* be damned," said Mendoza. "Just out of the blue?"

"Just out of the blue. Never laid eyes on him before. And first I said just what you did, I will be damned, I said. When

I got it through my head. And then I said the hell of a lot more, Lieutenant Mendoza. I said the country is in one hell of a state when government employees are out-and-out crooks, goddamn it, and while we'd be damn glad to get a big contract, any we get'll be strictly on our own, we don't operate underhand. And I told him to get the hell out of my office. The *hell* of a thing—cool as you damn please—a thousand bucks! If we wanted to operate that way, we could afford the hell of a lot bigger payoff than a measly grand, but we *don't* operate that way, and I damn well told him so, Lieutenant Mendoza."

"I will be—*¡caray!*" said Mendoza, light suddenly dawning. "Yes—but why, Mr. Drucker, didn't you do something about it? When was this, by the way?"

"When? Eight—nine months ago. Do something?"

"Yes. Why didn't you inform the police? That kind of thing's illegal, after all. Why didn't you call the local office of the Commerce Department, tell his superior? You thought he was a bona fide government employee?"

Drucker looked startled, cynical and amused all at once. He pounced on that last. "Wasn't he? I took it for granted—you mean—"

"But why didn't you?" And Mendoza knew the answer without hearing it.

"Why? Hell, man," said Drucker wearily, "if you'd been in business as long as I have, Lieutenant, you'd know how much of that goes on these days. Not like my dad's old machine shop. Something's happened to people—I don't know. But, the wheeling and dealing. I'm an honest man and so's Hansie Kraus. O.K. We're maybe the big exception. I tell you this—" he pointed a blunt forefinger at Mendoza. "Right then 'n' there, that smooth bastard doubletalking, I'd take a bet that nine out of ten men he fed the offer, they'd jump at it. And all of them honest men on the surface, Lieutenant. But

196

it's cutthroat all the way, a lot of men take it as they can get it. These days. Jump at it, by God—the nice government contract. I've got no doubt the same damn things went on just before the fall of Rome—you read Taylor Caldwell's *A Pillar of Iron?*" Mendoza said no, apologetically. "Great book —you ought to," said Drucker, running a hand through his hair. "I've got no doubt. Spiritual wickedness in high places —*and* low. You think I'm an idiot, Lieutenant? You think I don't know this Carson's boss at the local office was up to his neck in it too? How else'd Carson deliver on the pay-offs? And the police, my God, trying to get any solid evidence on federal employees—waste of time. My time and yours, damn it."

But what a beautiful racket, thought Mendoza. It burst on him in all its simple splendor, and he was fascinated. Endless varieties of the few basic con games, but this was new to him. If somebody hadn't taken Carson off prematurely, he might well have ended up as one of the great fraud artists. "He couldn't deliver, Mr. Drucker," he said amusedly. "He wasn't in any position to deliver anything. The con game pure and simple."

"What?" said Drucker.

"The federal government never knew anything about Carson except his Social Security number, and he wasn't reporting any of his profit. He just had those cards made up locally." Yes, and he'd been intending to go on the same game in Oregon—until he met Natalie. "It was strictly a one-call play. I wouldn't doubt—sad a situation as it is—that you're quite right. Nine out of ten men in your position— owners of smallish manufacturing companies—would have jumped at it. And not, as you say, turned a hair over the payoff bit. Way business gets done. These days. And he'd ask what he thought the traffic would bear—what sounded plausible. Five hundred on up. He—"

"You don't tell me he— I will be eternally *goddamned!*"
said Drucker. "Of all the nerve—my God, it never crossed my
mind—that kind of thing so damn common—"

"You'd never have seen or heard from him again," said
Mendoza. "Just fade away with your grand—a beautiful
racket. New to me. I wonder if it was original with him."

"Beautiful!" said Drucker wrathfully. "I could damn well
think of other names— I will be goddamned!"

"No wonder he'd X-ed out your name." Mendoza laughed.
"And no wonder that that Lamson was scared—maybe he
was a recent mark and still expecting the fat government contract, and afraid we'd foul it up. What a— Well, I'm much
obliged for your frankness, Mr. Drucker. Thank God for one
honest man left among us, anyway."

"This makes me all the madder," said Drucker. "And if you
think it's reassured me any about the essential honesty of
civil servants, you can think again. Known too many. Who
shot him, you find out yet?"

"That," said Mendoza, "seems to be the one thing we still
don't know, Mr. Drucker."

On the way back downtown, he meditated on the strange
lopsided beauty of the racket Carson had perfected. His one
steady gimmick. All the cynical Drucker had said was quite
true: unfortunately, the embattled and shortsighted busi-
nessmen, all too many of them, would jump at the promise of
the fat contract however obtained. And there must be liter-
ally thousands of such middling-sized businesses around here,
and what with the government in the market for anything
from office furniture to nuts and bolts, Carson's potential list
of marks had been legion. Academically, Mendoza wondered
how many he had hit since the brilliant notion occurred to
him. It was probable—possible?—that he'd only put down
addresses of that kind at the start of that career, latterly had
been more canny. . . . And there was also the fact that the

marks, in such a racket, were going to preserve absolute silence when they realized they'd been taken. Not a thing a man mentioned casually over a drink with friends.

But unfortunately it all said absolutely nothing about who had shot Carson, or why. That was still up in the air.

When he came into the office Lake said, "I traced that Donovan for you. At least his parents. They lived in Beverly Hills when he left that military academy three years ago," and he passed over the scribbled address.

"*Bien*," said Mendoza.

"Jase and George are just about finished getting those statements, I think."

Before Mendoza got to his office door Palliser came back and followed him in. "That dirty old female Andrews picked up," he said morosely, "might be or mightn't. On the Delaney girl. Who can say? Her rat hole was over on Darwin, same general area, the Delaney girl could have heard of her. But there'll never be any evidence. She's an old lush, and she's not talking."

"Helpful," said Mendoza. He looked at the papers on his desk. A new one—the medical report on Roderick Dover. Also helpful: he was on reefers, also on the H. "However, we have turned up a very interesting something on Carson. Not that it takes us any farther toward X. At least I don't see how it could." Hackett wandered in and said the inquest had ended in the expectable open verdict. "Yes," said Mendoza. "So now we know what Carson's sure gimmick was—and what a gimmick!" He told them about that, and they both laughed. "*Cómico*, maybe—but not really so funny, boys— comment on twentieth-century culture, maybe. I'll bet it was a nice living. But what the hell does it tell us about X? *Nada absolutamente*."

"And, damn it, it says nothing about those jewels," said Hackett, rubbing his jaw. Higgins came in and said Grace was getting the last of those statements about the bar brawl.

"Much ado about nothing," he added. "The corpse no loss—he had a long pedigree of D.-and-D., disturbing the peace, and so on, and the knifer not much better. Argument over brands of beer."

"People," said Mendoza.

"But you'll never believe this one, George," said Hackett. Carson's racket—" he started to tell him about that, and the inside phone rang on Mendoza's desk.

"Mendoza, Homicide."

"Carey," said the phone. "We've just got a new missing report and I thought I'd check with you, see if any of your recent corpses might match."

"Fire away," said Mendoza absently.

"One Edward Holly. His son filed a report just now. Age fifty-four, five nine, a hundred and fifty, blue eyes, gray-brown hair, white. He was a clerk at a chain market on Alvarado. Widower, lived alone—home address Crosby Lane, a little cul-de-sac in the Echo Park area—"

"Oh, yes?" said Mendoza. "Just a minute. George, does this sound like that corpse on the front porch yesterday morning?" He recited the statistics.

"On the nose," said Higgins.

"I thought it might. John, you're at loose ends—go see Carey in Missing Persons and try to get a positive ident from the relatives. Carey'll have the address."

Palliser went out muttering about the damned routine, and Mendoza picked up the slip of paper Lake had handed him.

"Jobs still to do. Suppose you go see these Donovans. See if son Colin is still living at home. He'll be accessory-before-and-after on Lister, probably. If he's the right Colin, and it's not a name you come across every day."

Hackett took the slip. "Beverly Hills again. And the military academy yet. It is getting on for lunchtime, of course. . . . That is the damndest thing, that racket of Carson's—

by the lock-box it was paying off, all right. What an idea."
He looked at his watch. "Try the parents before lunch,
George? We may have to split if they don't know where he
is."

"O.K.," said Higgins, getting up.

Lake looked in. "George," he said. "Your wife's on the
phone." Higgins shot out into the sergeants' office and picked
up the phone on his desk.

"Mary?"

"Well, it's positive. George, I feel so funny about it." She
laughed. "I mean, Laura's ten and—"

"Funny? It's—it's— Mary? The kids won't *mind?* I
mean—"

"Don't be silly. Probably be thrilled to death. So am I
really, but it's so—so—"

"It's fine," said Higgins. "It's just fine."

"Yes. Well—see you."

"See you."

Higgins went back to Mendoza's office. "Everything O.K.
at home?" asked Hackett casually.

"Everything," said Higgins, beaming, "is fine." And he
mightn't have said more if anybody else had been there, but
he and Hackett and Mendoza had worked together a long
time and knew each other inside out. "I don't quite believe
it myself," he said, "but I'm going to— I mean *Mary's* going
to have a baby. Just now. I mean we just, I mean *she* just
found out for sure. I hope the kids aren't going to mind. She
says not, but—"

"Well, congratulations!" said Hackett, surprised and
amused.

"I warn you, George," said Mendoza, "there are hazards
to starting a family at your age. The little monsters—"

"Don't be silly," said Higgins fondly. "It's fine. Just fine.
We never really—I mean, I didn't think Mary'd want—but
it'll be fine. Just fine. Doesn't matter which—I don't care

201

BURLINGAME
PUBLIC
LIBRARY

one way or the other—just hope Laura and Stevie won't mind, but they're old enough to—"

"Well, fond papa," said Hackett, grinning, "come on, we'll have an early lunch and I'll buy you a drink to celebrate."

"I don't need one," said Higgins. "I feel as if I'd had one already—but O.K., we'll do that. Luis?"

"Too early," said Mendoza. "I want to ruminate in peace. Congratulations, *hijo mío*. Keep up the good work." He grinned after them.

"Yes—that's him," said John Holly. "That's Dad." He swallowed.

The morgue attendant slid the cold tray shut silently. Palliser led Holly out to the corridor.

"I suppose you know there'll have to be an autopsy, sir. The way it looks now, we think your father was mugged—attacked in the street for what he had on him, and beaten, you know."

Holly looked at him in dull surprise. He was a thin young man in a rather shabby gray suit and wilted shirt; he was an accountant at a brokerage house down on Spring, where Palliser had found him. "On the street?" he said. "But that couldn't be. That can't be how it was. I can't—I can't take it in. Dad. *Killed*. That's—the kind of thing doesn't happen to people like us."

"I'm afraid it does sometimes," said Palliser sympathetically.

"But—Dad. It just doesn't make sense," said Holly numbly. "I—we always went to see him Sundays, you know. Sometimes brought him up to our place for dinner. We—and he wasn't *there*. We couldn't—he was always there. My wife—her folks are dead and she and Dad got on just fine. He was assistant manager of the market, you know, he could arrange his hours pretty much as he wanted. He was never on Sundays or nights. Never. Of course. They—they'd been pretty nice to him but he was going to have to retire in a couple of months. He knew that. I'm doing all right, we manage—he was going to move in with us. Mrs. Gilpin—the woman owns that house, where Dad rented the place in the rear—she didn't know anything. Said he came home the usual time on Saturday. Well, I don't know. Bonnie and I talked it over—Mrs. Gilpin let us into Dad's place and everything was just as usual, nothing different—only he wasn't there. And now he's *killed*. Like that. And you saying—" he shook his head, staring at Palliser. "That just doesn't make sense. Where—where was he found? You didn't say."

"On Crosby Place, Mr. Holly. That's—"

"Oh. But that's way the next block over," said Holly. "Mrs. Gilpin said he came home at the regular time on Saturday, five o'clock. You see, he never went out alone after dark. He couldn't. He—he was going blind. He could still just about do his work at the market, not checking anymore, but he couldn't have much longer. He never went out alone after dark. What was he doing over there, away from home at night?"

It was Palliser's turn to stare at him. Don't tell me, he thought, another little mystery?

"Really, that idiotic bird!" said Alison, taking the ham from the refrigerator.

"It just goes to show," said Mrs. MacTaggart, "that there's more to even a little bird than you'd expect, *achara*. I believe the creature's got fond of us for helping it."

"Well, if it has I'd just as soon it hadn't," said Alison. "You'd think any bird with a grain of sense would make tracks from a yard full of cats like greased lightning. Really—" She looked out the kitchen window to the back yard. Cedric was standing in the middle of the lawn wagging his tailless rump, the twins were shouting excitedly to each other and pointing up into the alder tree, and Bast was coiled up in the sun on the lowest back step, ostentatiously ignoring everybody. The other three cats were invisible but would be somewhere around.

When the mockingbird had finally taken off yesterday afternoon they had all thought they'd seen the last of it. The mockingbird had other ideas. An hour later it had reappeared, on the lowest limb of the alder tree, swearing at the cats and repeating its patriotic theme song. At intervals during the night and in the early dawn there had sounded from the alder tree the familiar repertoire, and now after another brief disappearance, *el pájaro* was back again.

"It's wonderful how intelligent they are," said Mrs. Mac-Taggart. "Picking up the different songs and all. Now it's back to flying it'll be safe enough from the cats."

"Well, if you think it shows intelligence," said Alison, "deliberately coming back to where four cats—" She put the ham into a large bowl and began to insert cloves into it. The windows were open, and there echoed into the kitchen the happy shouts of the twins and the mockingbird's raucous cry, and then his piercing imitation of the meadowlark's sweet call. That broke off to give way to "Yankee Doodle." Alison turned the ham, shoving cloves in firmly. "I wonder if we've got enough raisins for a raisin sauce? I—" The shouts from the yard rose to crescendo and she jumped. Cedric barked.

There was a gray-and-white flash and the mockingbird swooped and lit on the rose trellis outside the window. Its bright insolent eyes peered; it cocked its head this way and that, and said, "Tu-whoooo. Yankee Doodle came to town—"

"Of course it could be that the creature has a nest hereabouts," said Mrs. MacTaggart. "A mate and all. I suppose—"

Alison opened the cupboard and took down the bottle of cherry wine. She had her own special recipe for marinating ham, and cherry wine made all the difference. "I think it's a little early for them to be nesting, Mairí—" She jumped again.

The mockingbird swooped onto the windowsill screaming with rage. It beat its wings on the screen madly. "YAWK!" it shrieked, hopping up and down in fury. "YAWK!"

"Mercy!" said Mrs. MacTaggart, dropping the dishcloth. "YAWK!"

"There," said Alison, "you see! That damned bird's just missing its whiskey! It thinks any bottle's got whiskey in it, and we're stealing it. You see what you started."

"Guidness have mercy," said Mrs. MacTaggart, and began to laugh. "I do believe you're right—"

Alison recapped the bottle and the mockingbird beat its wings on the screen, frenzied, and shrieked again.

"And if you're thinking of putting some out for it, you know El Señor'd get it before *el pajáro*."

"Now I wouldn't be thinking of doing anything so foolish," said Mrs. MacTaggart, still laughing.

Alison put the bottle away and shut the cupboard. The bird fluttered on the sill; his *yawk* had a decidedly disappointed tone.

"If I know our luck," said Alison resignedly, "we're stuck with him for life. This kindness to dumb animals can be carried too far."

At two thirty Hackett called in and said they'd found Colin Donovan's parents at the Beverly Hills address. "Not a clue, Luis," he said. "It's kind of pathetic. Money, the father's something technical in films. Oh, they know Colin's a very *modern* boy, goes with a crowd of these young people with the modern ideas, all the in things—but young people always have fads, the long hair and all, it's just a phase. At twenty-one. All bewildered at *police* coming. Colin's a junior at U.C.L.A."

"Oh, yes," said Mendoza. "That kind."

"Yeah. We're going over to see if he's on campus. If he is, we'll fetch him in. . . . What do you know about George?

You know George, not exactly demonstrative, but if ever I saw a happy man—" Hackett laughed. "Kind of nice, Luis."

"*Ya lo creo*. And at least, Art, another one will have the good solid home and the tender loving care," said Mendoza. But he said it uncynically, and Hackett's laugh was in keeping.

"That's right. I'll call in if we have to go hunting."

"*Bueno*." Mendoza put the phone down. He lit a cigarette. He put out of his mind what Palliser had told him about their possible new mystery—Palliser and Grace were out on that, and Landers and Glasser on a new call, a knifing down on Main. The inquest tomorrow on the recent mass shooting. . . . He began to go over in his mind all they had turned up on the amateur con-man Rex Carson. The erstwhile CIA agent. The erstwhile Department of Commerce representative.

Amateur—*¡caray!* he thought. Like hell. Starting out amateur, allergic to the regular work, doing it when he had to, to eat. Preferring it, not the easier way—con-men had to be hustlers—but the underhand way. The amusing way. They always got a kick out of the game itself, that kind—enjoyed it for its own sake. *Pues, sí*. That latest lay of Carson's worthy of the real top artists. And undoubtedly profitable.

But—trace him back, the last few weeks, and nothing at all showed to point to why he'd been murdered or who had murdered him. He had got around and met people and done things, sure. And there were possibilities, but nothing very clear. He had this nice thing going for him—how long? No telling, at least a year, maybe longer. And then— He had taken Pike-Carter's heated threats seriously enough that he had made arrangements to run, change his base of operations and his name. (Evidently he'd used the aliases before, up in Oregon.) But by the time he'd met Natalie, followed her back here, he'd realized the threat was bluff. That was clear; that diamond solitaire he'd taken from Harry as payment of

206

the poker debt wouldn't have been in with the miscellaneous Victorian hoard he'd probably inherited from his mother, if he hadn't been back at the Alexandria Street address. All right. Harry. What about Harry?

Carson had dropped in on Patti Page on Sunday—before his date with Natalie. Hail and farewell. Leave 'em laughing. He had arranged a date with Rose Lamont for Monday night, and Mendoza would take a bet that that had been meant for hail and farewell too. One like Carson couldn't resist it—the theatricals. They got a kick out of it, just as much as out of the take. The honest types took up acting. Or preaching. Or, he thought cynically, politics. . . . Carson would have enjoyed putting on a last noble act for Rose, the brave CIA agent bid to another dangerous mission abroad. And the rest, silence. While he embarked on a new life with Natalie, in Florida. . . .

And damn it, all that said not one word about where to look for whoever used the gun on him. A week ago tonight. It was up in the air.

Still names in the address book they hadn't looked at. But —Harry? It was possible. It was possible that Carson had dickered with him for the jewels, and there'd been an argument. Harry had had a gun. But as to proving it, even to their own satisfaction—

Saul Goldberg, down in Robbery, was busy. He usually was. He'd had Sunday off, and now had a good deal to catch up on. In an area as large as his office covered, there was a lot of larceny. He was a little busier than usual that Monday, and it wasn't until about two thirty that he got round to reading the various reports on his desk.

He came to one that had been there since Saturday night and said, "That's a funny one."

"Hum?" said Sergeant Betts.

"I suppose it could be called burglary, in a way," said Goldberg, and sneezed, and got out Kleenex. "A very funny little thing. Damn allergies." And all of a sudden his mind made a leap—not on the gun, because he'd never heard about that, it was Homicide's concern, but on the address. He said, "By God, I do wonder—of *all* the funny things—" And he took up his phone and asked for an outside call. When he was connected, he asked questions, and the woman who'd answered said, "Oh, he's not here now. He's at work, naturally."

"Where?" asked Goldberg. He jotted down the address. A very peculiar little thing, a burglary you could call it, but the address— He just remembered Luis saying— Well, maybe do a little favor for Luis. If there was any connection.

He got up. No harm to go and ask a few questions.

FOURTEEN

Mendoza had just started down the hall for coffee, about three thirty, when Lake took a call and beckoned him. "Goldberg." Mendoza went back to his office and picked up the inside phone.

"Hello, Saul. What's on your mind?"

"Some of your business, actually," said Goldberg. "I think you'd better come down here. I may have got hold of something."

"What?"

"Come down," said Goldberg. "I want you to hear it personally. It's crazy, but it could make some sense to you."

"I'll be there." Intrigued, Mendoza went down the hall to the elevator and stepped into Goldberg's office three minutes later. Goldberg was leaning back in his desk chair, his long dark face sardonic: and one of the citizenry occupied the chair beside the desk—a man about forty, tall and lean and dark, in a decent if rather shabby navy-blue suit.

"Luis," said Goldberg. "Mr. Jerome Stewart. Lieutenant Mendoza. Sit down, Luis."

"¿Qué pasa, Saul?"

"Mr. Stewart," said Goldberg, "I'd like for you to tell Lieutenant Mendoza the little story you've told me. Just the same way."

"All over again? Him? Why? What—"

"Never mind, just tell him." There was, Mendoza saw suddenly, a revolver on Goldberg's desk. It was encased in the kind of plastic bag the laboratory used for evidence.

"Well," began Stewart obediently, "see, I live over on Bonnie Brae, up from Third. I've got a wife and a kid, and like we all know the crime rate's way up, and I worry. I work at the L. and G. Garage, days, but prices up and all, and I always had as a hobby, I play the piano, not bad if I do say, and I got this little combo together—piano, fiddle, accordion, and drums—we play three nights a week for this square-dance club. Auditorium over on Sunset."

"Yes?" Mendoza was at sea. He glanced at Goldberg. "So?"

"So, the wife and kid are alone. And even if I'm there—it's not just so good a district anymore. Right downtown, practically. A lot of break-ins and all that. So about a year ago, I got a gun. I got it secondhand, but it was reconditioned, good shape. And me, I'm a careful man. I grew up in the country, I know how to handle guns, but I took my wife up to that range in Flintridge, taught her how to handle it, see. And the gun I keep in the top bureau drawer in our bedroom, ready. In case. Loaded. What's the use of a gun unloaded, she wakes up to find a burglar in the place? Or even me waking up to the burglar?"

"All right. And?" said Goldberg, prodding him.

"Well, all *right*. My wife's a sensible woman. My kid's brought up strict, got orders never touch the gun. Usually I check it every so often, just look to see it's there and O.K. —you know. Saturday afternoon I come home from work—last Saturday this is—I take a shower, and while I'm getting dressed—we got a dance job to play that night—I look. Just casual. And there's a bullet gone from the gun."

"What?" Mendoza was startled.

"Yeah. I say what the hell, it was funny. I looked it over

and I couldn't say if it'd been fired or not, but one bullet was gone. I couldn't figure it."

Mendoza looked at the revolver on Goldberg's desk. "Just to be on the safe side," said Goldberg, "when I heard the story, we went to get the gun and I slid it into a lab bag. Thought—just on the outside chance—you might want it printed before you looked at it further."

"What's the gun?" asked Mendoza.

"Iver-Johnson Target, the four-and-a-half-inch barrel."

"¡Parece mentira!" said Mendoza softly. "You don't tell me."

Goldberg looked interested. "Does that tie up too? What I saw was the address. When you were sniffing around Harry you'd said something—"

"The—Bonnie Brae," said Mendoza. "Oh, yes, indeed, how nice. Five blocks from Crandall. How very—"

"I don't get what you mean. What— But anyway, I couldn't figure it. I asked the wife and she didn't know anything about it. The kid wouldn't touch it. And I thought— well, I'm all for being a responsible citizen, I just thought *somebody* ought to hear about it, so I called in."

"To the main desk," said Goldberg, blowing his nose. "And they sent a report up here—technically speaking it is a theft, you could say. One bullet."

"For an Iver-Johnson Target .22 revolver," agreed Mendoza, his long nose twitching. "When was the last time you looked at it before Saturday?"

"Oh, it'd be at least a week, maybe more. It was just there, you know. Yeah, it was O.K. then, a full load."

"Mmh. And what do you think is the answer?"

"How the hell should I know? That's why I called you—"

"Well, who knew you had the gun? Where you kept it?"

"My Lord, I couldn't say—most of the fellows at work know I've got one, I'd mentioned it casual—but they wouldn't know exactly where I kept it, of course. How'd I know who the wife might have mentioned it to?—not that May's any gossip, she'd know better than to go shooting off her mouth about it, for one thing the hoods are always looking for guns to steal." He shook his head. "I don't know."

"Who was in your apartment between the time you last checked the gun and the time you found a bullet missing?"

"Listen, I couldn't— Well, May's not out an awful lot, and only daytimes. We haven't been to a movie or anything, out evenings together, for a good month. One thing, it sure wasn't a break-in, like that, because nothing else's gone, and they'd—you know—go through everything, make a mess. Nothing like that. But people we know wouldn't— And it isn't as if we gave a lot of parties, had lots of people in. We're just quiet people, see. I don't know, I can't figure it. Mrs. Roccia, across the hall, she and May are kind of friendly, she might be in—cup of coffee, you know. And her kid, but he's only four or five. The landlady, Mrs. Lamont. But *she* wouldn't— Oh, May gave a shower for this girl getting married, she lives down the block, that was a week ago Wednesday or Thursday, I think, but—just neighborhood women, *they* wouldn't—and so far as I know none of those people knew the gun was there. I just can't—"

"You said you have a son? Would—"

"Daughter. Just the one. But the *kid* wouldn't—you can forget that. She's been raised strict, and I warned her plenty, leave it alone! Look, if she'd been a boy—well, you know what I mean—I'd have thought of that right away, boys just naturally curious about guns. But she's not. See what I mean. And she's too young to date—fourteen—we don't believe in letting her date, so it's not as if there'd be boys coming in. Around. She's not much interested yet anyways—she's kind of a brain, I guess, skipped one grade already. So it'd just be her girl friends at our place, times, and only a couple of those. Sue's kind of a loner, doesn't make many friends. What I say is, that's O.K., people got lots of friends, usually they're not real close friends, you know? There'd be that Margaret, and the Jewel kid, and that's about— But *kids*, I ask you, they wouldn't—"

Mendoza jerked upright. "Jewel?" he said. "Jewel?"

"Yeah. The Lamont kid. But school kids— I just can't figure it. Reason I thought I ought to call in—"

"*¿Qué es esto?*" said Mendoza blankly. "*¿Cómo dice? ¡Es un cuento absurdo!* What the hell—what the *hell?*"

When he came, fast, into his office, Hackett and Higgins were there, evidently just arrived. "Oh, Luis—we brought that Donovan in. He was in the campus cafeteria. He—"

"*No importa,*" said Mendoza. "This I don't believe—this I want to hear more about—but just possibly we've come up with something on Carson. I want some witnesses. Come on."

"What? What've you got?"

"I don't know," said Mendoza. "We're going to find out." In the elevator he told them what Goldberg had come up with. "I had the nagging little feeling I'd heard the man's name, just on the fringes of this somewhere—couldn't think where until he said—"

"But, Luis—"

They all got into the Ferarri and Mendoza gunned it out of the lot. "I know, I know," he said irritably. "A lot of questions—how and why. A mare's nest, maybe. But it's surely to God something to ask questions about. The gun is an Iver-Johnson Target .22."

"Now *that* you didn't say before," said Higgins, perched in the jump seat behind Hackett. "Where are we going? The school—"

"You've lost track of time, George."

The little café on Beverly Boulevard, at this hour of the afternoon, had only two customers: the same elderly man absorbed in a newspaper, and an amiable-looking young man, consuming pie and coffee, in a white jumpsuit with *Grandma's Pies* embroidered across the back. Rose Lamont was polishing the counter top with a damp cloth. She looked up as they came in, the bell attached to the doormat pealing shrilly. She gave Mendoza a tentative smile.

"Hello, sir."

Mendoza went up to the counter where she stood beside the cash register. "Mrs. Lamont. Is your daughter here?"

"Why, yes, like always. She helps out after school. To earn her allowance. You want to see Mary? Why? Oh, well, I guess—" She went down to the narrow door at the far end of the space behind the counter, a door probably leading to a washroom, premises where cleaning materials were kept; the cooking facilities were all in sight behind the counter. "Mary? Come on out a minute, dear."

"Has your daughter got a middle name, Mrs. Lamont?" asked Mendoza. "Does everybody call her Mary?"

"Well—" Rose Lamont tucked a stray lock of dark hair under the perky little linen cap that matched her blue smock. "Well, Mary *is* her middle name, if you're interested. I always called her by it since her dad died. It was his notion, name her after his sister who died. I never liked it. Jewel's a silly name, not a proper name at all. But legal-wise, she—"

The girl came toward them slowly, the lank dark girl with her Dutch bob and gawky figure. She had a book in one hand, closed over one finger marking her place. She had on a faded pair of blue cotton slacks and an ugly pink-and-blue striped knitted pullover. "What you want, Mama?"

"The officer wants to talk to you. I don't know—" Mrs. Lamont looked at them doubtfully, curiously. "Mary, you been reading all this time back there? I told you—"

"I know. I'll get it done," she said indifferently. She looked at Mendoza, at the two big men looming behind him, with faint curiosity.

"Mary—or do you like to be called Jewel?" he asked.

"Well, Jewel's my real name. Jewel Mary. Everybody at school calls me Jewel."

"Yes. You've got a girl friend named Sue Stewart."

"Sure," she said. "Why?" It wasn't a pretty face: it was still immature, unformed, a jaw too prominent, a too-high forehead even disguised by the bangs; but the dark eyes under the bangs were intelligent.

"And did you know," said Mendoza, "that Sue Stewart's father has a gun? Know where he keeps it, in their apartment?"

The dark eyes moved and dropped, and now she looked sullen. "Does he?"

"And there is now a bullet missing out of it. Do you know anything about police laboratory work, Jewel?"

"No," she said. Her voice was low, and he had kept his voice low; but the young man was looking up from his pie interestedly.

"Well, our laboratory will be taking a look at Mr. Stewart's gun. And they have ways of proving what gun a bullet was fired from. Definitely. Scientifically. Are they going to tell us that the bullet that killed Rex Carson was fired from Stewart's gun? Or maybe you can tell us now, Jewel."

"Oh, my God!" said Rose Lamont. She had been following this in bewilderment, slow comprehension. Now every vestige of color drained from her face. "Oh, my God—no! Oh, sweet Jesus—"

The girl didn't move or look up. "I rather think so," said Mendoza. He lifted the flap that led behind the counter and took Rose Lamont's weight as she half-collapsed toward the counter. "Art, we'd better—" he jerked his head at the two customers.

Hackett said briskly, "Sorry, gentlemen, this place is closing —you'll have to leave. Sorry. Out."

"Hey," said the young man, "I ain't finished—what gives?"

"Sorry!" Hackett shepherded them out, turned the sign on the door so it read *Closed*. "My God," he said to Higgins, "he *told* us. He tried to tell us—and we, like damned fools, had to complicate it and go off on a wild goose—"

Mendoza had Mrs. Lamont in a booth, her head down on her arms on the table. "No," she was saying dully. "No, I don't believe it, it's a lie, she's just a child, it's a lie, it couldn't be—"

The girl stood there unmoving, head down. The book she held, Hackett saw, was titled *Seven English Poets and Their Work*.

"What about it, Jewel?" said Mendoza, coming back to face her. She was silent. "What did Carson call you—Jewel or Mary? Well?"

She looked up at him slowly. Very carefully she laid the book down on the counter top and brushed back her thick dark hair in an automatic gesture. She said in her thin reedy voice, not quite a child's, not quite an adult's, "Is that true? I'm best at English, I don't know—an awful lot—about scientific things. What you said—about them telling which gun a bullet came from?"

"That's true," said Mendoza.

"Oh. Well, I don't see how that makes you think it was me."

"*Oh, my God—no, it can't be—*" Higgins went over to Mrs. Lamont.

"But you see, Jewel, he left us a note to say it was you," said Mendoza gently. "Only we've just—mmh—figured out what it meant."

"He *did?*" She was astonished. "Why, I thought—I was sure he was killed right *off*."

Hackett let out a breath, and Mendoza said, "You don't have to tell us about it, Jewel, unless you want to. You're a minor, and your mother will be informed of your rights as—"

She brushed her hair back impatiently. "I guess as long as you know, I might as well," she said, half-listless, half-sullen. "Can I—can I sit down?"

Mendoza glanced over at Mrs. Lamont, who was sobbing hysterically.

"I kind of think," said Hackett, "that we adjourn some-place else." And he sounded still as nakedly astonished as the girl.

She faced them there in a bare room at the Juvenile Hall. They had, in the end, to get an ambulance for Mrs. Lamont; they'd talk to her later. Meanwhile, a middle-aged matron sat by the girl, looking sane and shockproof. But Jewel Mary was possibly the coolest of them all.

"I never thought anybody'd know," she said. "I didn't see how they could. Ever. How did you—oh, you said he—Rex —wrote something down. That's funny. I always thought if somebody got shot in the head, they were killed right away."

"Not always," said Mendoza. "But why, Jewel? Why should you—?"

"He was stealing *my money!*" she shrilled. "The money Mama and I'd been saving ever since I can remember—my college money! He was a thief. Mama was too silly to see that, but I knew it right off—him talking all soft and silly, getting around Mama and her giving him our money—*my* money! As long as I can ever remember, all I wanted ever to do was teach in college—teach *English*—all the poetry and— And it costs an awful lot even if you get scholarships— And he— Mama—" she compressed her pale lips and there was impla-cable adult anger in her eyes. "Mama's so silly. He was just a thief. And—and he hadn't been around for awhile, I hoped he wouldn't come ever again. Mama talking about him all the time, Rex, Rex, Rex, how brave he was and all—silly—and then she said, that day, he'd been to the café and he'd be coming that night. And I just knew he'd be telling her some story again and she'd give him some more money." Suddenly she uttered one dry sob. "It wasn't *fair!* The money for my college—it's only four more years and I'll be graduated from high, and I want to go to Pepperdine and it's just awful expensive, the best there is, but nearly a thousand dollars a term. And I just couldn't stand it!" The matron gave her a handkerchief but she shook her head fiercely and found her own. "Mama might give him every cent we'd saved and it wasn't fair! He—he was a grown-up, grown-ups are supposed to *earn* their own money, not get it given to them by—by people like Mama!"

Out of the mouths of babes and sucklings, thought Mendoza wryly. "And so, Jewel?"

"So I—I—I could sort of see it going *on* and him coming and coming. He was *silly,* he tried to make up to me, make me like him, because of Mama, you know—I mean, make *Mama* think he liked me. He even called me Jewel instead of Mary even if she didn't like it—but he was *silly!* And I hated him because of the money—and—and Sue'd told me once about her father's gun, she knew where it was, but she was scared to touch it, her father's awful strict. But I thought of it. Then. Sue said it was all loaded and everything. And I made a good plan about it. I didn't see how anybody'd ever *know.* See, Mama said Rex'd be coming at nine o'clock. And I went to Sue's to do our homework together—we do a lot of times. Mr. and Mrs. Stewart were watching TV, it was easy as anything. I just said I was going to the bathroom and I went in their room afterward while the toilet was still flushing and I took the gun. It wasn't very big. I put it down under my slacks, I had an overblouse on and it didn't show. And Mr. Stewart never lets us go out alone after dark, I knew he'd walk me home, and I said I had to go at eight thirty, and he did. Only I knew he wanted to get back to his TV program, he just saw me up to the porch and went away, and I never went in. I just waited there. For Rex. And he came—I knew his car. He had a different one last year, this one was blue. And I went out and said hello as nice as I could and told him Mama said I should meet him, and she had to go see this friend of hers who was sick and I should ask him to drive there and bring her home, it wasn't far. I said I'd show him where. He never thought anything was wrong. I got in the car and he was all silly like always, pretending to be interested in me—" She tossed her head. "And I told him which way to go. Up that crooked street two blocks up. There's a deaf man lives in a place along there and he's always got his TV on awful loud. I thought if the gun made a lot of noise—" she stopped.

They looked at each other. As simple as that. *Finis* to the complexity of Rex Carson and his tangled trail. After all his plots, all his little schemings and greed and conniving, he had met an unexpected end because of somebody else's selfcenteredness. The half-child, half-adult with the welter of ambition and resentment churning in her—

And he had tried to tell them. After she had run away, back home, to come in all innocent from doing her homework with Sue, Carson—probably in shock, barely conscious, perhaps realizing he was dying or perhaps not—and still, probably, completely astonished—had made his one last effort to tell them. To get it down. Painfully scrawling the bare message—*Jewel shot me*— But he wouldn't have been seeing very clear, and he'd just got down the first letter of the second word when he collapsed. And a bunch of imaginative cops had taken it for the last letter of the first word.

When you knew, how simple. How very simple.

Of course there was an excuse; if they had ever heard the girl called by her first name— But they hadn't.

"And I just put the gun in my school bag, I always fix my own lunch because I've got a persnickety appetite Mama says and she makes sandwiches too thick, and I went home

219

from school with Sue on Tuesday and her mom went out to market so I just said about going to the bathroom again and I put the gun back. I didn't see how anybody'd ever know—" She looked at them blankly, and then overwhelming resentment came ugly and stark into her face, and she said in impotent, furious rage, "*Him!* Why'd he have to come *interfering?* And—and writing notes to *tell* you—stealing my money! He deserved getting shot—he—"

"My God," said Hackett. He drew a long breath, the night air fresh after the stale atmosphere in the old building. "My God, Luis. Fourteen. Who'd have— That poor damned woman."

"Yes," said Mendoza. "We can feel sorry for her. The hell of a lot of paper work to do on it yet—and do either of you care to guess at the outcome?"

"Well, she *is* a minor," said Higgins. "What else can they do? A hearing before the bench, and she'll be sent to some institution for wayward girls a few years, and then probation till she's twenty-one. And another hearing. By which time, don't say it, everybody including the judge will have forgotten Carson, and—"

"Who was no loss to humanity," said Mendoza sardonically.

"Well, fourteen, Luis. What else—"

"Nothing else," said Mendoza, shrugging. "In most—mmh—cultures, including that of our grandparents, *amigos*, fourteen is considered the age of reason. Of responsibility. All I'm thinking of is this. So there's another hearing when she's twenty-one, and she's let off. After the probation. The next time life rises up to thwart our Jewel some way—somebody else frustrates her ambitions—how's she going to react?"

"Yes," said Hackett, sighing. "There is that aspect."

"And the next fellow citizen she conceives a grudge on might not be so—unmissable a character as Carson," said Mendoza. "And for God's sake don't either of you try to feed me the Freudian doubletalk, she was jealous of her mother—"

"Who was going to? She said she thought he was silly and I'm inclined to think that's the plain truth," said Hackett thoughtfully. "The paper work, my God, yes—brief the D.A. —my God. And that poor damned woman, just because *she* was silly enough to be taken in by—"

"In a kind of way," said Higgins, "poetic justice." He looked at his watch in the entrance light of the big gloomy building. "And we've got other things still on hand. For to-morrow." It was getting on for seven o'clock. What with all the red tape at Juvenile Hall—

Mendoza passed a hand across his jaw; at this hour of the day he needed another shave. "So I'll take you back to your cars. *Dios,* that Donovan—we left him just sitting at the office."

"So we did. Damn," said Hackett. "All right, I'll be the fall guy and take him down and book him—material witness until we get something more."

"I never called Mary," said Higgins suddenly. "She'll be worried, damn it."

"Well, I was, a little," said Mary. "But I knew if anything *had* happened, I'd find out soon enough. Something break?"

"Something," said Higgins. "Never mind. We just cleaned up a case. Tell you later." It wasn't that he was superstitious exactly, all the old wives' tales, but after all she *was*— "You feeling all right?"

"Don't be silly. Fine." She'd come out to meet him at the garage when she heard the car. The little Scottie Brucie frisked around their legs, demanding attention. "George—I told Laura and Steve. They're absolutely thrilled. Laura wants a boy and Steve wants a girl."

"Well, *that's* all right then," said Higgins, immensely relieved.

"But, Art, how awful!" said Angel. "That poor woman!"

"Yes, and the devil of it is—I thought afterward—she'll probably stand by the girl. No choice really. And, as Luis said, what else might happen—one like that—God knows."

"You can't imagine it—how it'd be—as if it was Sheila."

"Oh, *Sheila!*" said Hackett. "Really, my Angel—"

"The worst of it is you never can *know*. Until it happens."

A faint cold finger moved up Hackett's spine. He laughed. "Don't be ridiculous. We're sane, sensible people and we—"

"Are human, Art," said Angel. "Just human. You never *know*. . . . But I'm so glad for the Higginses—that's nice, isn't it? You said he's so crazy about her—"

"Inconsistency, thy name is Woman," said Hackett.

"For the Lord's sweet sake," said Piggott. "For the—"

"I thought you'd like to hear," said Glasser. "The damnedest thing. A *kid*. And we were going around on all the complicated theories—"

At a quarter to midnight Galeano went out on a new call. When he came back he said to Schenke, "Well, a new little mystery for the lieutenant to consult his crystal ball on. Very funny. Couple coming home from the movies find a corpse in the alley where the garages are. A very fancy corpse, Bob. Young lady—blonde—all togged out in a green lace evening dress. Not a mark on her, but dead. Pretty recently dead, I'd say. Wonder what the autopsy'll say." He started to type up a report.

"That poor woman," said Mrs. MacTaggart. "I canna get her out of my mind. I'll be putting up some prayers for her. Och, she was foolish maybe—but most human creatures are, now and then." Shaking her head, she put down the fresh plate of toast and went back to the kitchen.

Alison poured Mendoza a fresh cup of coffee. "The gambles you take, having children— Awful. You're going to be late."

"I know, I know. I did some overtime last night," said Mendoza. He gulped coffee and looked around cautiously for cats before shoving his chair back. As a rule, whenever humans were eating or drinking, the cats were much in evidence. "Where's all the livestock?"

"I told you," said Alison. "Stuck with the creature for life. Everybody's out watching *el pájaro.* We're all birdwatchers now. Especially the cats."

"*El pájaro,*" said Mendoza, "had better watch out for Bast and El Señor. The other two typically female at fielding, but that pair—" He got up and reached for his hat. "Well, back to the salt mines. And what the hell I'm doing at the dirty thankless job—"

"You wouldn't know what to do with yourself," said Alison. "I'll come watch for hazards." She followed him out.

Cedric their shaggy dog was standing with the twins under the alder tree, amiable and uninterested. The twins were talking excitedly and looking up into the tree.

"*¡El pájaro, Mamacíta!* See?"

"*El pájaro lindo* come back!"

"Stuck with him for life," said Alison. "Kindness to dumb creatures—all because Mairí would feed him your whiskey—"

Bast came ambling across the lawn from the back porch, and without warning *el pájaro* went dive-bombing. A flash of gray and white, he swooped down like lightning, pecked her smartly on the rump, and flashed up to light in the alder tree. Bast jumped and swore, and the twins shouted.

"Well, isn't he the bold one?" said Mrs. MacTaggart from the back door.

223

"They always do it when they're starting to nest," said Alison, laughing. "Maybe he's found a wife."

Mendoza backed out the Ferrari under her watchful eye. And their erstwhile feathered friend came swooping down again to achieve a direct hit on a blameless Sheba strolling up from her morning dig in the rose garden.

"Bombs away," said Alison. "Have a good day, *amante*."

Mendoza backed the Ferrari into the street. The last glimpse he had, Alison, Mairí, and the twins were convulsed with laughter, the mockingbird was swooping down again, and Cedric was barking madly as Bast and Sheba fled for the shelter of the porch.

Unaware of the new little mystery awaiting him at the office, he said to himself, "Livestock!" and headed the Ferrari downtown.